D0495919

Twelve Sharp

Janet Evanovich

headline
review

First published in Great Britain in 2006
by HEADLINE REVIEW
An imprint of HEADLINE PUBLISHING GROUP

First published in paperback in Great Britain in 2007
by HEADLINE REVIEW
An imprint of HEADLINE PUBLISHING GROUP

1

ISBN 978 0 7553 3407 0 (B format)
ISBN 978 0 7553 2808 6 (A format)

Typeset in New Caledonia by Avon DataSet Ltd,
Bidford on Avon, Warwickshire

Printed and bound in Great Britain by
Mackays of Chatham plc, Chatham, Kent

Headline's policy is to use papers that are natural, renewable and
recyclable products and made from wood grown in sustainable forests.
The logging and manufacturing processes are expected to conform
to the environmental regulations of the country of origin.

HEADLINE PUBLISHING GROUP
A division of Hachette Livre UK Ltd
338 Euston Road
London NW1 3BH

www.reviewbooks.co.uk
www.hodderheadline.com

This book was gloriously edited by
SuperJen Enderlin.

Thanks to Deanne Waller for
suggesting the title for this book.

One

When I was twelve years old, I accidentally substituted salt for sugar in a cake recipe. I baked the cake, iced the cake, and served it up. It looked like a cake, but as soon as you cut into it and took a taste, you knew something else was going on. People are like that too. Sometimes you just can't tell what's on the inside from looking at the outside. Sometimes people are a big surprise, just like the salt cake. Sometimes the surprise turns out to be good. And sometimes the surprise turns out to be bad. And sometimes the surprise is just friggin' confusing.

Joe Morelli is one of those good surprises. He's two years older than I am, and for most of my school years, spending time with Morelli was like a visit to the dark side, alluring and frightening. He's a Trenton cop now, and he's my off-again, on-again boyfriend. He used to be the hair-raising part of my life, but my life has had a lot of changes, and now he's the normal part. He has a dog named Bob, and a nice little house, and a toaster. On the outside, Morelli is still street tough and dangerously alluring. On the inside, Morelli is now the sexy guy with the toaster. Go figure.

I have a hamster named Rex, a utilitarian apartment, and my toaster is broken. My name is Stephanie Plum, and I work as a bond enforcement agent, also known as bounty hunter, for my cousin Vinnie. It's not a great job, but it has its moments, and if I mooch food off my parents the job almost pays enough to get me through the month. It would pay a lot more but the truth is, I'm not all that good at it.

Sometimes I moonlight for a guy named Ranger who's extremely bad in an incredibly good way. He's a security expert, and a bounty hunter, and he moves like smoke. Ranger is milk chocolate on the outside . . . a delicious, tempting, forbidden pleasure. And no one knows what's on the inside. Ranger keeps his own counsel.

I work with two women I like a lot. Connie Rosolli is Vinnie's office manager and junkyard dog. She's a little older than I am. A little smarter. A little tougher. A little more Italian. She's got a lot more chest, and she dresses like Betty Boop.

The other woman is my sometimes-partner Lula. Lula was at this moment parading around in the bail bonds office, showing Connie and me her new outfit. Lula is a way-beyond-voluptuous black woman who was currently squashed into four-inch spike heels and a sparkly gold spandex dress that had been constructed for a *much* smaller woman. The neckline was low, and the only thing keeping Lula's big boobs from popping out was the fact that the material was snagged on her nipples. The skirt was stretched tight across her ass and hung two inches below the full moon.

With Connie and Lula you get what you see.

Lula bent to take a look at the heel on her shoe, and Connie was treated to a view of the night sky.

'Crikey,' Connie said. 'You need to put some underwear on.'

'I got underwear on,' Lula said. 'I'm wearing my best thong. Just 'cause I used to be a 'ho don't mean I'm cheap. Problem is that little thong stringy gets lost in all my derriere.'

'Tell me again what you're doing in this getup,' Connie said.

'I'm gonna be a rock-and-roll singer. I got a gig singing with Sally Sweet's new band. You heard of the *Who*? Well, we're gonna be the *What*.'

'You can't sing,' Connie said. 'I've heard you sing. You can't hold a tune to "Happy Birthday".'

'The hell I can't,' Lula said. 'I could sing your ass off. Besides, half those rock stars can't sing. They just open their big oversize mouths and yell. And you gotta admit, I look good in this here dress. Nobody gonna be paying attention to my singing when I'm wearing this dress.'

'She's got a point,' I said to Connie.

'No argument,' Connie said.

'I'm underrealized,' Lula said. 'I gotta lot of untapped potential. Yesterday my horoscope said I gotta expand my horizons.'

'You expand anymore in that dress, and you'll get yourself arrested,' Connie said.

The bonds office is on Hamilton Avenue, a couple blocks from St Francis Hospital. Handy for bonding out guys who've been shot. It's a small storefront office sandwiched between a beauty parlor and a used bookstore. There's an outer room with a scarred imitation leather couch, a couple folding chairs, Connie's desk and computer, and a bank of files. Vinnie's office is located in a room behind Connie's desk.

When I started working for Vinnie, he used his office to talk to his bookie and set up nooners with barnyard animals, but Vinnie has recently discovered the Internet, and now Vinnie uses his office to surf porn sites and online casinos. Behind the bank of file cabinets is a storeroom filled with the nuts and bolts of the bail bonds business. Confiscated televisions, DVD players, iPods, computers, a velvet painting of Elvis, a set of cookware, blenders, kids' bikes, engagement rings, a tricked-out Hog, a bunch of George Foreman grills, and God knows what else. Vinnie had some guns and ammo back there too. Plus a box of cuffs that he got on eBay. There's a small bathroom that Connie keeps spotless and a back door in case there's a need to sneak off.

'I hate to be a party pooper,' Connie said, 'but we're going to have to put the fashion show on hold because we have a problem.' She slid a stack of folders across her desk at me. 'These are all unresolved skips. If we don't find some of these guys we're going belly-up.'

Here's the way bail bonds works. If you're accused of a crime and you don't want to sit and rot in jail while you're waiting for your trial to come up, you can give the court a wad of money. The court takes the money and lets you walk, and you get the money back when you show up on your trial date. If you don't have that money stashed under your mattress, a bail bondsman can give the court the money on your behalf. He'll charge you a percentage of the money, maybe ten percent, and he'll keep that percentage whether you're proven guilty or not. If the accused shows up for court, the court gives the bail bondsman his money back. If the accused doesn't show up, the court keeps the money until the bondsman finds the accused and drags his sorry butt back to jail.

So you see the problem, right? Too much money going out and not enough money going in, and Vinnie might have to refinance his house. Or worse, the insurance company that backs Vinnie could yank the plug.

'Lula and I can't keep up with the skips,' I said to Connie. 'There are too many of them.'

'Yeah, and I'll tell you the problem,' Lula said. 'It used to be Ranger worked full time for you, but not anymore, he's got his own security business going, and he's not doing skip tracing. It's just Stephanie and me catching the bad guys these days.'

It was true. Ranger had moved most of his business toward the security side and only went into tracking mode when something came in that was over my head. There are some who might argue *everything* is over my head, but for practical purposes we've had to ignore that argument.

'I hate to say this,' I told Connie, 'but you need to hire another bond enforcement person.'

'It's not that easy,' Connie said. 'Remember when we had Joyce Barnhardt working here? That was a disaster. She screwed up all her busts doing her *big bad bounty hunter* routine. And then she stole everyone's skips. It's not like she's a team player.'

Joyce Barnhardt is my archenemy. I went all through school with her, and she was a misery. And before the ink was dry on my marriage license, she was in bed with my husband, who is now my ex-husband. Thank you, Joyce.

'We could put an ad in the paper,' Lula said. 'That's how I got my filing job here. Look at how good that turned out.'

Connie and I did eye rolls.

Lula was about the worst file clerk ever. Lula kept her job because no one else would tolerate Vinnie. The first time Vinnie made a grab at Lula, she clocked him on the side of the head with a five-pound phone book and told him she'd staple his nuts to the wall if he didn't show respect. And that was the end of sexual harassment in the bail bonds office.

Connie read the names off the files on her desk. 'Lonnie Johnson, Kevin Gallager, Leon James, Dooby Biagi, Caroline Scarzolli, Melvin Pickle, Charles Chin, Bernard Brown, Mary Lee Truk, Luis Queen, John Santos. These are all current. You already have half of them. The rest came in last night. Plus we have nine outstanding that we've relegated to the *temporarily lost cause* file. Vinnie's writing a lot of bond these days. Probably taking risks he shouldn't. The result is more than the normal FTAs.'

When someone doesn't show up for a court appearance we call them FTA. Failure to Appear. People fail to appear for a bunch of reasons. Hookers and pushers can make more money on the street than they can in jail so they only show up in court when you finally stop bonding them out. All other people just don't want to go to jail.

Connie gave me the new files, and it was like an elephant was sitting on my chest. Lonnie Johnson was wanted for armed robbery. Leon James was suspected of arson and attempted murder. Kevin Gallager was wanted for grand theft auto. Mary Lee Truk had inserted a carving knife into her husband's left buttock during a domestic disturbance. And Melvin Pickle was caught with his pants down in the third row of the multiplex.

Lula was looking over my shoulder, reading along with me.

'Melvin Pickle sounds like fun,' she said. 'I think we should start with Melvin.'

'Maybe a bond enforcement agent wanted ad in the paper isn't such a bad idea,' I said to Connie.

'Yeah,' Lula said, 'just be careful how you word it. You probably want to fib a little. Like you *don't* want to say we're looking for some gun-happy lunatic to take down a bunch of scumbags.'

'I'll keep that in mind when I write it up,' Connie said.

'I'm going down the street,' I told Lula. 'I need something to make me happy. We'll go to work when I get back.'

'You going to the drugstore?' Lula wanted to know.

'No. The bakery.'

'I wouldn't mind if you brought me back one of them cream-filled doughnuts with the chocolate frosting,' Lula said. 'I need to get happy too.'

At mid-morning the Garden State was heating up. Pavement was steaming under a cloudless sky, petrochemical plants were spewing to the north, and cars were emitting hydrocarbons statewide. By mid-afternoon I'd feel the toxic stew catch in the back of my throat, and I'd know it was truly summer in Jersey. For me, the stew is part of the Jersey experience. The stew has attitude. And it enhances the pull of Point Pleasant. How can you completely appreciate the Jersey shore if the air is safe to breathe in the interior parts of the state?

I swung into the bakery and went straight to the doughnut case. Marjorie Lando was behind the counter, filling cannoli for a customer. Fine by me. I could wait my turn. The bakery was always a soothing experience. My heart rate slowed in the presence of massive quantities of sugar and lard. My mind floated over the acres of cookies and cakes and doughnuts and cream pies topped with rainbow sprinkles, chocolate frosting, whipped cream, and meringue.

I was patiently contemplating my doughnut selection, when I sensed a familiar presence behind me. A hand brushed my hair back, and Ranger leaned into me and kissed me on the nape of my neck.

'I could get you to look at *me* like that if I had five minutes alone with you,' Ranger said.

'I'll give you five minutes alone with me if you'll take over half my skips.'

'Tempting,' Ranger said, 'but I'm on my way to the airport, and I'm not sure when I'll be back. Tank is in charge. Call him if you need help. And let him know if you decide to move into my apartment.'

Not that long ago I needed a safe place to stay and sort of commandeered Ranger's apartment when he was out of town. Ranger had come home and found me sleeping in his bed like Goldilocks. He'd very graciously not thrown me out the seventh-floor window. And in fact he'd allowed me to stay with a minimum of sexual harassment. Okay, maybe minimum isn't entirely accurate. Maybe it was a seven on a scale of ten, but he hadn't forced the issue.

'How did you know I was here?' I asked him.

'I stopped at the bonds office, and Lula told me you were on a doughnut mission.'

'Where are you going?'

'Miami.'

'Is this business or pleasure?'

'It's bad business.'

Marjorie finished with her customer and made her way over to me. 'What'll it be?' she wanted to know.

'A dozen Boston Cream doughnuts.'

'Babe,' Ranger said.

'They're not all for me.'

Ranger doesn't often smile. Mostly he thinks about smiling, and this was one of those thinking smile times. He wrapped his hand around my wrist, pulled me to him and kissed me. The kiss was warm and short. No tongue in front of the bakery lady, thank God. He turned and walked away. Tank was idling at the curb in a black SUV. Ranger got in and they drove off.

Marjorie was behind the counter with a cardboard box in her hand and her mouth dropped open. 'Wow,' she said.

That dragged a sigh out of me because she was right. Ranger was definitely a *wow*. He stood half a head taller than me. He was perfectly toned muscle, and he had classic Latino good looks. He always smelled great. He dressed only in black. His skin was dark. His eyes were dark. His hair was dark. His life was dark. Ranger had lots of secrets.

'It's a work relationship,' I told Marjorie.

'If he was in here any longer the chocolate would have melted off the eclairs.'

'I don't like this,' Lula said. 'I wanted to go after the pervert. I personally think it's a bad choice to go after the guy who likes guns.'

'He's got the highest bond. The fastest way to dig Vinnie out of the hole is to get the guy with the highest bond.'

We were in Lula's red Firebird, sitting across the street from Lonnie Johnson's last known address. It was a small clapboard bungalow in a depressed neighborhood that backed up to the hockey arena. It was close to noon and not a great time to roust a bad guy. If he's still in bed, it's because he's drunk and mean. If he's not in bed, it's most likely because he's at a bar getting drunk and mean.

'What's the plan?' Lula wanted to know. 'We gonna just bust in like gangsta bounty hunters and kick his ass?'

I looked at Lula. 'Have we *ever* done that?'

'Don't mean we can't.'

'We'd look like idiots. We're incompetent.'

'That's harsh,' Lula said. 'And I don't think we're *completely* incompetent. I think we're closer to eighty percent incompetent. Remember the time you wrestled that naked greased-up fat guy? You did a good job with that one.'

'Too early in the day to do the pizza-delivery routine,' I said.

'Can't do the flower delivery either. Nobody believe someone sending flowers to this dope.'

'If you hadn't changed clothes you could do the hooker-delivery routine,' I said to Lula. 'He would have opened the door to you in that gold thing.'

'Maybe we pretend we're selling cookies. Like Girl Scouts. All we gotta do is go back to the 7-Eleven and get some cookies.'

I looked Johnson's phone number up on the bond sheet and called him from my cell.

'Yeah?' a man said.

'Lonnie Johnson?'

'What the fuck you want? Fuckin' bitch calling me at this hour. You think I got nothin' better to do than answer this phone?' And he hung up.

'Well?' Lula asked.

'He didn't feel like talking. And he's angry.'

A shiny black Hummer with tinted windows and bling wheel covers rolled down the street and stopped in front of Johnson's house.

'Uh-oh,' Lula said. 'Company.'

The Hummer sat there for a moment and then opened fire on Johnson's house. Multiple weapons. At least one was automatic, firing continuous rounds. Windows blew out and the house was drilled with shots. Gunfire was returned from the house, and I saw the nose of a rocket launcher poke out a front window. Obviously, the Hummer saw it too because it laid rubber taking off.

'Maybe this isn't a good time,' I said to Lula.

'I *told* you to go for the pervert.'

Melvin Pickle worked in a shoe store. The store was part of the mall that attached to the multiplex where he'd been caught shaking hands with the devil. I didn't have a lot of enthusiasm for this capture, since I had some sympathetic feelings for Pickle. If I had to work in a shoe store all day I might go to the multiplex to whack off once in a while too.

'Not only is this going to be an easy catch,' Lula said, parking at the food-court entrance, 'but we can get pizza and go shopping.'

A half-hour later, we were full of pizza and had taken a couple new perfumes out for a test drive. We'd moseyed down the mall and were standing in front of Pickle's shoe store, scoping out the employees. I had a photo of Pickle that had come with his bond agreement.

'That's him,' Lula said, looking into the store. 'That's him on his knees, trying to sell that dumb woman those ugly-ass shoes.'

According to Pickle's paperwork he'd just turned forty. He had sandy-colored hair that looked like it had been cut in boot camp. His skin was pale, his eyes hidden behind round-rimmed glasses, his mouth accented by a big herpes sore. He was five-foot-seven and had an average build gone soft. His slacks and dress shirt were just short of shabby. He didn't look like he cared a whole lot if the woman bought the shoes.

I moved my cuffs from my shoulder bag to my jeans pocket. 'I can manage this,' I said to Lula. 'You stay here in case he bolts.'

'I don't think he looks like a bolter,' Lula said. 'I think he looks more like the walking dead.'

I agreed with Lula. Pickle looked like he was two steps away from putting a bullet in his brain. I moved behind him and waited for him to stand.

'I love this shoe,' the woman said. 'But I need a size nine.'

'I don't have a size nine,' Pickle said.

'Are you sure?'

'Yeah.'

'Maybe you should go back and look again.'

Pickle sucked air for a couple beats and nodded. 'Sure,' he said.

He stood and turned and bumped into me.

'You're going to leave, aren't you?' I said. 'I bet you're going to go out the back door and go home and never come back.'

'It's a recurring fantasy,' he said.

I glanced at my watch. It was twelve-thirty. 'Have you had lunch?' I asked him.

'No.'

'Take your lunch now and come with me, and I'll buy you a piece of pizza.'

'There's something wrong with this picture,' Pickle said. 'Are you one of those religious nuts who wants to save me?'

'No. I'm not a religious nut.' I held my hand out. 'Stephanie Plum.'

He automatically shook my hand. 'Melvin Pickle.'

'I work for Vincent Plum Bail Bonds,' I said. 'You missed a court date, and you need to reschedule.'

'Sure,' he said.

'Now.'

'I can't go now. I gotta work.'

'You can take your lunch break.'

'I had plans for lunch.'

Probably going to see a movie. I was still holding his hand, and with my other hand I clapped a bracelet on him.

He looked down at the cuff. 'What's this? You can't do this. People will ask questions. And then what will I tell them? I'll have to tell them I'm a pervert!'

Two women looked over at him and raised their eyebrows.

'No one will care,' I said. I turned to the women. 'You don't care, right?'

'Right,' they murmured and hurried out of the store.

'Just walk out into the mall quietly with me,' I said. 'I'll take you to court and get you rebonded.'

Actually, Vinnie would rebond him. Vinnie and Connie could write bond. Lula and I did the capture thing.

'Darn,' Pickle said. 'Darn it all.'

And he took off with the cuff dangling from his wrist. Lula stepped in front of him, but he had momentum and knocked her on her ass. He faltered for a moment, got his footing and ran off, into the mall. I was ten steps behind him. I stumbled over Lula, scrambled to my feet, and kept going. I chased him through the mall and up an escalator.

A hotel with an open atrium was attached to one end

of the mall. Pickle ran into the hotel and barreled through the fire door into the stairwell. I chased him up five flights of stairs and thought my lungs were going to explode. He exited the stairwell, and I dragged myself, gasping, to the door.

There were seven floors in the hotel. All rooms opened to a hallway that overlooked the hotel atrium. We were on the sixth floor. I staggered out of the stairwell and saw that Pickle had made it halfway around the atrium and was straddling the balcony railing.

'Don't come near me,' he yelled. 'I'll jump.'

'Fine with me,' I said. 'I get my money dead or alive.'

Pickle looked depressed at that fact. Or maybe Pickle just *always* looked depressed.

'You're in pretty good shape,' I said, still winded. 'How do you stay in such good shape?'

'My car got repossessed. I walk everywhere. And all day long I'm up and down with the shoes. At the end of the day my knees are killing me.'

I was talking to him, creeping closer. 'Why don't you get a different job? One that's easier on your knees.'

'Are you kidding me? I'm lucky to have *this* job. Look at me. I'm a loser. And now everybody's going to know I'm a pervert. I'm a pervert loser. And I have a big herpes. I'm a pervert loser with a herpes!'

'You need to get a grip. You don't have to be a pervert loser if you don't want to be.'

He sat on the railing and swung both legs over. 'Easy for you to say. You aren't named Melvin Pickle. And I bet you were a baton twirler in high school. You probably had friends. You probably date.'

'I don't exactly date, but I sort of have a boyfriend.'

'What does *sort of* mean?'

'It means that he looks like my boyfriend, but I don't say it out loud.'

'Why not?' Pickle wanted to know.

'It feels weird. I'm not sure why.' Okay, I knew *why*, but I wasn't going to say *that* out loud either. I had feelings for two men, and I didn't know how to choose between them. 'And I wish you wouldn't sit like that. It's creeping me out.'

'Are you afraid I'll fall? I thought you didn't care. Remember dead or alive?'

My cell phone was ringing in my bag.

'For crying out loud, answer it,' Pickle said. 'Don't worry about me, I'm only going to kill myself.'

I did an exaggerated eye roll and answered the phone.

'Hey,' Lula said. 'Where are you? I been looking all over.'

'I'm in the hotel at the end of the mall.'

'I'm right outside of that hotel. What are you doing there? Do you have Pickle?'

'I don't exactly *have* Pickle. We're on the sixth floor, and he's thinking about jumping off the balcony.'

I looked over the railing and saw Lula walk into the atrium. She looked up, and I waved at her.

'I see you,' Lula said. 'Tell Pickle he's gonna make a big mess if he jumps. This floor's marble, and his head's gonna crack open like a fresh egg, and there's gonna be brains and blood all over the place.'

I disconnected and relayed the message to Pickle.

'I have a plan,' he said. 'I'm going to jump feet first. That way my head won't make such an impact when I land.'

Pickle was getting noticed. People were dotted around the atrium, looking up at him. The elevator opened behind me and a man in a suit stepped out.

'What's going on here?' he wanted to know.

'Don't come near me!' Pickle yelled. 'If you come near me, I'll jump.'

'I'm the hotel manager,' the man said. 'Is there something I can do?'

'Do you have a giant net?' I asked him.

'Just go away,' Pickle said. 'I have big problems. I'm a pervert.'

'You don't look like a pervert,' the manager said.

'I whacked off in the multiplex,' Pickle told him.

'Everybody whacks off in the multiplex,' the manager said. 'I like to go when there's one of those chick flicks playing, and I wear my wife's panties and I—'

'Jeez,' Pickle said. 'Too much information.'

The manager disappeared behind the elevator doors and minutes later reappeared in the lobby. He stood in a small cluster of hotel employees, everyone with their head back, their eyes glued to Pickle.

'You're making a scene,' I said to Pickle.

'Yeah,' Pickle said. 'Pretty soon they're going to start yelling "*jump*". The human race is lacking. Have you noticed?'

'There are some good people,' I told him.

'Oh yeah? Who's the best person you know? Of all the people you know personally, is there anyone who has a sense of right and wrong and lives by it?'

This was a sticky question because it would have to be Ranger . . . but I suspected he occasionally killed people. Only *bad* people, of course, but still . . .

The crowd in the atrium was growing and now included some uniformed security guys and two Trenton cops. One of the cops was on his two-way, probably calling Morelli to tell him I was involved in yet another disaster. A cameraman and his assistant joined the crowd.

'We're on television,' I told Pickle.

Pickle looked down, waved at the camera, and everyone cheered.

'This is getting too weird,' I told Pickle. 'I'm leaving.'

'You can't leave. If you leave, I'll jump.'

'I don't care, remember?'

'Of course you care. You'll be responsible for my death.'

'Oh no. No, no, no.' I wagged my finger at him. 'That won't work with me. I grew up in the Burg. I was raised Catholic. I know guilt in and out. The first thirty years of my life were ruled by guilt. Not that guilt is an entirely bad thing. But you're not going to lay it on me. Whether you live or die is your choice. I have nothing to do with it. I'm not taking responsibility for the state of the pot roast anymore.'

'Pot roast?'

'Every Friday I'm expected for dinner at my parents' house. Every Friday my mom makes pot roast. If I'm late, the pot roast cooks too long and gets dry, and it's all my fault.'

'And?'

'And it's not my fault!'

'Of course it's your fault. You were late. They were nice enough to make a pot roast for you. Then they were nice enough to hold dinner for you even though it meant ruining the pot roast. Boy, you should learn some manners.'

My cell phone rang again. It was my Grandma Mazur. She lives with my mom and dad. She moved in when Grandpa Mazur sailed off in a heaven-bound gravy boat.

'You're on television,' she said. 'I was trying to find Judge Judy, and you popped up. They said you were breaking news. Are you trying to rescue that guy on the railing, or are you trying to get him to jump?'

'In the beginning I was trying to rescue him,' I said. 'But I'm starting to change my mind.'

'I gotta go now,' Grandma said. 'I gotta call Ruth Biablocki and tell her you're on television. She's always going on about her granddaughter and how she's got that good job at the bank. Well let's see her top this one. Her granddaughter don't get on television!'

'What are you so depressed about that you want to jump off this balcony?' I asked Pickle. 'Jumping to your death is pretty severe.'

'My life sucks! My wife left me and took everything, including my clothes and my dog. I got fired from my job and had to go to work in a shoe store. I have no money, so I had to move back home and live with my mother. And I got caught whacking off in a multiplex. Could it possibly get any worse?'

'You have your health.'

'I think I'm getting a cold. I have a *huge oozing cold sore!*'

My phone rang again.

'Cupcake,' Morelli said. 'I don't like finding you in a hotel with another guy.'

I looked down and saw Morelli standing next to Lula.

'He's a jumper,' I told Morelli.

'Yeah,' Morelli said. 'I can see that. What's the story?'

'He got caught whacking off in the multiplex and doesn't want to go to jail.'

'He won't get a lot of jail time for that,' Morelli said. 'Maybe a couple weekends of community service. It's not a big deal. Everyone whacks off in the multiplex.'

I relayed the message to Pickle.

'It's not just jail,' Pickle said. 'It's me. I'm a loser.'

Morelli was still on the phone. 'Now what?'

'He's a loser.'

'You're on your own with that one,' Morelli said. 'Are you going to need help with this?'

'Maybe you need . . . vitamins,' I said to Pickle.

Pickle looked at me. Hopeful. 'Do you think that could be it?'

'Yeah. If you get off the railing we could go to the health-food store and get some.'

'You're just saying that to get me off the railing.'

'True. When you get off the railing the police will probably arrest you for being a nut. You'll have to go to the station and wait for Vinnie to get there to bond you out again.'

'I can't afford to get bonded out again. I just walked off my job. I'm probably unemployed.'

'Oh for the love of everything holy.' I peeked at my watch. I didn't have time for this. I had other fish to fry.

'How about this. We need someone to do filing at the bonds office. Maybe I can get Vinnie to hire you so you can work off the fee to get bonded out.'

'Really? You'd do that for me?'

Morelli was still listening in. 'Okay, so far we've promised him community service, vitamins, and a job. The only thing left that he could possibly want is gorilla sex. And if you promise that to him I'm not going to be happy.'

I disconnected Morelli and put the phone back into my pocket.

'About the job,' Pickle said. 'Vinnie wouldn't mind that I'm a . . . you know, pervert?'

That was pretty funny. Vinnie minding that Pickle whacked off at the multiplex. 'It's probably the only thing you have going for you,' I told Pickle.

'Okay,' he said. 'But you're going to have to help me get off this railing. I'm terrified to move.'

I grabbed the back of his shirt and hauled him off the railing, and we both collapsed into a heap on the floor. The crowd reaction was mixed. Some cheers and some boos. We got to our feet, and I cuffed his hands behind his back and led him to the elevator.

Two

Morelli was waiting for me when the doors opened at the atrium level. He stepped in with two uniforms, and we all rode one floor down to the parking garage where a cruiser was idling. I got Pickle into the back seat and promised to get him rebonded.

'And the vitamins,' Pickle said. 'Don't forget the vitamins.'

'Sure.'

The cruiser took off, and I turned to Morelli. He was standing thumbs hooked into his jeans pockets, and he was smiling at me. Morelli is six feet tall and is all lean planes and angles and hard muscle. His complexion is Mediterranean. His hair is almost black and curls against his neck. His brown eyes are liquid chocolate when he's aroused.

'What?' I asked Morelli.

'Did you make any more promises after you hung up on me?'

'None you want to know about.'

The smile widened. 'Bob misses you. He hasn't seen you in a couple days.'

Bob is Morelli's big orange dog. And this is Morelli's ploy when he wants me to do a sleepover. Not that he needs a ploy.

'I'll have to call you later this afternoon,' I said. 'I don't know how my day will go. I'm on a mission to clean up a bunch of FTAs for Vinnie.'

He curled his fingers into my T-shirt, pulled me to him, and kissed me. There was a lot of tongue involved and some wandering hands. When he was done he held me at arm's length. 'Be careful,' he said.

'Too late,' I told him.

He moved me five steps backward into the elevator, pushed the button, and sent me up to the atrium where Lula was waiting.

'I'm not even going to guess what went on in that parking garage,' Lula said. 'But you better wipe that goofy smile off your face, or people are gonna get the right idea.'

I called Connie and told her about Pickle.

'Vinnie's out of town,' she said. 'I'll bond Pickle out. And before I forget, there was a woman in here asking for you. She said her name was Carmen.'

Offhand, I couldn't think of anyone I knew named Carmen. 'Did she say what she wanted?'

'She said it was personal. I'm guessing she was in her late twenties. Soft-spoken. Pretty. And crazy.'

Great. 'What kind of crazy are we talking about? Crazy stressed? Crazy dressed in clown shoes with a red rubber nose? Or crazy crazy?'

'Crazy stressed and crazy crazy. She was dressed all in black. Like Ranger. Black boots, black cargo pants, black T-shirt. And she was . . . intense. She said she would track you down. And then she asked about Ranger. I guess she's looking for him too.'

'We got choices to make,' Lula said when I put my phone away. 'We could cruise for shoes, or we could embarrass ourselves some more by pretending to be bounty hunters.'

'I think we're on a roll. I say we keep pretending to be bounty hunters.'

'I want to see the woman who stabbed her husband in the ass,' Lula said. 'Let's do her next.'

'She's in the Burg,' I said to Lula, pulling the file on Mary Lee Truk. 'I'll call my mom and see if she knows her.'

The Burg is a small chunk of Trenton just outside the center of the city. It's a working-class neighborhood that can't keep a secret and takes care of its own. My parents live in the Burg. My best friend Mary Lou Molnar lives in the Burg. Morelli's family is in the Burg. Morelli and I have moved out . . . but we haven't moved far.

Grandma Mazur answered the phone. 'Of course I know Mary Lee Truk,' Grandma said. 'I play bingo with her mother.'

'Does Mary Lee get along with her husband?'

'Not since she stabbed him in the behind. I understand he got real cranky about that and packed up and left.'

'Why did she stab him?'

'The story is that she asked him if he thought she was putting on weight, and he said *yes*, and then she stabbed him. It was one of them spontaneous acts. Mary Lee's going through the change, and everyone knows you don't just up and tell a menopausal woman she's getting fat. I swear some men have no brains at all.

'And by the way, I forgot to tell you before, but some woman came to the house this afternoon, looking for you. I said I didn't know exactly where you were, and she said that was okay, that she'd find you with or without anyone's help. And she was dressed like that hottie you work with, Ranger.'

Lula pulled the Firebird into the curb, and we sat looking at the Truk house.

'I don't have a good feeling about this,' Lula said.

'You were the one who wanted to do the butt stabber.'

'That was before I knew the menopause story. What if she has a hot flash while we're there and goes loony tunes?'

'Just don't turn your back on her. And don't comment on her weight.'

I got out of the car and walked to the door, and Lula followed. I was about to knock when the door was wrenched open, and Mary Lee glared out at me. She had short brown hair that looked like it had been styled with an electric mixer. She was fifty-two according to her bond papers. She was a couple inches shorter than me and a couple pounds heavier.

'What?' she asked.

'*Yow!*' Lula whispered to me.

I introduced myself and gave Mary Lee the routine about getting rebonded.

'I can't go with you,' she wailed. 'Look at my hair! I used to be so good with hair, but lately I can't do anything with this mess.'

'I use conditioner on mine,' Lula said. 'Have you tried that?'

We both looked at Lula's hair. It was orangutan orange and the texture of boar bristles.

'How about a hat?' I said.

'A hat,' Mary Lee sobbed. 'My hair's so bad I need a hat!' Mary Lee's face got red, and she stripped her T-shirt off. 'God, it's *hot* in here.' She was in her bra, sweating, and fanning herself with her shirt.

Lula put her finger to the side of her head and made circles. The international sign for *bats in her belfry*.

'I saw that!' Mary Lee said, eyes narrowed. 'You think I'm nuts. You think the big fatso is nuts!'

'Lady, you just took your shirt off,' Lula said. 'I used to do that but I made money on it.'

Mary Lee looked at the shirt in her hand. 'I don't remember taking it off.'

Mary Lee's face wasn't red anymore, and she'd stopped sweating, so I took the shirt and tugged it over her head. 'I can help you,' I said. 'I know just what you need.' I rummaged through my shoulder bag, found my baseball cap, and clapped it onto her head and tucked most of her hair in. I did a fast walk through the house to make sure it was locked up and Mary Lee hadn't accidentally put the cat in the oven, and then Lula and I steered Mary Lee out of the house and into the car.

Five minutes later, I had Mary Lee standing in front of the doughnut case at the bakery.

'Okay, take a deep breath and look over all the doughnuts,' I told her. 'Look at the strawberry doughnut with the rainbow sprinkles. Doesn't it make you happy?'

Mary Lee smiled at the doughnut. 'Pretty.'

'And the meringue that looks like a fluffy cloud. And the birthday cakes with the pink and yellow roses. And the chocolate cream pie.'

'This is very relaxing,' Mary Lee said.

I called Connie's cell phone. 'Are you still at the courthouse?' I asked her. 'I'm bringing Mary Lee Truk in and we're going to want to bond her out right away before she gets another hot flash.'

'I hate to break into the moment,' Marjorie Lando said. 'But what'll it be?'

'A dozen assorted doughnuts to go,' I told her.

Lula dropped me off in front of the bonds office. 'That wasn't so bad,' she said. 'We helped two lost souls today. That's real good for my horizon expanding and positive karma stockpile. Usually, we just piss people off, and that don't do me any good in the karma department. And it's only five o'clock. I got plenty of time to get to rehearsal. See you tomorrow.'

'See you tomorrow,' I said, and I waved Lula away and beeped my car open. I was driving a black and white Mini Cooper that I'd gotten from Honest Dan the Used Car Man. The interior space was a little cozy for carting bad guys off to jail, but the car had been the right price, and it was fun to drive. I slid behind the wheel and jumped when someone knocked on the driver's side window.

It was the woman dressed in black. She was young, maybe early twenties. And she was pretty in a normal kind of way. She had thick wavy brown hair that fell to her shoulders, blue eyes under long lashes, and full lips that looked like they could easily go pouty. She was maybe five feet five inches and had a nice shape with round breasts stretching the fabric of her black T-shirt.

I started the car and rolled the window down. 'You wanted to speak to me?' I asked the woman.

The woman looked in the window. 'You're Stephanie Plum?'

'Yes. And you would be . . .'

'My name is Carmen Manoso,' she said. 'I'm Ranger's wife.'

My stomach went into a free fall. If I'd been hit in the head with a baseball bat, I wouldn't have been more stunned. I suppose I had to assume there were women in Ranger's life, but I'd never seen any women. There'd never been mention of any women. And there had never been evidence of any women. Much less a wife! Ranger was a very sexy guy, but he was also a lone wolf.

'I understand you're sleeping with my husband,' the woman said.

'You're misinformed,' I told her. Okay, once! But it was a while ago, and she'd put the accusation into present tense.

'You were living with him.'

'I used his apartment as a safe house.'

'I don't believe you,' the woman said. 'Where is he now? Is he in *your* apartment? I've been to his office, and he isn't there.'

Keep calm I told myself. This doesn't feel right. This woman could be *anyone*.

'I'm going to need some identification,' I said to the woman.

She reached into a pocket on her black cargo pants and pulled out a slim credit card holder. It contained a Virginia driver's license issued to Carmen Manoso, plus two credit cards also issued to Carmen Manoso.

So this told me she was Carmen Manoso. It still didn't confirm that she was Ranger's wife.

'How long have you been married to Ranger?' I asked her.

'Almost six months. I knew he had an office here, and that he spent a lot of time here. I never had reason to think he was cheating. I trusted him. Until now.'

'And you don't trust him now, why?'

'He moved out. Like a thief in the night. Cleaned out our bank account and stripped the office of all the files and computer equipment.'

'When did this happen?'

'Last week. One minute he was in bed with me, telling me he was returning to Trenton in the morning. And then *poof*! Gone. His cell phone is no longer in service.'

I punched Ranger's number into my cell phone and got his message service. 'Call me,' I said.

Carmen's eyes narrowed. 'I knew you'd have a number for him. *Bitch!*' And she reached behind her and drew a gun.

I stomped on the gas and the Mini sprang off the curb and jumped forward. Carmen fired off two shots. One pinged off my rear fender.

Connie was right. Carmen Manoso was crazy. And maybe I was crazy too, because I was lost in a rush of insane emotions. Not the least of which was jealousy. Yikes, who would have thought *that* was hiding in the closet? Stephanie Plum, jealous of a woman claiming to be Ranger's wife. And the jealousy was mixed with anger and hurt feelings that this was kept from me. That Ranger had misrepresented himself. That this man I respected for his integrity and strength of character might be not at all what he'd seemed.

Okay, take a deep breath, I told myself. Don't go all hormonal. Get the facts straight. Have a mental dough-nut.

I live in a no-frills, three-story apartment building that is for the most part inhabited by the newly wed and the nearly dead . . . except for me. I live on the second floor with my apartment windows looking out on the parking lot. Handy for those times when I need to keep watch over my car because some pissed-off woman might be inclined to take an axe to it. The building is in a convenient location, a couple miles from the bond office and more important, just a couple miles from my mom's washer and dryer.

I rolled into the lot, parked, and got out to look at the damage. It wasn't bad, all things considered. A line slicing through the paint. A ding on point of impact. Considering that I once had a car smashed by a garbage truck, this hardly counted. I locked up and went into the building.

Mrs Bestler was in the elevator. She was in her eighties, and her own personal elevator didn't quite go all the way to the top anymore. 'Going up!' she sang out to me.

'Second floor,' I said.

She pushed the button and smiled at me. 'Second floor, ladies lingerie and better dresses. Watch your step, dear.'

I thanked Mrs Bestler for the ride and got out of the elevator. I walked the length of my hall and let myself into my apartment. One bedroom, one bath, kitchen, dining room, and living room. All beige, none of my choosing, redecorated by the building owner after an apartment fire. Beige walls, beige carpet, beige curtains. Total seventies orange and brown bathroom. My luck the fire didn't destroy the bathroom.

My hamster Rex lives in a glass cage on my beige kitchen counter. He poked his head out of his soup can when I came in. His whiskers twitched and his black button eyes were wide in expectation. I said *hello* and dropped a couple Cheerios into his food dish. He rushed out, shoved the Cheerios into his mouth and disappeared into his soup can. My kind of roommate.

I called Morelli and told him I'd be over in an hour. I took a shower, did the hair and makeup thing, put on some pretty undies, clean jeans, and a sexy little knit shirt and checked my messages. No Ranger.

This was a dilemma. I didn't know what to do about Carmen. My instincts told me she wasn't what she said. My curiosity had me in a state. And my hormones still had me a teensy bit jealous. Probably I wouldn't be bothered so much if she wasn't so pretty. Truth is, she looked like a woman Ranger might find attractive, except for the crazy part. I couldn't see Ranger with an irrational woman. Ranger was organized. Ranger didn't act on impulse.

Anyway, here she was, and I seemed to be in the middle of something. Whether or not she was Ranger's wife wasn't my most pressing problem. The fact that Carmen felt comfortable shooting at me put her beyond the nuisance category and into the *yikes* category. I was supposed to call Tank if I needed help, but I wasn't ready to push that button just yet. If Tank thought I was in danger he'd assign someone to follow me around whether I wanted it or not. My experience with Ranger's men is that this isn't desirable. They're big and hard to hide. And they're overly protective, since the fear is that Ranger might shoot them in the foot should they let anything bad happen to me.

I stuffed a change of clothes into my shoulder bag and locked my apartment up behind me. I headed out and did a fast check on my car before getting in. No spray-painted slogans suggesting I was a slut. Windows hadn't been broken by a sledgehammer. No ticking noises coming from the undercarriage. Looked to me like Carmen hadn't yet discovered my address.

I drove the short distance to Morelli's house and parked at the curb. Morelli lived in a pleasant neighborhood with narrow streets, small attached houses, and hard-working people. I spent enough time here that knocking wasn't a required formality. I let myself in and heard Bob galloping at me from the kitchen. He hurled himself against me, tail wagging, eyes bright. Bob was in theory a golden retriever, but his gene pool was questionable. He was big and orange and fluffy. He loved everybody, and he ate every*thing* . . . including table legs and upholstered chairs. I gave him a hug, he realized I didn't have any bakery bags, and he trotted away.

Morelli didn't gallop at me, but he didn't drag his feet either. He met me halfway to the kitchen, pressed me into the wall, plastered himself against me and kissed me. Morelli was off-duty in jeans and a T-shirt and bare feet. And the only weapon Morelli was currently carrying was pressed into my stomach.

'Bob really missed you,' he said, his mouth moving down my neck.

'Bob?'

'Yeah.' He hooked a finger into my shirt and slid it off

my shoulder so his mouth could kiss more of me. 'Bob's been nuts without you.'

'Sounds serious.'

'Fucking pathetic.'

His hands slid down to my waist, under my shirt, and in an instant the shirt was off.

'You aren't hungry, are you?' he asked.

'Not for what's in the kitchen.'

I was dressed in one of Morelli's shirts and a pair of his sweatpants. I was beside Morelli, on his couch, and we were eating cold pizza and watching a ball game.

'I had an interesting experience today,' I told him. 'A woman introduced herself to me as Ranger's wife. And then she pulled a gun on me and got two rounds off at my car.'

'Am I supposed to be surprised at this?'

There's a certain amount of professional respect between Morelli and Ranger. And from time to time they've worked together for the common good. Beyond that, Morelli thinks Ranger's a head case.

'Do you know anything about this woman?' I asked Morelli.

'No.'

'Ranger left for Miami today. Do you know anything about that?'

'No.'

'Do you know anything about anything?'

'I know a few things,' Morelli said. 'Tell me more about Ranger's wife.'

'Her name is Carmen. I saw a Virginia driver's license issued to Carmen Manoso. And two credit cards. She's pretty. Sort of curly brown hair, blue eyes, about five-foot-five, Caucasian, nice shape. Fake boobs.'

'How do you know the boobs are fake?'

'Actually, I'm just hoping they're fake. And she was dressed in black SWAT clothes.'

'That's cute,' Morelli said. 'Mr and Mrs Ranger clothes.'

'She said one minute they were in bed and then *poof*, he was gone. Cleaned out the bank account and emptied the office. And the cell number she has for him is out of service.'

'And your cell number for him?'

'It's in service, but he's not answering.'

'It doesn't work for me,' Morelli said. 'I can't see Ranger tying himself up in a marriage.'

I happened to know that Ranger had been married for about twenty minutes when he was in the military. He has a ten-year-old daughter from that marriage, and the daughter lives in Miami with her mother and stepfather. So far as I know, he's been careful to avoid entanglements since. At least, that's what I believed, until a couple hours ago.

'Who is this woman if she's not his wife?' I asked.

'Wacked-out bimbo? Paid assassin? Demented relative?'

'Get serious.'

'I *am* serious.'

'Okay, different subject. Did you do the report on Melvin Pickle? Do you know his status?'

'Oswald did the report. Pickle shouldn't have any problem getting rebonded. Probably have to go through some kind of mental health screening.' Morelli eyed the last piece of pizza. 'Do you want it?' he asked.

'You can have it,' I told him, 'but it'll cost you.'

'What's the price?'

'How about running Carmen Manoso through the system?'

'I'd need more than a piece of pizza for that,' Morelli said. 'I'd need a night of balls-to-the-wall sex.'

'You're going to get that anyway,' I told him.

Morelli was already out of the house when I dragged myself down the stairs and into the kitchen. I gave Bob a hug, scooped some coffee into the coffeemaker, added water, pushed the button, and listened to the magical gurgle of coffee brewing. Morelli had a loaf of raisin bread out on the counter. I considered toasting a slice, but it seemed like unnecessary work, so I ate a slice raw. I drank my coffee and read the paper Morelli left behind.

'Gotta go to work,' I said to Bob, pushing back from the table.

Bob didn't look like he cared a lot. Bob had found a patch of sun on the kitchen floor and was soaking it up.

I showered and got dressed in clean jeans and a little knit shirt. I swiped some mascara on my lashes and took off. I had two files pulled from the pack on the seat next to me. Leon James, the arsonist. And Lonnie Johnson. Both high bonds.

I drove the short distance to Hamilton and parked in front of the office. I got out of the Mini and looked across the street at the black SUV with Virginia plates and tinted windows. Carmen was on the job. I stuck my head into the office. Lula was on the couch reading a movie star magazine. Connie was at her desk.

'How long's the SUV been across the street?' I asked.

'It was there when I opened the office,' Connie said.

'Anybody come in to say hello?'

'Nope.'

I turned and walked across the street and rapped on the driver's side window of the SUV.

The window rolled down, and Carmen looked out at me. 'Looks to me like you spent the night with someone,' she said. 'Like maybe you spent the night with my husband.'

'I spent the night with my boyfriend. Not that it's any of your business.'

'I'm going to stick to you like nothing you've ever seen. I know you're going to lead me to the son of a bitch. And when I find him, I'm going to kill him. And then I'm going to kill you.'

Carmen Manoso had said this with eyes narrowed and teeth clenched. And I realized that the jealousy I felt over her and Ranger was nothing compared to the jealousy she felt toward me. Like it or not, fact or fiction, I was the other woman.

'Maybe we should talk this over,' I said. 'There are some things that don't add up for me. Maybe I can help you. And I have a couple questions.'

The gun appeared, pointed at a spot in the middle of my forehead. 'I'm not answering any more questions,' Carmen said.

I stepped to the rear of the SUV and got the plate. Then I hustled across the street and into the office.

'Well?' Connie asked.

'It's Carmen, the woman in black. She claims to be Ranger's wife. I've seen her driver's license. It reads Carmen Manoso. Her story is that he walked out on her last week, and she's looking for him.'

'Holy crap,' Lula said.

Connie started punching information into her computer. 'Do you know anything else? Address?'

'Arlington. I didn't see her driver's license long enough to get more,' I told her. 'And I have the plate.' I scribbled it on a piece of paper for her. 'Supposedly, Ranger had an office in the area, closed it without warning and disappeared.'

This is the age of instant access. Connie had computer programs that pulled everything from credit history to medical history to high school grades and movie preferences. Connie could find out if you were constipated in 1994.

'Here she is,' Connie said. 'Carmen Manoso. Twenty-two years old. Maiden name, Carmen Cruz. Married to Ricardo Carlos Manoso. Blah, blah, blah. I don't see anything especially interesting. She's originally from Lanham, Maryland, and then Springfield, Virginia. No children. No history of mental illness. No criminal history that I can see. Unimpressive work history. Mostly in retail sales. Waited tables at a bar in Springfield and most recently lists herself as self-employed, bounty hunter. Some financial information. The SUV is leased. Lives in a rental in Arlington. I can go deeper, but it'll take a day or two.'

'What about Ranger? Can you run a check on him?'

'Connie and me try to run a check on him all the time,' Lula said. 'It's like he doesn't exist.'

I looked at Connie. 'Is that true?'

'I'm surprised his name showed up in Carmen's data base,' Connie said. 'He has a way of erasing himself.'

I redialed Ranger's cell number and got his service

again. 'Hey, man of mystery,' I said, 'your wife is here, and she's looking for you with a gun in her hand.'

'That would get my attention,' Lula said.

'Only if you were near a cell tower,' I told her. 'And sometimes Ranger goes places where no cell tower has gone before. Let's saddle up. I want to see what Lonnie Johnson's house looks like today. See if anyone's shooting at him.'

Lula's Firebird was parked in the small back lot, so we left through the back door and took her car. After a couple blocks I called Connie.

'Is Carmen still at the curb?'

'Yep. She didn't see your rear exit. Guess bounty hunter skills aren't high on the list for things you learn when you're married to Ranger.'

I hung up, and Lula cruised down Hamilton and hooked a right turn into Johnson's neighborhood. We were a block away when we saw the lone fire truck. It was parked in front of Johnson's house . . . or at least, what was left of it.

'Hunh,' Lula said, creeping in for a closer look. 'Hope he had insurance.'

Johnson's house was a pile of blackened rubble.

I got out of the car and walked to the fire truck where two firemen were checking a form off on a clipboard.

'What happened?' I asked.

'The house burned down,' one of them said.

They looked at each other and laughed. Fireman humor.

'Anyone hurt?'

'No. Everyone got out. Are you a friend?'

'I knew Lonnie Johnson. Do you know where he went?'

'No, but he went there fast. Left his girlfriend behind to sort through the mess. She said it was a kitchen fire, but there was no way.'

How about this: maybe the *firebomb* landed in the kitchen.

I got back into the car and slouched in my seat.

'Look on the bright side,' Lula said. 'Nobody's shooting. And I don't see no rocket launcher.'

Three

'I think we'll file Lonnie Johnson in the lost cause file,' I said to Lula. 'If he has any sense at all, he's on a bus out of town.'

'Good idea,' Lula said. 'Who we got next up?'

I'd planned to do the arsonist next, but he'd lost some appeal now that I had my nose clogged with barbecued house. I got the stack of files from the back seat and fingered through them.

Luis Queen had been picked up for solicitation. Not a high bond, but he'd be easy to find. I hauled Luis Queen in all the time. Unfortunately, it was too early for Queen. He wouldn't be on his corner turning tricks until midafternoon. Queen liked to sleep in.

Caroline Scarzolli held some potential. She was a low-bond shoplifter. First-time offender. Worked in a lingerie and gadget shop. I handed the file to Lula. 'How about this one?'

'I like this one,' Lula said. 'Scarzolli will be at work

now, and I've been wanting to take a look at this store. I gave up being a 'ho, but I still like to keep up on the technology.'

Pleasure Treasures was on a side street in the middle of the city. The name on the front of the store was written in hot-pink neon light. The lingerie displayed in the window was exotic. Crotchless panties trimmed in faux fur, sequined thongs, nipple pasties, animal-print garter belts.

Lula parked in the small lot adjacent to the store, and we sauntered up to the front door. Actually, Lula was the only one sauntering. I was skulking, head down, hoping no one was looking.

An older woman walked by with her dog and our eyes met.

'I'm a bounty hunter, looking for someone,' I said to her. 'I'm not buying anything here. I've never even been here before.'

The woman hurried on, and Lula shook her head at me.

'That is so sad,' Lula said. 'That shows low self-esteem. That shows you got no pride in your sexual side. You should've told that woman you were going in to get a vibrator and edible massage oils. This here's the twenty-first century. Just 'cause we're women don't mean we can't be sick as men.'

'It's not the twenty-first century in the Burg. My

mother would get an eye twitch if she heard I was shopping in the Pleasure Treasures.'

'Yeah, but I bet your Grandma Mazur shops here all the time,' Lula said, walking into the store, going into browse mode. 'Look at all those dildos. A whole wall of dildos.' Lula picked one off a shelf and pushed a button and it started to hum and rotate. 'This here's a good one,' she said. 'It can sing and dance.'

I had no frame of reference for dildos. 'Yeah,' I said, 'it's . . . nice.'

'It ain't nice!' Lula said, obviously impressed. 'It's a nasty bugger.'

'That's what I meant. Nice and nasty.'

She handed me the dancing dildo. 'Here, you hold it for me while I look around. I want to check out the DVD selection.'

I followed Lula to the DVDs.

'They got a good selection,' Lula said. 'They got all the classics like *Debbie Does Dallas* and *Horny Little People*. And here's my personal favorite, *Big Boys*. Have you seen *Big Boys*?'

I shook my head, no.

'You gotta see *Big Boys*. It'll change your life. I'm gonna buy *Big Boys* for you.'

'That's okay, I don't—'

'It's a present from me.' She handed me the DVD. 'Hang onto it while I keep looking.'

'We're supposed to be working,' I said. 'Remember how we came in here to apprehend Caroline Scarzolli?'

'Yeah, but that's her over there behind the counter, and she don't look like she's going anywhere. She looks just like her picture. I bet she's wearing a wig. Don't it look like a wig to you?'

Caroline was seventy-two years old, according to her bond sheet. She had skin like an alligator and bleached blond hair that was teased into a rat's nest. If it was a wig, she got swindled no matter what she paid. She was wearing orthopedic shoes, fishnet stockings, a tight spandex miniskirt, and a skimpy tank top that showed a lot of wrinkled cleavage. I was guessing she smoked three packs a day and slept naked in a tanning bed.

I glanced at my watch.

'Okay, I can see you're all antsy to make this bust. How about we check out, and then we give her the bad news?'

'Deal.'

Lula took the dildo and the DVD to the register and handed Caroline her credit card.

'We're having a two-for-one sale on dildos,' Caroline said. 'Don't you want to pick out a second?'

'Hear that?' Lula said to me. 'Two-for-one sale. Go get yourself a dildo.'

'I don't actually need—'

'Two for one!' Lula said. 'Pick one, for crying out loud. How many times in life do you get offered a free dildo?'

I took the first one I saw and brought it to Lula.

'That's a beauty,' Caroline said. 'You have good taste. It's our precision replica of the famous adult movie star Herbert Horsecock. It weighs five pounds and it's solid rubber. It's one of our few uncircumsized dildos. It even comes in a special-edition red velvet drawstring carrying sack.'

Lula got her credit card back and took possession of the dildos. 'Okay,' she said to me. 'Do your thing.'

I gave Caroline my card and introduced myself and gave her the baloney about rebonding.

'Who's going to watch the store if I leave now?' she asked.

'Is there someone you can call to come in and babysit?'

'What, like my ninety-year-old mother?'

'You're not exactly doing a lot of business,' I told her.

'Sweetie, I just sold over a hundred dollars worth of shit.'

'You sold it to Lula!'

'Yeah,' Caroline said in her deep smoker's voice. 'Life is good.'

'It isn't *that* good,' I told her. 'You're going to have to come with me. Now.'

'Okay,' she said. 'Just let me get something.' And she dipped behind the counter.

'What are you getting?' I asked.

She reappeared with a sawed-off shotgun. 'This big

gun,' she said. 'That's what I'm getting. Take your dildos and march your ass out of my store.'

Lula and I speed-walked out of the store and rammed ourselves into the Firebird.

'Look on the bright side,' Lula said. 'You got a free dildo. And you got a great movie. Happy birthday early.'

'I don't need a dildo.'

'Sure you do. You never know when it might come in handy. And this Herbert Horsecock dildo's got some heft to it. You could use it as a doorstop, or a paperweight, or you could decorate it with those little twinkle lights at Christmas.'

'I need an apprehension. Vinnie isn't the only one worried about money. I need rent money.' I shuffled through the files. 'I want to do phone work on some of these. Make some calls to verify employment. See if anyone's at the home address. Let's go back to the office.'

'Where am I supposed to park?' Lula wanted to know. 'There's not supposed to be people parked in this lot back here. This is a private lot for the bonds office. We should call the cops on these people.' She circled around the block and looked for a spot on the street. 'I swear I've never seen so many cars. They must be having a party at the beauty parlor.'

'Carmen hasn't moved from her spot,' I said.

Lula glanced over as she crept down the street, looking

for a parking space. 'She's hunkered in. Ranger really pissed her off.'

I was still having a hard time believing Carmen's story. I couldn't see Ranger married. And I couldn't see Ranger cleaning out the bank account. Ranger played a little loose with the law, but he had a very firm moral code. And from what I could see, he wasn't hurting for money.

I checked my phone to make sure it was on, and I hadn't missed a call.

'Still haven't heard from him?' Lula asked.

'No. He must be underground.'

He'd only been gone for twenty-four hours. It was too early to be worried about his safety. But I was worried all the same. It was all too weird.

Lula parked two cars down from me, and we walked to the office. I watched the black SUV for a protruding gun barrel but saw none. When we got to the office we realized it was packed with people.

'What the heck?' Lula said, pushing through the mob to Connie.

Connie was at her desk, trying to talk to the people crowded directly in front of her.

'I ran an ad in the paper this morning for the bond enforcement agent job,' she said to me. 'And this is the response. And the phone hasn't stopped ringing. I had to turn it over to the answering service so I could try to clear this out.'

'Looks like they emptied out the funny farm and everyone came here,' Lula said. 'Who *are* these people? They look like movie extras. They all look like that bounty hunter guy on television, only most of them have better hair. I tell you, they should take that TV bounty hunter guy to the beauty parlor.'

Connie handed me a steno pad and pen. 'You take the front of the room, and I'll take the back. Get names and phone numbers and some work information and tell them we'll be in touch. Put a star by anyone who has potential.'

Forty-five minutes later, the last of the BEA wannabes walked out the door, and Connie hung out a CLOSED sign. Two people were left sitting on the couch. Joyce Barnhardt and Melvin Pickle.

Joyce was dressed in black leather, her eyes heavily lined in black, her red hair teased and lacquered, her lips artificially inflated and painted red to match her hair. She had her arms crossed, and her legs crossed, and her foot jiggled impatiently in stiletto-heeled boots.

Joyce was a flesh-eating fungus. She'd been through more husbands than I could count, and each time she chewed them up and spit them out, she got richer. Three months of marriage to Joyce, and a man was willing to bankrupt himself to get free. When I was in first grade, Joyce threw my crayons in the toilet. When I was in second grade, she spit in my lunch. In third grade she told everybody I didn't wear underpants. In fourth grade she said I had three nipples. In high school she somehow took a picture of me in the girls' locker room and had it made into a flyer and distributed two hundred.

'I am *very* insulted by this whole piece of shit,' Joyce said. 'If you needed another bounty hunter, why didn't you call me? You *know* Vinnie brings me in when he needs help.'

'First off,' Connie said, 'Vinnie doesn't bring you in when he needs help. He brings you in when he needs to fornicate with a barnyard animal. And second, I didn't call you because we all hate you.'

'And?' Joyce said.

'And that's it,' Connie said.

'So why didn't you call me?'

Melvin Pickle was sitting beside Joyce. He looked like he was trying to be invisible.

'Who's this little turd?' Joyce said, turning to Pickle.

'He's going to be doing some filing for us,' Connie said.

'Why did he get a job, and I didn't get a job?' Joyce wanted to know. 'What's so special about him?'

'I'm a pervert,' Pickle said.

'And?' Joyce said. *Hello-o-o.* What am I, chopped liver?'

'Why don't you let her work the LC file?' I said to Connie. 'The one you keep in your bottom drawer.'

'What's LC stand for?' Joyce asked.

'Large cash,' I told her. Also, lost cause, but she probably didn't want to be bothered knowing that.

Connie pulled seven folders out of her bottom desk drawer and gave the top three to Joyce. 'Here you go,' she said to Joyce. 'Good luck. Nice seeing you. Mazel tov.'

Joyce took the folders and looked down at Pickle. 'Love the herpes. Adds color to your face.'

'Thank you,' Pickle said, his hand to his mouth, covering the herpes. 'Have a nice day.'

Connie locked the door after her. 'I swear she's the Antichrist. I always smell sulfur burning when she's in the office.'

'Maybe it's the salve I put on my cold sore,' Pickle said.

'I don't want to be mean about it,' Lula said to Pickle, 'but you might want to think about wearing a mask and rubber gloves when you do the filing.'

'It's going away,' Pickle said.

We all gave an involuntary shudder.

'I'll go through the list of freaks and line up some interviews,' Connie said to me. 'I'll schedule them for tomorrow morning. I'd like you to be here to help.'

'Sure.' I looked at my watch. One o'clock. Luis Queen would be on his corner. 'New game plan,' I said to Lula. 'Let's go get Luis, and then I'll do my phone work from home.'

Luis Queen is a slim, five-foot-four-inch Hispanic sweetie pie. He turns tricks for a living and doesn't discriminate between male and female. I've been told he'll do *anything,* and I prefer not to think about that too much. He works the corner across from the train station. The police have pretty much cleaned that area out, except for Luis Queen. Luis refuses to leave. Which is why he got picked up for soliciting.

Luis was wearing a pristine white tank top today, the better to show the muscle definition in his arms and his freshly shaved chest. He was in tight jeans, trimmed out in a wide belt decorated with rhinestones. And he was strutting his stuff in his trademark black lizard-skin cowboy boots.

Lula pulled to the curb, and I rolled my window down to talk to him.

'Look who's here,' Luis said, big smile. 'My favorite bounty hunters. You girls need something from Luis? I got a few minutes for you. You need to get relaxed?'

'Tempting,' I said, 'but I had other plans for you. You missed your court date. You need to rebond. Get in the car, and we'll give you a ride.'

'Oh man,' Luis said. 'You gonna ruin my business day. This is my housewife time. They come for a little tickle from Luis before the kiddies get out of school.'

'Are you going to make me come out there and get you?'

'You think you could take me?' Luis said, still smiling. 'Bring it on, momma. I do Pilates. I'm toned perfection.'

'I've got two inches and ten pounds on you. And if I

have Lula get out of the car you'll be nothing but a grease spot on the pavement.'

Luis did a frustrated arm flap and slid into the back seat. 'I don't know why you bust my balls. I'm just out here making a living.'

'You need a new corner.'

'I like this corner. It got sunshine.'

'It's also got cops.'

'I know, but I can't move until I tell all my regulars.'

'You need a mailing list,' Lula said, heading for the courthouse. 'You should get a Web site.'

Luis opened the Pleasure Treasures bag on the back seat. 'Looks like you ladies been shopping. Whoa, baby, that's a monster. I think I'm blushing.'

'You can drop me at the office,' I told Lula. 'Then you can pick Connie up and take her to the courthouse with you and Luis, so she can get him released again.'

Fifteen minutes later I swapped seats with Connie.

'Don't forget your toys,' Luis said, handing me the bag.

I took the bag, waved Luis and Connie and Lula away and crossed the street to the SUV. The window slid down, and Carmen looked out at me.

I decided to try friendly. 'How's it going?'

Carmen didn't say anything.

'Can I get you something? Lunch? Water?'

Nothing.

'I'd really like to ask you a few questions. I don't think—'

The gun came up.

'Okay then,' I said. 'Good talk.'

I crossed the street, angled into the Mini, cranked it over, and eased into traffic. I drove two blocks on Hamilton and turned into the Burg at the hospital with Carmen close on my bumper.

I've had occasion to lose people, and I had a route that worked. I wound through the Burg, took Chambers to Liberty and returned to the Burg. Between traffic and lights and the back alleys of the Burg I was always able to lose the faint of heart. And I lost Carmen. Probably she'd eventually go to my apartment building, but I thought *eventually* was better than *now*.

Four

I had the phone beside me while I worked at the dining room table. I was prioritizing the skips, making calls to check on addresses and employment histories, trying to determine who was where. And I was hoping for a call from Ranger. The call that finally came in was from my grandmother.

'Big news,' she said. 'The funeral parlor is having a viewing tonight. It's the first viewing with the new owners. Catherine Machenko is getting laid out. Dolly did her hair, and she gave me all the dirt. She said the new owners are from Jersey City. Never owned a funeral parlor before. Fresh out of mortuary school. Dolly said they were a nice young gay couple. Dave and Scooter. Dave is the mortician, and Scooter makes the cookies for the viewings. Isn't that something?'

Some communities have country clubs, some have senior centers, some have shopping malls and movie theaters. The Burg has two funeral parlors. Only

Thursday night bingo occasionally draws a bigger crowd than a well-run viewing in the Burg.

'I tell you, those homosexuals are all over the place,' Grandma said. 'And they get all the good jobs, too. They get to be cowboys and morticians. I never wanted to be a homosexual, but I *always* wanted to be a cowboy. What do you suppose it's like to be a homosexual? Do you think their privates look different?'

'*All* privates look different,' I told her.

'I haven't seen too many. Mostly your grandfather's . . . and that wasn't a real pretty sight. I wouldn't mind seeing some others. I'd like to see some minority privates and maybe some blue ones. I was listening to one of them late-night radio shows and they were talking about blue balls. I thought that sounded colorful. I wouldn't mind seeing some blue balls.'

My mother groaned in the background.

'Hold on, dear,' Grandma Mazur said. 'Your mother wants to talk to you.'

'I'll do your laundry if you take your grandmother to the viewing,' my mother said. 'And I'll iron it if you make sure she doesn't get into trouble. If it's closed casket, I don't want her trying to get it open.'

Grandma thinks if she made an effort to come out to a viewing the least they can do is let her take a look at the dead guy. I guess I understand her point of view, but it makes for a scene when the lid is nailed down.

'That's asking a lot,' I said to my mother. 'I'll give her a ride, but I can't guarantee no trouble.'

'Please,' my mother said. 'I'm begging you.'

Carmen was in my lot when I exited the building. She was parked one space over from my Mini, and her windows were down to allow air into the car.

I waved when I walked past. 'I'm going to pick up my grandmother,' I said. 'I'm taking her to a viewing on Hamilton. Then I'll take her home and probably stop in to see Morelli.'

Carmen didn't say anything. She was wearing mirrored lenses, and she wasn't smiling. She followed me out of the lot, into the Burg, and she parked half a block down while I went in to get Grandma.

Grandma was at the door when I arrived. Her grey hair was tightly curled. Her face was powdered. Her nails were newly manicured and matched her red lipstick. She was wearing a navy dress and low-heeled patent leather pumps. She was ready to go.

'Isn't this exciting,' Grandma said. 'A new funeral director! Catherine is lucky to be his first. There'll be a real crowd there tonight.'

My mother was in the foyer with my grandmother. 'Try to behave yourself,' she said to my grandmother. 'Constantine had years of experience. He knew how to manage all the little disasters that happen when people get together. These two young men are brand new at this.'

For as long as I can remember, Constantine Stiva owned the funeral parlor. He was a pillar of the community and the funeral director of choice for the Burg bereaved. As it turned out, he was also a little insane and had a homicidal past, and he's now spending his remaining years in maximum security at Rahway prison.

I've heard rumors that Con prefers prison life to seeing Grandma Mazur walk through his front door, but I'm not sure they're true.

My father was in the living room watching television. His eyes never left the screen, but he mumbled something that sounded like 'poor unsuspecting bastard funeral director'.

My father used to keep an old army-issue .45 in the house as protection against intruders. When Grandma Mazur moved in, my mother quietly got rid of the .45, fearing someday my father would lose patience and blow Grandma away. If it had been me, I would have also gotten rid of sharp knives. Personally, I think Grandma Mazur is a hoot. But then, I don't have to live with her.

'We'll be fine,' I said to my mother. 'Don't worry.'

My mother made the sign of the cross and bit into her lower lip.

I drove the short distance to the funeral parlor and

dropped Grandma in front of the building. 'I'll find a parking place and meet you in there,' I said.

Grandma tottered up the stairs to the big wide front porch, and I motored slowly down the street, followed by Carmen. I parked one block north, Carmen chugged past me, hooked a U-turn, and parked across the street.

I was in no rush to get back to the funeral parlor, so I called Ranger again. 'Hi,' I said to his answering service, 'it's me. Things are looking up. Your wife is tailing me, but she hasn't shot at me yet today, so that's a good thing, right? And you need to answer your damn phone calls.'

I cracked my knuckles and looked at my watch. I hated viewings. I hated the cloying smell of too many flowers. I hated the small talk I'd be forced to make. I hated the inevitable dead person. Maybe I could procrastinate with another phone call.

I called Morelli and told him I might be stopping around after the viewing. He said he'd take a nap in anticipation. That didn't take up nearly enough time so I called my best friend, Mary Lou.

'What?' she yelled into the phone. 'I can't hear you. I'm putting the kids to bed.'

Bedlam in the background.

'I'll call some other time,' I said.

I disconnected Mary Lou and called my sister Valerie. 'I'm feeding the baby,' she said. 'Is it important?'

'Just checking in,' I said. 'Nothing that can't wait.'

Since I couldn't think of anyone else to call, I left the comfort of my Mini and trudged off to the funeral parlor.

I worked my way through the crush of people to slumber room number one where Catherine Machenko was laid to rest. Grandma was close to the casket, not wanting to miss any of the action. She was with Catherine Machenko's sisters and two young men dressed in black.

'This is the new funeral director,' Grandma said to me. 'Dave Nelson. And this is his partner Scooter.'

Dave looked like Paul Bunyan in a suit. He was huge. Dark hair, slightly receding. Head insignificant on his tree-trunk neck. Barrel-chested. Thighs bulging against his pants fabric.

'Dave used to be a wrestler,' Grandma said.

No shit.

Scooter and Dave were yin and yang. Scooter was average height, slight build, blond hair nicely cut, pale blue eyes. Very Norwegian. Or maybe German. Definitely Nordic. I was guessing his suit was Armani and probably his tie cost more than my car.

They were wearing wedding bands. And when they looked at each other you knew they liked being together. I was a little jealous. Again. But in an entirely different way. I wondered if I ever looked like that when I was with Morelli.

Lucky for Dave and Scooter, the Burg wouldn't care about their sexual orientation as long as the cookies were good and they had some expertise at plugging the occasional bullet hole.

Both Dave and Scooter were beaming, proud of their first viewing, flushed with the success of the party. Very different from the calm, cool solicitous demeanor always displayed by Constantine Stiva.

'I just heard they have one of those alerts out here in Trenton for a kidnapping,' Grandma said to me. 'A little girl was kidnapped in Florida, and they think she might be here in Trenton, because she was kidnapped by her father, and her father lives here. I bet you could find her.'

'The little girl's name is Julie Martine,' Scooter said. 'It's all over the television. She's ten years old. And they think she's with her birth father, Carlos Manoso.'

My heart stuttered in my chest, and for a moment there was no air around me. Ranger's legal name is Ricardo Carlos Manoso, but he never uses the Ricardo.

'What else did they say on television?' I asked him.

'That was mostly it. They showed a picture of the man from when he was in the army. Special Forces. And they showed a picture of the little girl.'

I looked at my watch. 'We can't stay much longer,' I said to Grandma. 'I promised Joe I'd come over tonight.'

'That works perfectly for me,' Grandma said. 'I've seen everything, and there's a television show on in a half-hour that I like to watch. It's a rerun of the *Crocodile Hunter*. That crocodile guy is a real cutie in those little shorts.'

'Make sure you get a cookie before you leave,' Scooter said. 'I baked them myself. Chocolate chip and oatmeal raisin.'

We hit the cookie table on the way out.

'Look at this,' Grandma said, taking two cookies, 'Scooter put them on doilies and everything. Such a nice young man. You can entrust your loved one to a funeral parlor that takes the time to use doilies.'

I dropped Grandma off, and I went home to my apartment. I said hello to Rex, hung my bag and jacket on a hook in the hall, and went straight to my computer. I surfed a couple news sites and then went to the site for missing children. The little girl was pretty with an infectious smile. She had brown hair pulled into a ponytail and big brown eyes. She lived with her mom and stepdad in Miami. She was picked up on her way home from school and not seen since. She was with two girlfriends who said she got into a car with a man police believe to be her birth father. The description of the man that the girls gave to the police fit Ranger. And the photo shown was of Ranger.

I shut the computer down and called Morelli. 'Have you gotten the missing child alert?' I asked him.

'Oswald just called me.'

'Do you know anything I don't know?'

'Oswald got all his information from television.'

'What do you think?'

'Ranger's not my favorite person. I think his wiring isn't code. And it wouldn't surprise me to hear he's kidnapped his daughter, but I'd be very surprised if he didn't have a good reason. Are you still planning on coming over?'

'I don't know. I'm really thrown by this. Carmen showing up, and now the little girl getting kidnapped.'

'I have a cake,' Morelli said. 'Got it just for you.'

'You don't!'

'Only one way to find out.'

'Okay, I'll be there in ten minutes.'

I hung up and called Tank.

'What's going on?' I asked him.

'Business as usual.'

'What's going on with Ranger?'

'He's off-line.'

'And?'

'Keep the faith.'

I disconnected and made a mental note not to call Tank unless I was bleeding profusely, and he was the only other person on earth.

Five

Morelli was slow to kill the alarm on his clock radio.

'You purposely let that ring, so I'd wake up,' I said to him.

'I didn't want you to miss anything.'

'Such as . . . oh God, give me a break. What time is it? It's still dark out.'

'There's this thing that happens when I wake up next to you,' Morelli said. 'It's very uncomfortable . . . in a good way.'

'What about the cake you promised?'

'It's baking.'

That was obvious.

'Can't you go back to sleep and pick this up in an hour or two?' I asked Morelli.

'I have to be at my desk in an hour or two. And my body doesn't work like that. Once the cake's in the oven, it keeps baking until it's done.'

'I'm tired. Maybe this is one of those times when you can have your cake and eat it too. You know, all by yourself.'

'Do you want to watch?'

'No! I want to sleep.'

Morelli nibbled on my neck, and his hand snaked around to my breast. 'Okay,' he said with his voice all soft and old-whiskey smooth. 'Go back to sleep. We'll do this some other time.'

I blew out a sigh. 'What kind of cake is it?' I asked. 'Coffee cake? Birthday cake?'

We were lying spoon fashion, and I could feel Morelli laughing behind me.

'It's a cannoli,' he said.

'Oh boy,' Lula said when I swung into the office. 'Only one thing puts *that* kind of smile on your face.'

'I had cake for breakfast.'

'Must have been damn good cake.'

Melvin Pickle was working at filing. 'I can't eat cake for breakfast,' he said. 'It's bad for my blood sugar level.'

'She didn't mean *cake* cake,' Lula said. 'That was one of them double entendre things. Boy, you're awful slow on the pickup for a pervert.'

'Did you hear about Ranger?' I asked Connie and Lula.

'It came up on my news service this morning,' Connie said.

'What did the service say? Have they found him or his daughter?'

'No. It just said she was picked up after school by a man who met Ranger's description and not seen since. I tried paging him but he's not answering.'

I glanced out the front window. 'I see Carmen is back at the curb.'

'This just gets weirder and weirder,' Lula said. 'This is like *Twilight Zone* shit.'

Connie gave me a clipboard and then gave one to Lula. 'I don't have time to think about it this morning. We have people coming in for the BEA job. I cut the group of applicants in half by eliminating everyone with a criminal record,' she said. 'The rest have been divided into three groups. I'm calling those groups Best, Okay, and God Help Us. Hopefully, we'll find someone before we get to God Help Us. The Best group is coming in this morning. We're going to give everyone a fifteen-minute interview, so this shouldn't take all day. I know you're anxious to go out there and round up some bad guys.'

'Yeah, I can't wait,' Lula said. 'I need to look like an idiot at least twice a day to keep myself humble.'

My clipboard had seven bios on it. Connie had run simple background checks on today's group and gotten the basics. First up was George Panko. He was scheduled for a nine o'clock interview. At nine-fifteen we ripped his sheet off the clipboard.

'Guess he changed his mind,' Lula said. 'Probably decided to get a good job . . . like feeding lions or cleaning kennel cages.'

Becky Willard strolled in at nine-twenty-five. 'I figured you'd be running late,' she said. 'So I stopped for a latte, and the moron behind the counter took *so* long. And then he didn't put the right kind of milk in it. I asked for a skim milk latte, and I *know* he gave me regular milk. I mean, do I look stupid? So he had to make it over. And he took *so* long again.' She looked around. 'This office is *so* dreary. Would I have to spend much time here? And I get a company car, right? I mean, you don't expect me to use my own car to apprehend fugitives, do you?'

When Willard left, Connie ripped Willard's sheet off the clipboard. 'Two down.'

The nine-thirty interview was precisely on time. He was dressed in head-to-toe black leather and had a six-shooter strapped to his leg.

'That gun looks vintage,' Lula said. 'Is it real?'

'You bet your ass,' he said. And he pulled the gun, twirled it around on his finger, and shot a hole in the front panel of Connie's desk. 'Oops,' he said. 'Sorry about that. Slipsies.'

Another sheet got ripped off the board. Four to go.

Anton Rudder was next in the hot seat. 'I can do this job,' he said. 'I'll go out there and get those motherfuckers. They won't even know what hit them. I'll have their law-breakin' ass in the trunk of my car . . .'

'Actually, we almost never transport someone in the trunk,' I said.

'Yeah, but that's because you're pussy,' Anton said. 'This whole office is pussy. I figure that's why I got the callback. You need a real man here.'

'If we needed a real man we wouldn't have called your runt ass,' Lula said.

'No offense,' Anton said. 'I like pussy. I especially like fat black pussy. But it's not like pussy can do the same job a man can do. Everybody knows that. That's a scientific fact.'

Lula was on her feet, rooting through her shoulder bag. 'Excuse me? Did you just imply I was fat? Is that what I heard?'

'Probably you should leave before Lula finds her gun,' I said to Anton.

Lula had her head in her bag. 'It's in here somewhere.'

Anton hustled out the door, and Connie ripped his sheet off her clipboard.

Three interviews left, and I was having a hard time concentrating. I was in a state over Ranger.

Martin Dorn arrived for his interview looking relatively normal with the exception of a mustache drawn onto his upper lip with a black Magic Marker.

'It's always been my lifelong dream to be a bounty

hunter,' Dorn said. 'I watch all the television shows. And I went to bounty hunter school on the Internet. You could ask me anything about being a bounty hunter, and I bet I know the answer.'

'That's promising,' Connie said. 'Do you know you have a Magic Marker mustache on your upper lip?'

'I tried to grow a real one, but I didn't have any luck at it,' he said. 'I'm good with a Magic Marker. I used one to draw a lightening bolt on my penis. Would you like to see it?'

Melvin Pickle was filing reports on the other side of the bank of cabinets. He popped his head up to take a look at Dorn, and Connie ripped Dorn's sheet off her clipboard.

The sixth applicant was a no-show.

The seventh was Brendan Yalenowski.

'I need to know my rights,' Brendan said. 'Am I allowed to shoot people? Suppose I shot someone while I was in the act of making an apprehension. Only suppose that person wasn't actually the guy I was looking for. Suppose it was someone who looked a little like the guy. And suppose he wasn't armed. And this is just theoretical, but suppose it turned out that I knew him and owed him money . . .'

Connie slouched in her seat when Brendan left. 'Is it too early in the day to start drinking?'

'This was a big bust,' Lula said. 'Who'd think this would be so hard? It's not like we were gonna be picky. I mean, look what you got doing this job, a former 'ho and someone who used to sell cheap ladies' panties.'

'I was a buyer,' I said. 'The job wasn't *that* bad.'

'Yeah, but you got fired.'

'Laid off. It wasn't my fault.'

Vinnie's office door was closed. 'Where's Vinnie?' I asked Connie. 'I haven't seen him all week.'

'He's in Biloxi. Bail bonds conference. And I hate to bring this up, but you need to bring in a couple of the high bonds. We need Lonnie Johnson and Leon James.'

'I made some phone calls last night, and I couldn't get anything on Johnson. Someone a lot scarier than I am is after him, and he's on the run. I'll try Leon James today.'

'I'll go with you,' Lula said. 'Only I gotta be careful because I just got my nails done, and I don't want to ruin them. This is my big night. I'm making my debut with the What tonight. We're gonna be at that bar on Third Street. The Hole.'

'That's a pretty rough bar. I didn't know they had bands,' I said to Lula.

'We're the first. They're trying something new. They said they wanted to expand their clientele.'

'I hope Sally isn't going in drag to that bar.'

'He's got a dress that's like mine only his is in red on account of he don't look good in gold. People be disappointed if Sally wasn't in drag. That's his thing. He's famous for his accessorizing.'

Salvatore Sweet is a good friend in a constant state of reinvention. He's played lead guitar with a bunch of bands. The Funky Butts, the Pitts, Beggar Boys, and Howling Dogs. When I met him he was playing in drag for the first time with the Lovelies, and that was where he hit the jackpot. Actually, it was just a local jackpot, but it was more success than he'd ever seen. When the band broke up Sally continued to perform in drag. He's currently driving a school bus days and playing guitar nights. His bands are always a collection of misfits. Good musicians most of the time who for one reason or another don't fit in anywhere else. In a bizarre way, Lula would be a perfect addition.

'If he goes in drag to the Hole he's going to be accessorizing in the hospital,' Connie said.

'Something to think about,' Lula said.

I glanced out the front window at the SUV. 'Does she ever get out?' I asked Connie. 'Just to stretch? Walk around?'

'I haven't seen her out since that first time when she came into the office looking for you.'

'I have a sick stomach over this Ranger thing,' I told Connie. 'I think we should get some background on Julie Martine's mother and stepfather. And maybe you could poke around in Arlington. I'd like to know more about Ranger's business there.'

Ten minutes later, we were in Lula's car, on the way to

Leon James's last known address, and I was on the phone with Morelli.

'I need some help,' I told him. 'I'd like to know the captures Ranger made through his Virginia office. And it would be helpful if I could get a photograph of the Virginia Ranger.'

'The captures I should be able to get for you. The photo will only happen if he has a mug shot or a Virginia driver's license.'

'Good enough. And remember, it's Friday, and we're expected for dinner at my parents' house.'

'I'll be there,' Morelli said.

Lula parked in front of a two-story brick row house in a neighborhood adjacent to the Burg. 'Here it is,' she said. 'This is the address on the file.'

Leon James had listed the house as his residence and had also used it to secure the bond. He was a penny-ante hitman, selling his services to anyone with a grudge. Usually evidence is scarce against him. And witnesses have been known to recant stories and occasionally to disappear. He was wanted for arson and attempted murder. He was a third-time offender, and this was going to be an ugly capture.

'How are we going to do this?' Lula wanted to know. 'This isn't a nice guy. He kills people and burns down houses.'

'I think we'll have to be tricky.'

'Yeah, tricky. I like the sound of that.'

'First thing, we need to get him out of his house and into someplace public. Then we need to distract him until we can get him cuffed.'

'Okay,' Lula said. 'I'm with you.'

'That's it. That's all I've got.'

'That's not much,' Lula said.

'Suppose one of us calls him and says she wants to hire him to do a job. And then she could set up a meeting.'

'Good thinking. That's going to be you doing the calling, right? You're a way better liar than I am.'

I cut my eyes to Lula. 'You're an *excellent* liar.'

'Maybe, but I gotta be saving myself for tonight. I can't afford to use my voice too much.'

'That is so lame,' I said to Lula.

'It's the best I could come up with.'

I punched Leon's number into my cell phone. 'I'd like to speak to Leon James,' I said to the guy who answered.

'Speaking.'

'I think I might need some help in solving a problem.'

'Un hunh.'

'You were recommended.'

'Oh yeah. Who recommended me?'

'Butchy.'

'I don't know any Butchy.'

'Well, he knows you. And he recommended you.'

'What sort of problem we talking about?'

'I don't want to say on the phone.'

'That sounds promising already,' James said.

'I was hoping we could meet somewhere. I need to solve this problem fast.'

'It'll cost you.'

'I don't care. Just solve my friggin' problem, okay?'

I'd agreed to meet Leon James in a small park in the Burg. The park wasn't much more than a patch of grass half a block in size. It had a couple trees and a couple benches and that was it. Once in a while an old guy would sit on a bench and soak up sun. And once in a while a couple kids would sit on a bench and smoke some weed. And once in a while someone would walk his dog in the park.

Lula and I had driven to Morelli's house and commandeered Bob. The plan was that I'd meet Leon James at the bench, and while we were talking, Lula would mosey by with Bob. Then when James was distracted, one of us would zap him with a stun gun.

I dropped Lula and Bob off on a side street, turned a corner, and parked not far from the bench. I walked to the bench and sat down with my purse in my lap. After five minutes a car pulled up behind Lula's Firebird, and James got out. He looked around, straightened his jacket, and walked toward me. It was eighty degrees out, and there was only one reason to be wearing a jacket.

James was five-foot-nine and stocky. The fact that he'd been caught numerous times for arson put him in the not-too-bright category. Arson is a respected profession among certain subcultures in Jersey, and the good ones don't get caught. The good ones channel lightning and mysterious acts of spontaneous combustion.

I fought stage fright as I watched James cut across the grass. My heart was racing, and I could feel panic sticking in my throat. Deep breath, I told myself. Be calm. Be cool.

'You looking for a problem solver?' James said, coming up to the bench.

'I might be.'

He sat down. 'What kind of problem you got?'

'A cheating husband.'

'And?'

'I'm told it would be cheaper to pay you to take care of the bastard than it would be to divorce him and lose half of everything.'

'Works for me.'

James was turned toward me, and I could see Lula and Bob coming up behind him. Bob was straining at the leash, wanting to run, but with Lula at the other end it was like pulling a refrigerator.

'Are you interested, or what?'

'Sure. I'm a professional. I don't need to know *why*. I just need to know you'll pay.'

'Good. Then it's settled. We just have to agree on a price.'

'I don't negotiate price. My price is fixed. Ten big ones. Five now and five when the job is completed.'

'Nobody told me that part,' I said. 'I don't have a lot of money on me.'

'Then you have a problem.'

'Do you take credit cards?'

'Lady, I'm not the Gap.'

'How about a check?'

'How about cash,' he said.

'Wait a minute, let me think. I just have to go to the bank. Can you wait while I go to the bank?'

'Sorry, no can do. I have a visibility problem.'

Lula was about twenty feet away, and Bob was chugging like a freight train, pulling against his collar, trying to get to me.

James turned to see what was making all that noise behind him, I slipped the stun gun out of my bag, pushed the button, and the little *on* light didn't go on.

James turned back to me and saw the stun gun. 'What the fuck?'

I looked at Lula in utter panic.

Lula let go of Bob's leash. Bob bounded over and took a flying leap for me, knocking me off the bench. James reached for his gun. And Lula roundhoused James on the side of the head with her purse. I still had the stun gun in my hand and suddenly the light blinked on. I shoved Bob out of the way, scrambled to grabbing distance of James, and caught him in the ankle with the prongs of the stun gun. James squeaked, slumped over, and slid to the ground.

I flopped over and lay spread-eagle on my back, hand to my heart for a moment. I was breathing hard, and I was leaking nervous fear, sweating in places I didn't think had sweat glands.

'What the heck was that?' Lula wanted to know. 'You had a expression on your face like you just had an irritable bowel experience.'

I looked at the stun gun. The light was off again. 'Low battery,' I said.

'Don't you hate when that happens?'

'What have you got in your purse? It sounded like you hit him with a frying pan.'

'I got my gun in there. And I got a couple rolls of quarters for meters. And I got a Maglite. And a stun gun. And cuffs.' She pulled the cuffs out and handed them to me. 'I guess you should cuff him, except it seems like a shame to ruin Bob's fun.'

Bob was jumping around on James, trying to get him to play. He'd snuffle James, and then he'd jump up and land on James with all four feet and do a growly thing, and then he'd jump around some more.

'Gonna be hard to explain all those muddy Bob-sized

footprints on him,' Lula said. 'Gonna be even harder to explain all the dog slobber on his crotch.'

I dragged Bob off, and I cuffed James behind his back and stood. 'Do you have any shackles?'

'I got shackles in the trunk,' Lula said. 'You babysit, and I'll go get them.'

James moaned and sucked in some air and squinted up at me. 'Fuck. What happened?'

'Bond enforcement,' I said. 'Lula hit you with her purse.'

He sat up and looked at his slacks.

'What's all over my pants? Why are my pants wet?'

'Lula fell in love,' I told him. I thought that would put him in a better mood than telling him it was Bob slime.

Six

'Are we hot, or what?' Lula said. 'We captured Leon James.'

We'd done a drive-through at Cluck-in-a-Bucket to celebrate our success, and then we'd processed James, picked up our body receipt, and now we were back in the office.

Connie was smiling. 'The morning was a downer, but the rest of the day was good. That was a big bond. And it turns out Melvin Pickle is a filing demon.'

Bob was sitting on my foot, pressing his body against my leg. He'd gone for a walk, eaten two pieces of chicken, slurped up a bowl of water, and now he was ready to nap.

'I'm taking Bob home,' I told Connie. 'If any information comes in on Ranger give me a call on my cell.'

'Yeah, and I'm going home too,' Lula said. 'I gotta get ready for tonight.'

'We have another batch of job applicants coming in tomorrow,' Connie said. 'Starting at nine o'clock.'

I loaded Bob into the back seat of the Mini and rolled the window down so he could stick his head out. The car was wall-to-wall dog, but Bob looked happy on the cushy leather.

I turned the engine over and moved into the stream of traffic with my eyes on Carmen, expecting her to follow. When I stopped for the light at the corner, the SUV was still at the curb, no sign of life. Carmen had probably fallen asleep at the wheel. Or maybe she'd gone for a walk. Or maybe she was in a second car, using the SUV as a decoy. I wound through the Burg watching my rearview mirror for a tail. No tail appeared, so I drove to Morelli's.

I deposited Bob in the house, locked up, and got back into the Mini. I motored the short distance to my apartment, parked, and rode the elevator with Mrs Bestler.

'How was your day, dear?' she asked, pressing the button for the second floor.

'Very good. And yours?'

'My day was excellent. I visited the chiropodist this morning. That's always exciting.' The doors opened, and Mrs Bestler sang out, 'Second floor, ladies lounge.'

Here's the thing about my apartment: no matter how chaotic my day has been, my apartment is usually calm and silent. There was a time when my answering machine would be filled with messages when I came home, but my answering machine broke and was never replaced, so now everyone calls my cell. Rex is happy about this, since no one disturbs him while he's sleeping. I don't cook, so the kitchen is never messy. My furnishings are sparse, since the clutter went up in flames with the fire. And the bathroom doesn't count. The bathroom is always a wreck.

I filled Rex's food dish with hamster crunchies, a peanut, a green bean, and a piece of pretzel. I gave him fresh water. I said, 'Hello.'

Rex backed out of his soup can, stuffed the green bean and pretzel into his cheek, and rushed back into his can.

It was four o'clock, and I had to be at my parents' house at six. I turned my computer on and surfed the net for news of Ranger. I went to the site for missing children and I visited some of the news sites. No information beyond what was initially released.

Vinnie belongs to PBUS. Professional Bail Agents of the United States. PBUS shares information and loosely links agencies nationwide. A couple months ago a Virginia agency needed help locating a guy who'd skipped out of their area and was believed to be in Trenton. I found the guy and held him until the agency could get someone to Trenton to take possession. I had a business card from John Nash, the agent who collected the FTA, and I thought he might be willing to do me a favor.

I emailed Nash and asked if he knew anything about Ranger. Bail bonds is a small world. Agents know when new competition pops up in their neighborhood.

I ran through my spam box and deleted sixty-four ads

for penis enhancement, seventeen ads for animal porn sites, and two ads for cheap credit.

Beautification was next on my list. I jumped into the shower, did what I could to improve on nature by way of makeup and hair gel, got dressed in my best jeans and sexy little shirt, and took off for my parents' house.

Morelli arrived a beat after I did.

'Everyone to the table,' my mother said. 'Stephanie, you get the mashed potatoes from the kitchen.'

Dinner in my parents' house happens precisely at six o'clock. Five minutes late, and it could all be ruined. Burned pot roast, cold potatoes, overcooked green beans. A disaster of biblical proportions.

My father was first to sit. He had his fork in hand and his attention focused on the kitchen door, waiting for my mother to emerge with the pot roast. Grandma Mazur set the beans on the table and took her place across from Morelli and me. My mother followed with the meat, and we all dug in.

If a man attended enough pot roast dinners in the presence of a single woman and her family, it was a marriage in the eyes of the Burg, if not God. And Morelli was dangerously close to marriage by pot roast. There's a part of me that likes the comfortable intimacy between Morelli and me at the table. I like the way his knee snuggles against mine. And I like the way he accepts my family. And I like the way he looks with a glass of red wine in his hand, relaxed and confident, his dark eyes not missing anything. In fact, there isn't a lot *not* to like about Morelli. So the hesitancy I have to commit is confusing. I suppose it has something to do with the fact that I'm horribly attracted to Ranger. Not that I would ever commit to Ranger. Ranger is an accident waiting to happen. Still, the heat is there.

'I was talking to Merle Greber today,' Grandma Mazar said. 'She lives two houses down from Mary Lee Truk, and she said Mary Lee's feeling much better. I guess she's got the hot flashes under control. And the stitches came out on her husband's behind from where she stabbed him, and word is he's thinking about dropping the charges against her and moving back home. Merle said, only problem now is it looks like Mary Lee's putting on weight.'

The unfortunate result of acquiring happiness at the bakery.

'Anyone hear anything about that little girl who was kidnapped?' Grandma asked.

'She's still missing,' I said.

'People are saying Ranger took her. I hope for her sake that's true, because he wouldn't hurt her. It's still a terrible thing.'

We all lapsed into silence after that. Not that silence was abnormal at my parents' table. We tended not to multitask body functions. When we sat down to eat, we got to it.

* * *

'Oh man, you're kidding,' Morelli said. 'You want me to do what?'

It was eight-thirty, and we were walking Bob around Morelli's neighborhood, so Bob could do one last tinkle.

'I want you to go to the Hole with me. Lula's singing there tonight, and I feel like I should be supportive. And I thought it wouldn't hurt to have an armed cop in the room.'

'Lula can't sing. I've heard her sing. She's tone-deaf.'

'Yeah, but she looks good in her dress.' As long as she doesn't bend over. 'And she's singing with Sally Sweet and his band. None of them can sing. They just play loud enough to drown themselves out.'

'I had plans for tonight,' Morelli said.

'Would those be the same plans you had for last night?'

'The basic plan is the same, but I have a few variations I thought I'd throw in.'

'Look on the positive side. You could try to get me liquored up at the Hole, and I might come up with some of my own variations. I'm an animal when I'm liquored up.'

Morelli smiled at me. 'Good point.'

'Did you have any luck getting information for me on Ranger?'

'No photo. He doesn't have a Virginia driver's license. And no captures on record. Sorry.'

'That's okay. I suspected there wouldn't be anything, but I thought it was worth a try.'

'What about the woman? Have you talked to her?' Morelli asked.

'Carmen? I can hear her release the safety on her Glock when I get within two feet of her.'

'Do you want me to roust her?'

'No. At least this way I know where to find her. And as long as there's distance between us, I don't think she's dangerous. She's not exactly a sharpshooter.'

We took Bob back to the house, locked up, and headed off in Morelli's SUV. Morelli used to have a truck, but he traded it in so Bob could ride with him and be more comfy in bad weather.

The Hole was on Third, in an area top-loaded with bars and pawnshops and adult video stores. Sandwiched between the bottom-feeder businesses were bedraggled drug stores, convenience stores, rooming houses, and fast-food franchises.

Morelli drove around three blocks, looking for a parking space, finding none. He turned into the alley behind the Hole and found a space reserved for employees.

'It's good to be a cop,' I said to him.

'Sometimes.'

We entered through the back door, skirted around the kitchen, walked past the restrooms, and stepped into a large room, packed with people. The stagnant air was saturated with kitchen grease and smelled like beer and booze and weed. There was a small stage at one end. The stage was set with amps and standup mics. A mahogany bar stretched the length of one wall, and everywhere else there were round tables crammed with chairs. There was at least one person sitting in every chair. The noise level was set at *roar*. Most of the women were in tube tops and shorts. The men wore jeans and muscle shirts, chains and tattoos. I was still in my jeans and little T-shirt. Morelli was wearing a gun on his ankle and at his back, both covered by clothes.

Morelli snagged a waitress by the strap on her tank top, gave her a twenty, and ordered two Coronas.

'You're disturbingly good at this,' I said to Morelli.

'I had a wild youth.'

That was an understatement. Morelli had been a womanizer and a bar brawler of the first magnitude. I slipped my hand into his, and we smiled at each other, and it was one of those moments of understanding that happens between people with a long history together.

I chugged down a cold Corona and stood close to Morelli. The lights blinked, and the What appeared onstage. There was a guy on drums, a guy on keyboard, and a guy on bass. They set up and rapped out a fanfare. No one on the floor paid any attention. And then Lula and Sally came out and everyone turned and gaped.

Lula was wearing the gold dress and spike-heeled

shoes, and Sally was wearing his guitar, dangly red sparkly earrings, four-inch red sequined heels with two-inch platform soles, and a red-sequined thong. He'd foregone his usual platinum Marilyn Monroe wig and was au naturel in his shoulder-length, kinky curled black hair. His big, gangly, hairy body ambled up to the mic, and he gave a loud strum on the guitar that brought the house down.

'I usually wear a dress,' Sally said. 'But people told me it might not go over here, so I wore this thong instead. What do you think?'

Everyone whistled and hooted. Morelli had his arm around me and a grin on his face. I was smiling too, but I was afraid the good mood of the audience wasn't going to last. It looked to me like this was a crowd with a short attention span.

Sally Sweet has been punk, funk, rock, country western, and everything in between. This band looked to me like a seventies cover band since the first song was 'Love Machine'.

Lula had a handheld mic and was doing a routine somewhere between Tina Turner and a Baptist revival meeting. It wasn't bad, but every time she raised her arms the skimpy gold dress would hike up, and she'd have to tug it back down over her ass. Halfway through the song Lula lost her place and gave up on the lyrics and started singing, 'Love machine, la la la la love machine.' Not that it mattered. The entire audience was mesmerized by the fleeting glimpses of Lula's size XXX large leopard thong.

When the song ended, someone yelled out that he wanted to hear 'Love Shack'.

'No way,' came back from the other side of the room. '"Disco Inferno".'

'"Disco Inferno" is gay,' the first guy yelled. 'Only pussies like "Disco Inferno".'

'Pussy this,' the Disco Inferno guy said. And he threw a beer bottle at the Love Shack guy.

'You better stop that,' Lula said to the Disco guy. 'That's rude behavior.'

An onion ring came sailing out of the audience, hit Lula in the head and dropped onto her chest.

'Now I'm getting mad,' Lula said. 'Who did that? I got a big grease spot on my dress now. You're getting my dry cleaning bill.'

'Hey,' someone yelled to Lula, 'show us the rest of those big tits. I want to see your tits.'

'How about you want to see my foot up your ass,' Lula said.

A show-us-your-tits chant went up and a bunch of the women flashed headlights.

The drunk next to me grabbed my shirt and attempted to pull it over my head. 'Show me *your* tits,' he said.

And that was the last thing he said because Morelli shoved his fist into the guy's face.

It pretty much went downhill after that. Beer bottles were flying, and the room looked like a WWE cage match with a frenzied mob smashing furniture, scratching and clawing and punching each other out.

Sally went off the stage with a war whoop, wading into the mess, whacking guys with his guitar, and Lula crawled under a table. Morelli wrapped an arm around my middle, lifted me two inches off the floor, and fought his way toward the hall leading to the restrooms and rear door, laying waste to anyone in his way. He got me outside, and he went back in for Lula. He shoved Lula out the rear door just as the police arrived, front and rear.

Eddie Gazarra was in one of the squad cars angled behind Morelli's SUV. He was a good friend, and he was married to my cousin, Shirley the Whiner. He was with three other cops, and they all had big smiles when they saw Morelli and Lula and me.

'What's going on?' Gazarra wanted to know, working hard not to totally crack up.

'I got hit with an onion ring,' Lula said.

'Anything else?' he asked Morelli.

'Nope, that's about it,' Morelli said, hands loose at his side, knuckles scraped and bleeding, bruise flowering on his right cheekbone. 'Be nice if you'd move your car, so we could get out of here. And when you go inside you might look for a guy in a red thong. He's with us.'

* * *

Morelli was slouched on the couch, holding an ice pack to his bruised cheek, taking in the last minutes of a West Coast ball game.

'It could have been worse,' I said.

'It could have been a *lot* worse. We could have had to listen to another set of songs.'

'We'd probably be sitting in jail right now if you weren't a cop.'

'My being a cop had nothing to do with it. Gazarra would never arrest you. I went along for the ride on this one.'

'You don't talk much about being a cop anymore.'

Morelli tossed the ice pack to the floor. 'I'm working homicide. There's not much I'd want to talk about. I'm up to my armpits in gang-related killings. The only decent part is usually they kill each other.' He clicked the game off. 'This game is boring. I bet we can find more interesting things to look at if we go upstairs.'

The first applicant was already in the office when I arrived. He was wearing chaps, and he had a sawed-off strapped to his back.

'We don't actually dress like bounty hunters in this office,' Connie was explaining to him. 'We find it's . . . too obvious.'

'Yeah, and chaps makes your ass look big,' Lula said. 'You go around looking like that and the fashion police gonna come after you.'

'I always dress like this,' the guy said. 'I ride a Hog.'

'What about the sawed-off?' Connie asked.

'What about it?'

Two more applicants came and went after the guy with the chaps. I cracked my knuckles through both of them, wanting to move on. I had three FTAs targeted for today, plus Caroline Scarzolli was still at large. And Lonnie Johnson was out there, somewhere. And the truth was, I didn't want to find any of these people. I wanted to find Ranger.

When the last applicant walked out the door, Connie wrenched her bottom drawer open, unscrewed a bottle of Jack Daniel's, and chugged some down.

'Okay,' she said. 'I feel better now.'

'I like this job interviewing shit,' Lula said. 'It's a real boost to my self-esteem. Even with my damaged early years, I'm looking good up against these freaks.'

'Where's Pickle?' I asked Connie.

'He's working Monday through Friday. Since we usually only work half-day on Saturday anyway, I gave him weekends off.'

I looked out the front window at the black SUV. It was starting to feel eerie. No one ever saw Carmen. Just the tinted black windows.

'The SUV is still out there,' I said. 'When was the last time anyone saw that SUV move?'

'It was here when I arrived this morning, and I guess it was here when I left last night,' Connie said.

I took a slurp of booze from Connie's bottle. 'I need to take a look at the car.'

I crossed the street, and I knocked on the driver's side window but nothing happened. I looked in through the windshield. Nobody home. Blood everywhere. I turned and slid down the car until I reached pavement. I sat there with my head between my knees until the nausea was under control and the noise subsided in my head. I got to my knees, waited a moment for the fog to clear, and then got to my feet. I walked to the rear of the SUV where the smell of decomposing flesh was strong. I put my face to the glass and squinted through the tinted window. A tarp had been pulled across the cargo area.

I took my cell phone out and called Morelli. 'You might want to get over here,' I said. 'I think I have a body for you.'

Seven

Connie and Lula and I waited across the street in front of the bonds office, while the police did their thing. I was so terrified at what would be found that my fingers were numb, and I could feel tears welling behind my eyes. I suspected Carmen was in the back of the SUV, but it could as easily be Ranger or his little girl, Julie.

Morelli stood to the side watching while a uniform opened the back hatch and slid the tarp aside. Morelli's eyes flicked to the body in the cargo area and then to me. *Carmen,* he mouthed to me.

I wasn't sure what I felt. A mixture of emotion. Horror for Carmen and relief that it wasn't Ranger or the child.

'Did we get information back on Julie's mother and stepfather?' I asked Connie. 'Anything on the Virginia business?'

'I saw reports come in, but I didn't read them.'

We went into the office, and Connie pulled up the

reports. Rachel Martine had no work history. High school graduate. Lived her whole life in Miami. Nothing derogatory in her credit file. Her banking history showed a steady money stream from Ranger. No criminal history. She married Ronald Martine eight years ago. They bought a house shortly after they were married, and they were still at that same address. Ronald Martine was seven years older than his wife. Also a high school graduate. No college, but he had gone to school to repair air-conditioning systems and had been working at his trade for eighteen years. Both seemed to be very stable. There were two other Martine children, a seven-year-old girl and a four-year-old boy. They attended the local Catholic Church. You couldn't get much cleaner than Rachel and Ronald Martine.

Rangemanoso showed up on the Virginia business report. Described as bail enforcement and fugitive apprehension. The business had leased office space in Arlington. The proprietor was Rxyzzlo Xnelos Zzuvemo. In six months of operation it had incurred a long list of delinquent bills.

'I love the way he's coded his name every time it pops up in a data base,' Lula said. 'It's genius.'

'This doesn't sound right,' Connie said. 'Ranger runs a tight business. He pays his bills on time.'

'I saw a TV show on identity theft,' Lula said. 'Maybe someone's posing as Ranger.' I'd actually been thinking the same thing for some time. And the fact that Ranger's name is always in code probably helped to hide the theft.

I dialed Tank. I'd sworn I'd never again dial Tank, but I couldn't help myself. I didn't know what else to do.

'They just found Carmen Manoso dead in her SUV in front of the bonds office,' I told him. 'If Ranger's looking for his body double, there's a good chance he's here in Trenton.'

'Ten four.' And Tank hung up.

'So you don't think Ranger offed Carmen?' Lula asked.

'Ranger wouldn't have left her in front of the bonds office for us to find. Ranger would have made her disappear, never to be found again. Ranger likes to keep things tidy.'

Morelli stuck his head in the office and crooked his finger at me. 'Can I see you outside?'

I left the bonds office, and we stood by the side of the building.

'Her driver's license identifies her as Carmen Manoso,' Morelli said. 'She seems to be the woman you described to me. I didn't think you'd want to see for yourself. She's been dead a while. It's not good. A single bullet in the head.'

'Could it have been self-inflicted?'

'No. Her gun was unfired on the driver's side floor.'

'I have a theory.'

'Oh boy.'

103

I gave Morelli a copy of the Virginia business report. 'I think some nut is posing as Ranger.'

'Identity theft.'

'Yeah, only maybe it's not that simple. Maybe this guy is wacked-out. He got married as Ranger. That's carrying identity theft a little far.'

'You still haven't heard from Ranger?'

'No. I've talked to Tank a couple times, but that's like talking to a wall.'

'What about the kid? Any more theories?'

'I think one of the Rangers took her.'

'And?'

'And I think it's the wrong one. The little girl's parents look solid. And Ranger's been regularly sending child support. I don't think he'd take the girl without telling her mom. A while ago, Ranger mentioned that he had a daughter, but I got the impression it wasn't common knowledge. So either it's someone who was at one time very close to Ranger, or else it's someone close to the little girl or her family.'

'And I want to know this because . . .'

'Because you want to close Carmen's case, and it's possible she was shot by the Un-Ranger.'

'Something I've learned with police work,' Morelli said. 'It's good to have theories, but don't lock yourself into them. In the end, it's facts that count, not theories. Carmen could have been killed by some random maniac.

And Ranger could easily be leading his own double life. No one knows what's in Ranger's head. There are too many times a crime doesn't get solved because the investigator followed an obvious but wrong lead and ignored looking for anything else until it was too late and all other leads were cold.'

'Point taken,' I said.

'Well?' Lula asked when I returned to the office.

'A single bullet to the head,' I told her. 'Not self-inflicted.'

'Right in front of the office,' Lula said. 'Gives me the creeps.'

'I'm feeling stressed,' Connie said. 'This has been a really shitty morning.'

'I bet I got something that'll cheer you up,' Lula said. 'This here specialty shop I know about was open this morning, and I stopped on my way to the office. I got another singing gig tonight, and I needed a new outfit. Everybody wait here, and I'll try it on.'

Five minutes later, Lula swung out of the bathroom and paraded around the bonds office in a one-piece jumpsuit-type thing made out of glaring white vinyl. The bottom was short-shorts that sort of got lost in Lula's ass, and the top was strapless, squishing her boobs up so they bulged out everywhere. The outfit was accessorized with four-inch-spike-heeled white vinyl boots that came to just below her knee.

'Now when someone hits me with a onion ring and it leaves a grease spot I can just wipe it off with Lysol,' Lula said.

'Smart,' I said to Lula. 'Are you sure you want to do this?'

'Fuckin' A. I'm expanding my horizons, remember? This could be a whole new career for me. Not that I don't like bounty huntering, but I feel this is a time when I should be open to new opportunities. Anyways, the What's got a job lined up at the Golden Times Senior Center in Mercerville tonight.'

Connie and I were speechless. Lula was going to perform in a white vinyl Band-Aid in front of a bunch of impaired senior citizens.

'I know what you're probably thinking,' Lula said.

'You're thinking I probably don't have to worry about them throwing onion rings . . . but you never know. Some of those old people are real feisty.'

'That's not what I was thinking,' Connie said. 'I was thinking you're going to give them all a heart attack if you wear that getup.'

Lula looked down at herself. 'You think it's too much?'

'I think it's not enough,' Connie said.

'What's Sally wearing?' I asked Lula.

'I got him a matching thong.' Lula glanced down at her watch. 'I gotta go. We got a rehearsal this afternoon, and then we're playing at six o'clock on account of the old folks don't stay up real late.'

'Life just gets weirder and weirder,' Connie said, taking in the full rear view of Lula running off to the bathroom to change.

I grabbed my shoulder bag and headed for the door. 'See you Monday.'

'Don't be late,' Connie said. 'We have the last group of mutants to interview Monday morning.'

Goody. Goody.

Morelli was still standing across the street, hands on hips, keeping watch over the crime scene. The medical examiner had arrived, along with the meat wagon. A tech truck was angled into the curb, the back doors open. A squad car was double-parked, strobe flashing. A uniform was keeping traffic moving.

I didn't often see Morelli at work, and I was struck by a few things that I already knew but didn't always think about. He was movie-star handsome in a rugged, lean and muscled way. He was good at his job. He carried more responsibility than I could manage. And his job was really crappy. Every day he slogged through death and misery, seeing the worst side of society. I suppose once in a while good people walked through his life, but I didn't think it was the norm.

I slid behind the wheel of the Mini and motored off. In a few minutes I was back at my condo. I went straight to my computer and brought my e-mail up. Five more ads for penis enhancement, three ads for big-busted women, two ads for cheap mortgage money, and an answer from Nash in Virginia.

The email from Nash read:

> know the guy you're looking for. one of those idiots dressing in black, tearing posters off the post office wall. had a one-room office in a strip mall but it's closed up. i checked for you. don't know any more than that. met him once while i was on a stakeout and he wandered onto my turf. i told him he was poaching and he left.

So I was more and more convinced there was a guy out there pretending to be Ranger. What I didn't have was a name for the guy. Or a face. He obviously resembled Ranger in build and coloring and had to be close in age. He was able to get a fake ID. Not a hard thing to do. Every sixteen-year-old kid has a fake ID.

Ranger was probably riding the wind, looking for the guy. And any well-adjusted person would walk away and let Ranger do his thing. Unfortunately, I wasn't that well adjusted. I possess an abnormal amount of curiosity, undoubtedly a Grandma Mazur gene. And dwarfing the curiosity was concern. I was worried. Really worried. Not to mention I had all these hormonal Ranger feelings that I hadn't a clue how to control.

I'd exhausted all my search possibilities, but I knew

where there was more information. Ranger's computer. I'd worked for Ranger for a brief amount of time, running searches in the RangeMan office. I knew the programs available, and I knew how they worked. Connie had good programs, but Ranger had better. And I suspected Ranger had a way of recognizing his own name.

I had a key to Ranger's apartment, but I couldn't get into it without Tank knowing. Ranger resided on the seventh floor of his office building. The building was secure, from the sidewalk in front to the rooftop. Every inch, with the exception of the interior of the apartments, was monitored.

I could go to Tank and tell him I was using Ranger's apartment, but the thought practically made me break out in hives. Tank was intimidating. I had no real relationship with Tank. And I was pretty sure he thought I was a pain in the ass.

Well, what the hell, half the people in New Jersey probably thought I was a pain in the ass. A girl can't let something like that stand in her way, can she? Besides, this was all Ranger's fault for not returning my calls.

I made myself a peanut butter and olive sandwich, washed it down with a diet soda, beefed up my courage by adding another layer of mascara to my lashes, and set out for Range-Man headquarters.

Ranger's building was on a quiet side street in city center. It was an unremarkable building. Neatly maintained. Only identified by a small plaque by the front door and the security cameras at the entrance to the underground garage. I pulled the Mini up to the garage entrance and flashed my key pass. The gate opened and I whipped the Mini into one of Ranger's four parking places. Ranger drove a Porsche Turbo, a Porsche Cayenne, and a big-ass truck. All three were parked. I waved at the security camera facing me and stepped into the elevator. I used my key to get to the seventh floor and stepped out into the small foyer.

I dialed Tank on my cell phone.

'Tank here.'

'Are you in the control center?' I asked him.

'Yeah.'

'Then you know I'm upstairs in the foyer. I thought I'd call and make sure Ranger wasn't inside and naked.'

Silence. Tank didn't know what to say to this.

'I'm taking your silence as an affirmative that it's okay to go in,' I said to Tank.

'Let me know if you need anything,' Tank said.

I unlocked Ranger's lair, opened the door, and stepped over the threshold. I closed and locked the door behind me and took a moment to let the cool calm wash over me. Ranger's apartment was tastefully decorated by a professional and perfectly kept by a housekeeper. It was masculine and sophisticated and slightly Zen. Everything had a place, and I'd spent some time as Ranger's guest so

I knew the routine. Keys went in a dish on the sideboard in the front entrance hall. Also on the sideboard were fresh flowers in a small glass vase. Probably the flowers were never once noticed by Ranger. Mail was stacked in a silver tray.

I leafed through the mail, checking the postmarks. It looked like Ranger hadn't been in his apartment since I saw him in the bakery. I called 'hello,' just in case. No one answered.

I walked past the kitchen, dining area, and small living room and went to Ranger's office just off the bedroom. I sat at his desk and turned his computer on. This felt invasive but I didn't know what else to do. I couldn't just sit on my hands while Ranger was suspected of kidnapping and possibly murder.

I stood and stretched and looked at my watch. It was almost seven o'clock, and I still hadn't found what I was looking for. I couldn't track the Un-Ranger because I couldn't decode Ranger's name. And Carmen and Rangemanoso always came to a dead end. I went to the kitchen and looked through the cupboards and fridge. Not a lot I was interested in. Ranger didn't exactly keep a ton of food on hand. There'd be sandwiches downstairs in the control center kitchen, but I didn't want to go there. I finally settled on a beer and some cheese and crackers.

I went back to the computer and looked around

Ranger's office. No photographs. No personal doo-dads. Only articles selected by the housekeeper or the decorator. This was a place where Ranger slept and worked. This was the Batcave. This wasn't his home. I knew Ranger had other properties. And one of those properties was home. I hadn't a clue where it was located or what it looked like.

I slouched back in the leather desk chair and closed my eyes. Let's go at this from a different direction, I thought. Straight computer searches weren't working. Pretend Ranger's an FTA. What do I know? He was going to Miami. Why? Not on normal BEA business. He would have told me. And Tank wouldn't be this uncommunicative. Ranger had said it was 'bad business.'

So just to choose a direction, let's assume the Un-Ranger popped up on the radar screen. Ranger would have shut him down . . . professionally and personally. Possibly permanently. Since it doesn't look like that happened, the next assumption would be that the Un-Ranger moved on before Ranger got to him in Virginia. And maybe he moved to Miami. And that would be his undoing, because there was a RangeMan office in Miami. And Ranger's computer guru was at that office. His name was Silvio, and I was betting he knew how to decode Ranger's name.

So let's assume the Un-Ranger tried to set up shop in Miami and Silvio found out. And Ranger took off for

Miami to take care of the Un-Ranger. But before Ranger got to the Un-Ranger, the little girl was kidnapped. And now Ranger was looking for both of them.

Lots of assumptions. Still no facts. Still no name. No Un-Ranger face. I went into Ranger's mail program. The in-box was empty. 'Sent items' was empty. Nothing in 'Deleted Items'. Ranger kept things clean. I went to his hard drive and started opening files. This took some time because Ranger numbered his files but didn't name them. File XB112 contained two JPGs. I opened the JPGs and there was the Un-Ranger. Both photos had clearly been taken without the man's knowledge. He was walking toward a car. The shots were full frontal and head turned slightly.

The man was dressed in black. He was a little less muscular than Ranger. Maybe a little wider in the hip. His hair was colored and styled like Ranger's. Sideburns cut at an angle. His skin tone was close. Maybe a half-shade lighter than Ranger. Facial features were startlingly similar. It was easy to see how a description of this man would fit Ranger. The foliage in the background was tropical. Florida plates on the cars in the photo.

I printed both JPGs and then e-mailed the JPGs to myself. Then I permanently erased the e-mail from 'Sent items'.

My cell phone rang and was so startling in the silent apartment, it had me out of my seat.

'I'm still at work,' Morelli said. 'This is going to be a late night.'

'That's okay,' I said. 'I'm at work, too. Maybe I'll see you tomorrow.'

I didn't have a name, but I had a picture. And I knew Ranger was on top of it all. I shut his computer down, shut the lights off, and locked up behind myself. I rode the elevator to the garage, waved good-bye at the security camera, and drove away.

I stopped at Pino's on the way home and picked up a pizza and a six-pack. Then I rode past the bonds office out of morbid curiosity. Not much to see, thank heaven. The car had been removed.

I carted the pizza and beer upstairs, opened my door, and realised the lights were on in my apartment. I experienced a nanosecond of terror until I saw Ranger sitting in my living room.

'*Jeez!*' I said. 'You scared the crap out of me. I thought you were in Florida.'

Ranger unfolded himself and closed the space between us. 'I just got back.'

He took the pizza box and the beer and carried them to the kitchen. We each took a beer and a slice of pizza and ate standing at the counter.

'Did you water my plants?' Ranger wanted to know.

'Ella waters your plants.'

He went to my shoulder bag, rummaged around in it,

and pulled out the two pieces of paper with the Un-Ranger pictures.

'I'm impressed. Where did you find them?' he asked.

'In a file in your hard drive. I couldn't get anything else because I couldn't decode your name. If I'd been really desperate, I would have called Silvio.'

'Tank wasn't helpful?'

'Tank's entire vocabulary consists of seven words. Ten, tops. You could have returned a phone call and saved me a lot of trouble,' I said.

'People can listen in on phone calls.'

Ranger took an unheard-of third piece of pizza.

'Wow,' I said. 'You must be hungry.'

His eyes were dark when he looked at me. 'Babe, you don't want to go there.'

My heart skipped a beat. 'Probably not,' I said. I picked the Un-Ranger picture off the counter. 'Do you know who this is?'

'No name. Just this photo. It was taken two days before the kidnapping. We thought it was simple identity theft and didn't have him under twenty-four-hour surveillance. Big mistake, because he checked out of his motel in the middle of the night and the next day he kidnapped Julie. We've been two steps behind him ever since.'

'Everyone thinks *you* kidnapped Julie.'

'Not everyone. Rachel and Ron know I didn't take her. I have a good relationship with them. And the lead agency man knows. We made a decision to go this route and hope the kidnapper feels comfortable enough to get sloppy. The downside is my picture's been all over the media and now my movement is limited. So I could use some help.'

'Why don't you just go blond?'

'I've been blond. When I go blond I look like I should be singing with the Village People.'

I burst out laughing. The visual was so perfect.

'You have a sense of humor,' I said to him. 'Who would have thought?'

'There are lots of things you don't know about me.'

'Just about everything.' I gave Rex a piece of pizza crust. 'Your cars were all parked at RangeMan.'

'I can't drive them. Every poser cowboy bounty hunter in the country is looking for me, along with a lot of law enforcement. I've got a green Explorer parked on the street.'

'And a new wardrobe.'

Ranger was total Abercrombie in jeans, olive-drab T-shirt, and a loose-fitting button-down shirt, worn untucked.

'You aren't going to give me grief over this, are you?' he asked.

I smiled at him. 'You look cute.'

'*Cute*,' Ranger repeated. 'That just dropped my testosterone level.'

The Pleasure Treasures bag was sitting forgotten on my counter. 'Looks like I'm not the only one who's been shopping,' Ranger said, reaching for the bag.

'*No!* Don't touch that.'

Too late. He had it in his hands.

'This is embarrassing,' I said. 'Give me the bag.'

Ranger held the bag out of my reach. 'Want to wrestle me for it?'

At another time this exchange might have felt flirty. Tonight there was an edge to Ranger. Anger simmering just below the surface. And I thought it wouldn't take too much provocation for him to rearrange someone's face. Not mine, of course. He liked my face. Still, he was a little scary.

I narrowed my eyes at him. 'Just give me the damn bag.'

'I let you snoop in my computer,' Ranger said. 'The least you can do is let me see in this bag.'

'I don't think so.'

'Not much you can do about it, babe.'

'I'll be mad at you.'

'You can't be mad at me,' Ranger said. 'I'm cute. I might even be adorable.'

'Try *jerk* on for size.'

'Sticks and stones.' He looked in the bag and gave a single soft bark of laughter. 'Nice,' he said, taking the dildo out, setting it on the counter, balls down, shaft up, like a giant pink rubber mushroom.

I'm not one of those women who blushes easily, but I could feel my ears burning.

'Having problems with Morelli?' Ranger asked, the edge gone. Anger replaced by something much softer . . . amusement, exhaustion, affection.

'The woman working in the Pleasure Treasures store went FTA, and Lula and I went in to make an apprehension, and Lula got this dancing dildo, but they were having a two-for-one-sale, and somehow I ended up with this. It's the Herbert Horsecock model.'

'It's impressive.'

'It's frightening,' I told him.

He took the DVD out of the bag. '*Big Boys*,' he said. 'I'm seeing a theme here.'

'Lula said it would change my life.'

Ranger put the dildo and the DVD back in the bag. 'Does your life need changing?'

'I don't know. I thought so a while ago, but it feels comfortable now ... except for a commitment dilemma.'

He pulled me to him and kissed me in a way that more than made up for the benign kiss in the bakery. 'Let me know when you figure it out,' he said.

I realized that sometime during the kiss I'd inserted my leg between his and had plastered myself to him in all the strategic places. I inched away and smoothed out the wrinkles I'd made when I gripped his shirt.

'Is there something I should be doing tonight to find Julie?' I asked him.

'Not tonight, but I have some legwork for you to do tomorrow if you have time.'

'Of course I have time. Are you managing this okay?'

'It's not the first time I've had to find someone important to me. You learn to keep moving forward. And you go deep into denial.'

'Are you scared?'

'Yeah,' Ranger said. 'I'm scared for Julie.'

'Do you have a place to stay?'

'I have a safe house in north Trenton. I'll pick you up tomorrow morning at eight.' He reached out to kiss me again, but I jumped away. Another kiss like the last one and he wouldn't leave . . . I'd make sure of it.

'Still think I'm cute?' Ranger asked with the almost nonexistent smile curving the corners of his mouth. And he left.

Eight

I opened an eye and squinted at my bedside clock. Six-thirty. In the morning! My alarm wasn't set to go off for another hour, but something had dragged me awake. I opened the other eye and did some deep breathing, sucking in the smell of coffee brewing. I rolled out of bed and shuffled into the dining room.

Ranger was at the table, using my laptop.

'Unh,' I said.

'Coffee's in the kitchen.'

'What are you doing here?'

'No computer in the safe house, and I thought this was easier than getting Tank to try to get a laptop to me. I had some things I wanted to run down.'

'I don't have very good programs.'

'I don't need programs. Silvio is sending me information from Miami.'

'How long have you been here?'

'About an hour.' He stood and stretched and headed

for the kitchen. He got two mugs out of the cabinet, filled them with coffee, added milk, and gave one to me.

I was wearing short cotton pajama bottoms and a knit tank top, and I could see Ranger was enjoying the tank top.

'I'm feeling self-conscious,' I said to him.

'That's not what I'm feeling.'

No kidding! 'Go back to work,' I told him. 'I'm going to take my coffee into the shower. I'll be ready to go in a half-hour.'

Ranger had parked on a side street a block away from my building. He left through the front door and walked to his car. I left through the back door, got into the Mini, and drove around three blocks until I was sure I wasn't being followed. I parked behind Ranger, beeped the Mini locked, and slipped into the green Explorer.

'Now what?' I asked.

Ranger pulled into traffic and went north on Hamilton. 'I want you to canvas a neighborhood for me.'

Ranger isn't an especially talkative guy. He doesn't do small talk, and he doesn't usually initiate conversation, but he'll talk about the job if he feels there's a genuine interest. In this case, I definitely had interest.

'I'd really like to know the history on this,' I said to him. 'I've only got bits and pieces.'

'Two weeks ago someone started using a credit card

issued to Rangemanoso Enterprises with my name on it. Silvio found it during a routine scan. Silvio traced down Rangemanoso and to the best of our knowledge this guy appeared in Arlington six months ago and set up shop. I was about to go to Arlington and shut him down when we discovered he'd moved on. And then all of a sudden he started using the card in Miami. We assumed he was there reestablishing himself, but in retrospect, I think he was there to get Julie.'

'So you went to Miami to find this guy and before you got to him he took Julie.'

'Yes. And until you called Tank and told him someone smoked Carmen we had no reason to think he was in Jersey. We thought either he hunkered down somewhere in Florida or else he was in a car moving around. We didn't think he'd be able to get Julie through security and onto a plane. And the FBI was combing passenger lists for Julie Martine and Carlos Manoso and not finding anything.'

'If he stole your identity, I guess he could steal others.'

'Two others turned up when Silvio ran through the Rangemanoso credit history. He paid some early bills with cards issued to Steve Scullen and Dale Small. Silvio had been watching passenger lists for both those identities, but nothing there either.'

'No leads in Miami from the crime scene?'

'Miami went cold. Julie got picked up in a stolen car. It

was found abandoned two blocks from the pickup point. The police issued a bulletin, and they're doing the follow-up on calls coming in.'

'It was my impression that not many people knew you had a daughter.'

'You and Tank and relatives.'

'And Julie's mother and stepfather.'

'Rachel and Ron are working with the people in Miami, trying to trace down anyone who might have known about me. They didn't hide the fact that Ron was Julie's stepfather, but they didn't tell a lot of people the details. Julie knew. My name is on her birth certificate, but Ron adopted her, and she's always thought of herself as Julie Martine.'

'Is that painful?'

'It might be painful if she wasn't happy, but Rachel and Ron are good parents. Rachel is a nice Catholic girl I took advantage of one night on leave when I was in the military. She got pregnant, and I married her and gave the baby my name and financial support. We divorced after the baby was born. I'm involved only as much as Rachel wants me to be.'

'She didn't want you to stick around and be a permanent husband?'

'That was never an option either of us would have considered.'

We were on Route I, driving north. It was early Sunday

morning and traffic was light. I was in my usual uniform of jeans and T-shirt. Ranger was in homeboy clothes.

'From the way you're dressed, I'd guess we were canvasing the ghetto today,' I said to Ranger.

'You'd guess right.'

His jeans were loose-fit but not falling off his ass. 'Think you can pull it off in those jeans?'

'They'll have to do. You can't chase someone down if your pants are around your ankles.'

True enough. I'd actually chased guys who'd literally run out of their pants.

'And I'm a little old for the homey look. I was shooting for Latino Gap,' Ranger said. 'I don't plan to get out of the car, but just in case, I wanted to blend.'

Ranger took the turnpike and got off at the Newark exit. When they nicknamed New Jersey the Garden State they weren't talking about Newark. The neighborhoods we drove through were bleak by anyone's standards. If I'd been with anyone other than Ranger I'd have turned tail and gotten back on the turnpike.

'This is a scary neighborhood,' I said, taking in the graffiti, the occasional condemned building, the sullen faces of the kids hanging on street corners.

'I grew up here,' Ranger said. 'It hasn't changed much in twenty years.'

'Were you one of those guys on the corner?'

Ranger cut his eyes to a group of teens. 'Eventually. When I was a kid, I was little and I didn't fit, so I got beat up a lot. My skin color was too light for the blacks and too dark for the Cubans. And I had straight brown hair that made me look like a girl.'

'How awful.'

Ranger shrugged. 'I found out I could survive a beating. And I learned to be quick, and to watch my back, and to fight dirty.'

'All good skills,' I said.

'For street thugs and bounty hunters.'

'I thought you lived in Miami for a while.'

'When I was fourteen I got arrested for stealing a car and spent some time in juvie. When I got out, my parents sent me to Miami to live with my grandmother. I went to high school in Miami. I moved back to Jersey to take a shot at college, and then I came back when I got out of the army.'

Ranger found a place at the curb in front of a deli. 'My parents live on the next block,' Ranger said. 'This neighborhood we're in right now really isn't so bad. It's actually the Cuban equivalent to the Burg. Problem is, you have to go through the bad neighborhood to get anywhere, including the school.'

Ranger clipped a little gizmo onto my jeans waistband. 'Panic button. If you have a problem, just push it, and I'll come to you. I want you to take the photo you got from my computer and see if someone knows this guy. He has to have some association with me.'

'All the signs are in Spanish. Will I be able to talk to anyone?'

'Everyone speaks English. Except for my Grandma Rosa, and we're going to try hard not to run into her.'

I left Ranger sitting in the SUV and took the picture into the deli. It was a little mom-and-pop business. A butcher in the back behind a glass case filled with sausages and pork roasts and chicken parts. Shelves filled with sacks of rice, spices, cereals, canned goods. Baskets of vegetables. More shelves with breads and packaged cakes and cookies.

A middle-aged woman was at the register. I waited for her to check out a customer before introducing myself.

'I'm looking for this man,' I said, showing her the photo. 'Do you know him?'

'Yes, I know him,' the woman behind the counter said. 'This is Carlos Manoso.'

'No,' I said to her. 'I know Carlos, and this isn't him.'

I showed the picture to the butcher and to a woman waiting to have a pork roast boned and rolled. They both thought it was Carlos Manoso, the man the police were looking for. They said they'd seen his photo on television.

It was close to noon when I returned to the green Explorer. My nose was sunburned, and I had sweat running in a river down my breastbone.

'Nothing,' I said to Ranger. 'Everyone thinks it's you.'

Ranger looked at the picture. 'I need to get back to the gym.'

'It's not the body. It's the clothes and the face. He's spent some time studying you. He's got the clothes down. And he's had his hair cut like yours. Hard to tell from this picture if the skin tone is the same or if he's tanned himself to mimic your coloring.'

'This is the third day, and I still haven't got anything,' Ranger said. 'We worked Miami really hard. Mostly talking to relatives and neighbors, going with the idea that he knew me, that he was close enough to someone in my circle to know about Julie.'

'Is this the first you've started looking in Jersey?'

'We went to relatives and friends right away. This is the first neighborhood search. And this is the only neighborhood where he'd pick up information on Julie. It would have to come from one of my relatives. No one in Trenton knew.'

'Okay, so we seem to be at a dead end on the Ranger connection. Let's go in another direction. He married Carmen Cruz from Springfield, Virginia, and he set up an office in Arlington. Maybe that's where he originates. Not in Arlington but close enough to feel comfortable with the area. Maybe we should talk to Carmen's parents.'

Ranger put the SUV in gear and called Tank. 'Run Carmen Cruz in Springfield, Virginia, and get Stephanie and me on a train out of Newark going to northern Virginia. I'll be traveling as Marc Pardo.'

'Stolen identity?' I asked him.

'No. It's all mine.'

'Wouldn't it be faster to fly?'

'I can't take a gun on a plane.'

Ranger left the green SUV in the train-station parking lot. Good luck with that one. One of his guys was supposed to pick it up, but I was giving it a half-hour tops before it was on the way to a chop shop.

I was sitting next to Ranger, I had a box of food in front of me from the café car, and the rocking of the train was hypnotic and soothing and exciting all at the same time. We were rolling through the country's backyards, seeing America with its pants down.

Ranger was on the phone with Tank, taking down information on Carmen Cruz and arranging for a rental car.

'About the cell phone,' I said, when Ranger disconnected. 'Why is it okay to talk to Tank when you couldn't call me?'

'Tank has a secure phone.'

'Like it's scrambled?'

'No. They're just phones under different names. It's a way to make sure no one's listening. If someone's trying to get a line on me, they're not going to tap Larry Baker's phone.'

'Spending time with you is always a learning experience.'

'There are other things I could teach you,' Ranger said.

It was four o'clock by the time we picked up the rental car and rolled out of Union Station. Ranger had the GPS gadget set to take us to the Cruz house in Springfield, and it was talking us through downtown Washington.

'Turn left in twenty feet,' the mechanical voice told us. 'Move to the left lane. Take a right at the bottom of the off-ramp. Merge into traffic.'

'This thing's giving me an eye twitch,' Ranger said. 'Can you get the sound off?'

I started pressing buttons and the screen went blank.

'How's that?' I asked.

'Babe, you shut the system down.'

'Yes, but the sound is off.'

'Reprogram it.'

'No need to get testy,' I told him.

'I don't know where I'm going.'

'I have a map. You just get on I-95 south and take the Springfield exit.'

'And then what?'

'Then you'll have to pull over and reprogram the GPS.'

Ranger cut his eyes to me and there was the tiniest of smiles on his mouth. I was amusing him.

'You're a very strange man,' I told him.

'Yeah,' he said. 'That's what I hear.'

I had my cell phone clipped to my waist, and I could feel it buzzing. I looked at the screen. Morelli.

'Howdy,' I said to Morelli.

'Can I buy you dinner and a movie and a room at Hotel Morelli?'

'Sounds good but I'm working.'

'After work.'

'After work will be late,' I said.

'How late?'

'Monday or Tuesday.'

'Where are you?' Morelli wanted to know.

'I can't tell you that,' I said.

'Goddamn it, you're with Ranger, aren't you? I should have known. He's up to his armpits in murder and kidnapping, and he's going to drag you into it with him.'

Ranger reached over, grabbed my phone, and shut it down.

'Hey!' I said. 'That was Morelli.'

'If you stay on too long it can be traced down. I'm sure he understands.'

'Yeah, he understands. If he knew where we were, you'd be seeing his Kojak light in your rearview mirror.'

'Then I'm glad he doesn't know where we are because I wouldn't want to have to square off with Morelli. It wouldn't end well for either of us.'

We moved onto I-95 south, and I tightened my seat

belt. Driving out of DC into northern Virginia is like NASCAR on a flat straight track, racing bumper-to-bumper six wide, twenty miles deep. And attached to that is another identical race going six wide in the opposite direction. Two-story-high sound barriers rise out of the breakdown lanes, and form a cement canyon filled with wall-to-wall noise and insanity. We hurtled forward to the appropriate exit, catapulted ourselves down the chute, and peeled off toward Springfield.

Ranger pulled onto the shoulder and reprogrammed the GPS system.

'Lucky for you, you look good in a T-shirt,' Ranger said.

'Lucky for you, I don't have a gun on me.'

Ranger turned to me. His voice was low and even, but there was a whisper of incredulous disbelief. 'You're not carrying a gun?'

'Didn't seem necessary for us *both* to have one.'

Nine

It was a little after five o'clock when we drove past the Cruz house. We were in a development of middle-income homes, mostly little ranches sitting on small plots of land. Every third house was the same. From the maturity of trees and shrubs, I'd have guessed the houses were maybe ten years old.

The Cruz house was pale yellow with white trim and a teal-green front door. The landscaping was economy grade but neat. There were several cars in the driveway and two at the curb. I imagined friends and relatives were sharing the Cruz's grief over their daughter.

Ranger drove two blocks over and parked. We were in front of a small public access to a bike path that wound through a narrow greenbelt behind the houses.

'I'm going to wait here,' he said. 'You take the car and go do your thing.'

'Are you sure you want to give me the car after making

sexist remarks about my mechanical skills? I might not come back for you.'

'I'd find you,' Ranger said. He took my hand, kissed the palm, and got out of the car.

I exchanged seats, put the car in gear, and drove back to the Cruzes'. I parked at the curb and blew out a sigh. I was going to feel like a real shit for intruding at a time like this. I set off for the house, and just as I got to the porch two young women came out to have a cigarette. They lit up, took a deep drag, and sat down on the step to enjoy the rest in comfort.

I extended my hand. 'Stephanie Plum,' I said. 'Were you friends with Carmen?'

They both nodded.

'I'm Sasha,' one said.

'Lorraine.'

'I'm part of the task force investigating the crime,' I told them. 'Would you mind if I asked some questions?'

Lorraine looked down at my jeans.

'You're going to have to excuse my dress,' I said. 'I was called in on my day off, and I didn't get a chance to change.'

'What do you want to know?'

'Do you know her husband?'

'Carmen talked about him in the beginning. Ranger, Ranger, Ranger. I mean, how lame is that? Who calls himself Ranger?'

'Did she ever mention his real name?'

'Carlos.'

'Would you recognize him if you saw a picture?'

'No. None of us actually saw him. And then all of a sudden she was married and living in Arlington and she sort of fell off the earth.'

'Is he from this area?'

'I don't know where he's originally from,' Lorraine said. 'He was working as a security guard at Potomac Mills Mall when she met him. He told her it was only a temporary job until his business took off.'

'What business was that?'

'He was a bounty hunter. Carmen thought that was real cool. From what I hear, she cashed in an insurance policy so they could buy computers and shit.' A tear ran down Lorraine's cheek, and she wiped her nose with the back of her hand. 'The people on television are saying the bastard shot her.'

'Thanks,' I said. 'This has been helpful.'

I got directions to the mall, drove back to the bike path, and picked Ranger up.

'When Carmen met this guy he was working as a security guard at Potomac Mills. It's a mall off I-95 a couple miles south of here,' I told Ranger.

Ranger punched Potomac Mills into the GPS. 'Okay, sweetheart,' he said to the GPS. 'Talk to me.'

* * *

If you entered Potomac Mills at one end and stared down the length of the mall, you would be sure it ended in Kansas. We were standing in front of a mall map getting the lay of the land, looking for the security office and not finding it.

'The mall closes at seven,' Ranger said. 'We've got a little over an hour to get someone to ID our man. I'm going to have Tank see if he can do something by phone. Meanwhile, you try to find security people to talk to. I'll be fifty paces behind you.'

I looked down the mall and saw two uniformed guards standing back on their heels watching the shoppers. Man and woman. In their twenties. The woman looked like she'd gained some weight since they'd issued her uniform. Her partner was tall and gangly. Bad complexion. I was guessing they ate a lot of meals at the food court.

I came up to them with a smile. Friendly. Needing assistance.

'Excuse me,' I said. 'I'm looking for a guy who used to work as a security guard here. I can't remember his name but he was medium build, dark brown hair, kind of nice-looking. Caucasian, I think, but with dark skin. Probably hasn't been here for maybe six months.'

'Doesn't ring a bell,' the woman said. 'Did he work weekends? We only work weekends.'

'I'm not sure.'

'You should talk to Dan,' she said. 'He's been here

forever. He knows everyone. He's sort of heavyset and balding, and he's probably down toward the other end. He might be around Linens-N-Things, unless he got a call.'

I wasn't sure where Linens-N-Things was located, but with the way this mall was looking it could be a couple miles. I took off at a fast walk, trying not to be distracted by the stores. I made it past Banana Republic and the Gap but instinctively stopped in front of Victoria's Secret.

I felt Ranger at my back, his hand warm on my waist. 'If you buy something you have to model it,' he said.

I got a rush at the thought, panic followed . . . and then guilt. 'Just looking,' I said.

'I hate to ruin this moment, but there's a guard at three o'clock.'

'Is he overweight and balding?'

'Hard to tell if he's balding from here, but he's overweight. He's standing by the kiosk, four or five stores down.'

'I see him.'

I read his name tag as I approached him. Dan Whitten. 'Excuse me,' I said. 'I'm looking for a guy who used to be a security guard here. I can't remember his name. Medium build. Caucasian but sort of dark skin. Dark brown hair.'

'That's a pretty broad description. What do you want with him?'

'I met him in a bar a couple days ago, and he walked away with my iPod. We were comparing MP3 players, and he got a phone call and had to leave. I didn't realize until too late that he'd walked off with my iPod and left me with his piece of junk. Anyway, all I remembered was that he said he used to work here. And he said now he was working as a bounty hunter.'

'Edward Scrog. You should kiss that iPod goodbye. The guy is a nutcase. He got fired for harassment.'

'You mean sexual harassment?'

'*All* kinds of harassment. Some guys go power-goofy when they get a badge and a uniform. This guy thinks he's Wyatt Earp or something. Walked around with his hand on his flashlight like it was a gun.' He broke into a smile. 'Scrog used to pat women down. He'd claim they looked suspicious. That was ultimately his undoing. Tried to do a pat-down on a fed. She pulled a move on him and had him on the floor with her foot on his neck. Then she filed charges.'

'I don't suppose you know where I can find him?'

'No. It wasn't like we were friends.'

'Well, thanks,' I said. 'This has been helpful.'

'Let me give you some advice you didn't ask for. Stay away from Scrog. He's got a screw loose. When they fired him, they walked him to his locker, made him clean it out and leave the premises. I was there to make sure he left, and I saw what was in the locker. He had it filled with guns and ammo. And he had pictures pasted on the door like a kid does with baseball stars and then later on with girls with big hooters. Only this guy had pictures of SWAT guys taking people down. It's like he's seen too many cop movies. When he first came on the job he was applying to all the local police academies, only no one would give him a call back.

'After he was here a couple months he started talking about the bounty hunter thing. Watched all the shows on television. Apparently, he was hooked on some bounty hunter in Jersey who was supposed to be a real hotshot, and he said he was studying him. Used to take off weekends so he could "observe" this guy. So maybe he's in Jersey now. Good for Virginia, that's my opinion.

'You look like a nice girl,' he said. 'Take my advice and buy yourself a new iPod.'

I walked back to Ranger and gave him the whole story. 'I imagine the hotshot Jersey bounty hunter would be you,' I said to Ranger.

Ranger called Tank and gave him the name. 'Run an address history for me,' Ranger said. 'I want to know what's open.'

We found the food court and sat at a table while we ate pizza and waited for Tank to call back. The call came in at five minutes to seven. Ranger took two addresses down and disconnected.

'We have Scrog's parents' house in Fairfax and an apartment in Dale City.'

'Did you ever search his office or the apartment he shared with Carmen?'

'We went through the office in Arlington on the first pass. He didn't leave anything. Same with the apartment. He didn't leave on an impulse. He'd removed everything that could identify him. There were some clothes hanging in the closet and some things in the dresser. Everything else belonged to Carmen.'

Scrog's Dale City apartment building was a two-story cinderblock bunker with a parking lot and a close-up view of the interstate. Scrog was on the second floor. Unit 209. Ten units to a floor. Stained carpet. Strong burrito aroma coming out of 206.

Ranger knocked on the door of 209. No answer. He tried the knob. Locked. 'I don't suppose you have anything helpful in your bag?' he asked me.

'Like a set of burglary tools? No.'

Ranger put his foot to the door, kicked it open, and stepped inside. I followed behind him and tried to get the door to stay closed.

'Don't worry about it,' Ranger said, flipping the light on. 'We won't be in here long. There's not a lot to see.'

It was a one-bath studio apartment with a small kitchenette along one wall. The blinds were drawn on the single window. There was a sofa bed open and un-made, a small table with two wooden ladder-back chairs, a two-drawer metal file cabinet, and two laundry baskets holding a computer and accessories.

'This guy travels light,' Ranger said.

'Maybe he has stuff stored with his parents.'

Ranger opened a closet and a bunch of guns fell out. He stepped over the guns and squatted in front of the file cabinet and opened the top drawer.

'He has a file labeled "Captures" but it's empty. He also has a file labeled "Wanted", and it's filled with pictures he's ripped off federal bulletin boards.'

Ranger pulled the bottom drawer open, removed a scrapbook, and handed it over to me. 'I have a bad feeling about this scrapbook. Scan it while I look through the cupboards.'

'Your bad feeling is justified,' I said, flipping pages. 'This is homage to Ranger. It looks to me like he was following you around. There are pictures in here of your office building and your cars. There are pictures of you. Pictures of you with me. Pictures of . . . omigod.'

It was a picture of Carmen naked. The handwriting on the bottom read: OUR WEDDING NIGHT. PRACTICING FOR THE REAL THING. And it was followed by a snapshot of me. And for the first time, I saw the resemblance between Carmen and me. Not that we'd pass for twins, more that we were similar in coloring and build.

Ranger looked over my shoulder. 'This guy is sick.'

'Do you think he married Carmen because she looks a little like me?'

'Yes. I think he's trying to move into my life.'

'He left her behind and killed her.'

'Guess he's done practicing,' Ranger said.

The next page had a picture of Ranger in front of the Martines' house, talking to Ron. The caption read: RANGER MAKES A MYSTERIOUS VISIT AND I KNOW HIS SECRET. This was followed by pictures of Julie.

Ranger went dead still. He stared at the pictures of his daughter and his face showed no emotion, but he wasn't breathing. It was as if the oxygen had been sucked out of the room. His hands were loose at his sides and his eyes were focused on the pictures. He was looking at a little girl with silky brown hair, intelligent brown eyes, and flawless light brown skin . . . the image of her father. I slipped my hand in his and waited for him to pull himself together.

'She'll be okay,' I said. 'He's playing a role. He's going to act like he's her dad.'

Ranger nodded. 'I'd like to think that was true. Let's pack up. I'm going to take the computer and the scrapbook. I don't see anything else of value to us.'

We carted Scrog's stuff downstairs and out to the car and put it in the trunk. The sun had set, and the parking lot was dark. Traffic noise carried over the apartment building.

'Now what?' I said to Ranger. 'Do you want to talk to his parents?'

'No. I have what I need. Let's go home.'

We took 95 north to the beltway, driving in silence, Ranger in his zone. We were following taillights in the dark, gliding through the night like disembodied spirits. We were between time and place, encapsulated in steel and fiberglass. All this much more poetic than the reality of the moment, which was that my ass was falling asleep. I'd like to say I was in a zone like Ranger, but the truth was, I'd never in my life achieved a zone. In fact, I couldn't even imagine a zone, and didn't really know what one was. If I had to describe my condition, I'd have to say I was freaked.

I fell asleep somewhere in Maryland and didn't wake up until we were on Broad Street. I stretched and looked at Ranger. His hand was loose on the wheel. His breathing was even. At first glance, he seemed relaxed. If you looked more closely, the tension around his eyes and the corners of his mouth was visible. I wondered what was really inside him. And at what cost he kept it hidden.

He parked in my lot and got out of the car. 'I'm going to see you upstairs,' he said.

'Not necessary.'

He beeped the car locked and moved me toward the building. 'It is necessary. There's some psycho running around wanting to add you to his Ranger memorabilia.'

'You're right,' I said. 'Thanks. I'm happy to be escorted.'

We got upstairs without incident, Ranger opened the door to my apartment and flicked the lights on. Rex was quietly running on his wheel.

'The attack hamster is on the job,' Ranger said.

I dropped a peanut into Rex's cage and turned back to Ranger. He looked tired under the kitchen light. He had dark smudges under his eyes and his mouth was tight, fighting sleep. 'You look exhausted,' I said to him.

'Long day.'

'You have another half-hour drive to get to your safe house. Would you like to stay here tonight?'

'Yes.'

'This isn't a sexual invitation,' I said.

'I know. The couch will be fine.'

Ten

I woke up slowly. I opened my eyes and saw there was a bar of light shining through the crack in my bedroom curtains. It was morning. And I was in my own bed, feeling incredibly comfy. I looked down and realized there was a man's arm thrown across my chest, the hand lightly curled around my breast.

Ranger.

I moved my head ever so slightly on the pillow and looked over at him. He was still asleep. He had a decent beard growth going and his hair had fallen across his forehead. I was pretty sure he wasn't in my bed when I fell asleep. I looked under the covers. I was wearing my knit tank top and short pajama bottoms. Ranger was wearing briefs. Could be worse, I thought.

'Hey,' I said.

He wrapped his arms around me and cuddled me into him, his eyes still closed.

'Ranger!'

'Mmm.'

'What are you doing in my bed?'

'So far I'm not doing anything, but that could change.'

'You said you were going to sleep on the couch.'

'I lied.'

This was bad because he felt *way* too good. I looked beyond him to the clock. Nine o'clock, 'I have to go to work,' I said. 'I'm already late.'

He drew me in a little closer and stroked his thumb across my breast. 'Are you *sure* you want to go to work now?'

I got a rush that was so strong it might have been an orgasm, and I think I might have moaned a little. Mentally, I was working hard to be faithful to Morelli, but the physical part of me wasn't cooperating.

Ranger kissed my shoulder, and the phone rang. Ordinarily, at a time like this you'd rip the phone line out of the wall. But these were scary days, and we both went still at the sound.

'Let me get it,' I said, reaching across Ranger.

There was a lot of noise at the other end, and then Melvin's voice came on. 'Thank God, you answered,' he yelled into the phone. 'I'm all alone here, and this mob's getting ugly. And Joyce Barnhardt is here, and she's frightening me!'

'Where're Connie and Lula?'

'I don't know where Lula is. Connie had to go bond someone out.'

I heard a gun go off in the background, Melvin shrieked and the line went dead. I pushed away from Ranger, and I rolled out of bed. 'I have to go. Melvin's alone at the bonds office, and he's got problems.'

I grabbed some clothes and ran into the bathroom.

'Who's Melvin?' Ranger said to my back.

I slid to a stop in front of the bonds office and jumped out of the Mini. The plate-glass window was filled with lettering advertising bail bonds. Beyond the lettering, I could see that the small front office was filled with people dressed like the television bounty hunters. I pushed through the door and shouted for Melvin.

'Here,' he yelled back. 'Under the desk.'

I plowed through the crowd and looked under the desk at Melvin. 'Why are all these people here? I thought they were scheduled throughout the morning.'

'Something got messed up, and they were all told to come in at nine.'

'What was the gunshot I heard?'

'Two guys were playing quick draw and one of them accidentally shot the phone.'

I glanced over at the phone. Shot dead.

I reached into the petty cash drawer and took out a wad of money. 'Hey!' I said. 'Listen up.'

No one listened, so I climbed onto the desk and tried again. *'Hey!'* I yelled. 'Everyone shut the fuck up and listen to me.'

This got their attention.

'I'm very sorry but the appointments got screwed up,' I told them. 'I'm going to reschedule you, and I'm going to give everyone five dollars to go have breakfast while you wait for your appointment time. So I want everyone to line up single file.'

Pandemonium. Everyone wanted to be first. Someone got knocked to the ground, and someone got punched in the face. And there was a lot of cussing and shouting and eye gouging and biting.

I got Connie's gun out of her desk drawer and fired a round into the ceiling. A chunk of plaster fell onto the desktop and plaster dust sifted onto my hair and shoulders.

'If you don't get in line nicely, I'm going to shoot you,' I said.

This got them to sullenly line up with just a minimum amount of pushing and shoving. I gave out fifteen-minute appointments to eleven people. They each got five dollars. All but one left.

'You can come out from under the desk now,' I told Melvin. 'What happened to Joyce? I thought Joyce was here.'

'She left. She said she'd be back later this morning. She

was real mad. Something about getting sent on a wild goose chase.'

I dragged a folding chair over to the desk and told the first bounty hunter impersonator to sit down. The folding chair was old and scarred and said STIVA FUNERAL HOME on the back. I sat in Connie's chair and called Lula on my cell.

'Where the heck are you?' I asked Lula.

'I had to go shopping. We were a big hit at the old people's home, and we got a new gig out of it. And I need a new outfit.'

'You're supposed to be here helping with the interviews.'

'I figured you didn't need me. They're all losers, anyway.'

I looked at the guy in the folding chair. He was dressed in black leather pants and a black leather vest that showed a lot of chest hair. A roll of fat oozed out from under the vest and spilled over his belt buckle. He'd accessorized with black leather wristbands that were studded with the metal things you see on Rottweiler collars. And he was wearing a blond mullet wig.

'You're right,' I said to Lula. 'Happy shopping.'

'So,' I said to the guy in front of me, 'what makes you qualified to be a bond enforcement agent?'

'I watch all the television shows, and I know I could do this. I don't take shit from anyone, and I got a gun.'

'That would be the one that's strapped to your leg?'

'Yeah. And I'm not afraid to use it. I don't take crap from blacks, spics, chinks, pollacks or commies. I swear, I'll kill all the motherfuckers if I have to.'

'Good to know,' I said. 'You can go get breakfast now.'

Connie rolled in while I was interviewing idiot number 5. 'How's it going?' she asked. 'Sorry I'm late. I had to bond someone out. Is that a bullet in my phone?'

'We had some problems in the beginning, but it's all straightened out now,' I told her. 'So far I've seen two psychos, one gay hut, a guy who got a boner talking about guns, and this gentleman here who seems to be wearing black leather chaps, cowboy boots, and nothing else.'

Connie looked down at the guy in the chair. 'Nice boots,' she said to him.

When he left we sprayed the chair with Lysol and invited the next candidate to sit.

'I'm here on a mission from God,' he said. 'I'm here to save your immortal souls.'

'I thought you were here for the bond enforcement position,' Connie said.

'God loves sinners and what better place to find them?'

'He's got a point,' I said to Connie.

Connie ripped his application off her clipboard.

Lula bustled in as the last guy was leaving. 'I can't

believe how hard it is to find clothes when you're a rock star. It's not like us singers can wear just any old thing. And now Sally and me are getting famous for dressing together, and so I gotta find something that'll match up with a thong for him. I tell you, it's not easy.'

'Why can't you wear the white outfit again?' I asked her.

'It turns out all that shiny white isn't good for the old folks. They got macular shit and cataracts, and they were getting seizures from the light reflection off my ass.' Lula pulled a wad of pink feathers out of her shopping bag. 'I finally found this here flamingo feather dress. Only thing is, I couldn't find a flamingo feather thong, so I got a boa, and I figure we can sew some of it on a jock strap or something.'

'That's a lot of flamingo feathers,' Connie said. 'They aren't real, are they?'

'It says here they're genuine farm-raised dyed fowl. You want me to try it on?'

'No!' Connie and I said in unison.

Lula looked a little put off, so I told her it was just that we were starving, and maybe she'd show us after lunch.

'I'm hungry, too,' Lula said. 'I'm feeling like spaghetti and meatballs.'

'I could go for some spaghetti,' Connie said. 'I'll get Pino's to deliver.'

'I want a meatball sub,' I told her.

'And a side of potato salad,' Lula said. 'And a piece of their chocolate cake. Now that I'm doing all this entertaining I gotta keep my strength up.'

'Melvin?' Connie yelled out. 'We're ordering from Pino's. Do you want something?'

'No,' Melvin said from behind the first bank of file cabinets. 'I brought my lunch. I have to save my money in case I go to jail. I hear if you can't afford to buy cigarettes for everyone you have to be someone's bitch.'

'Is that why you didn't show up for your trial?' Lula asked. 'On account of you didn't want to be someone's bitch?'

'Yeah. I know I'm a pervert and all, but I'm not that *kind* of a pervert. I'm sort of a specialist. I'm like a do-it-yourself pervert.'

'I hear you,' Lula said. 'I've shopped in that aisle.'

Connie put the order in and shoved a stack of files to the middle of her desk. 'We have to pick one of these . . . for lack of a better word, *people*.'

'These *people* all gonna lower the quality of our work,' Lula said. 'And God knows it's already pretty low.'

'How are we doing?' I asked Connie. 'Are we catching up enough to do without a third person?'

'The problem is, you catch up but then we get a couple new FTAs in, and we're behind the curve again. I'm going to divide these files between us and everyone has to pick the best person in their stack. Then we'll choose one of those three people.'

We were still reading through the files when the Pino's guy arrived. We set the files aside, spread the food out on Connie's desk, and pulled up more of the funeral home folding chairs. I had my sub in my hand when Joyce Barnhardt stormed in and threw a file on the table, splattering Lula's spaghetti sauce.

'What the fuck's the matter with you?' Lula said. 'You got a problem?'

'Yeah, I got a problem, fatso. I don't like getting sent off on a goddamn wild goose chase with those LC files. I bet you all thought it was funny. See if Joyce can find Willie Reese, right?'

'What's wrong with finding Willie Reese?' Connie asked. 'Those were legitimate files I gave you.'

'He's friggin' dead. He's been friggin' dead for almost a year. What do you want me to do, dig him up and cart him in here?'

'No,' Connie said. 'I want you to bring me a copy of his death certificate, so we can close the case and get our money back.'

'Oh,' Joyce said. 'I didn't know I could do that.'

'I don't like being called a fatso,' Lula said. 'I think you should apologize.'

'If the shoe fits,' Joyce said. 'Or in your case, if nothing but a *tent* fits . . .'

'I'm not that fat,' Lula said. 'I'm just a big woman. I'm Rubenesque. You wouldn't know that because you're ignorant. I know all about it because I took an art course at the community college last semester.'

'I know fat,' Joyce said. 'And you're fat.'

I didn't like Joyce frightening Melvin Pickle. And I didn't like Joyce calling Lula fat. And I *really hated* that Joyce was able to find stupid dead Willie Reese when I hadn't been able to find him.

'Hey Joyce,' I said.

Joyce turned to look at me, and I threw one of my meatballs at her. It hit her square in the forehead and left a big splotch of marinara sauce.

'Bitch,' Joyce said, narrowing her eyes at me.

I narrowed my eyes back. 'Slut.'

'Skank.'

'Hag.'

Joyce grabbed Lula's spaghetti and dumped it on my head. 'I am *not* a hag,' she said.

'That was my lunch!' Lula said to Joyce. And she dumped Connie's chocolate milkshake down Joyce's cleavage.

Joyce pulled a gun on Lula, and Lula pulled a gun on Joyce, and they stood there pointing guns at each other.

'I'm going to fucking kill you,' Joyce said.

'Yeah, maybe, but I got a better gun than you,' Lula said.

'Your gun's a piece of shit compared to my gun,' Joyce said.

'I got a big whup-ass gun,' Lula said.

'Puleeze,' Joyce said. 'I've got dildos bigger than that gun.'

'Oh yeah? Well I bet Stephanie could out-dildo you any day of the week. She's got a Herbert Horsecock.'

'Are you shitting me?'

'No, honest to God. Tell her, Stephanie. You got a genuine Herbert Horsecock, right?'

'It was a two-for-one sale,' I said.

Melvin had managed to crawl under Connie's desk while all this was going on. I looked down and saw him reach out and tag Joyce in the leg with a stun gun. Joyce gave a squeak, went limp, and crumpled to the floor.

'I hope it was okay that I did that,' Melvin said. 'I was afraid she was going to shoot someone. I've never used one of those before. Will she be all right?'

'You did good,' Lula said. 'And don't worry about Joyce. We zap her all the time. When she opens her eyes, we'll tell her she slipped in the marinara sauce and knocked herself out hitting her head on the desk.'

I had noodles in my hair and noodles hanging off my ears and noodles sliding down my face.

'You're a magnet for mess,' Lula said to me. 'I've never seen anything like it.'

I picked some noodles off my shirt and dropped them

on Joyce. 'I have to go home to change. I'll be back later to go through my stack of losers.'

It was hard to go out through the bonds office front door and not look across the street. Even if I didn't look, if I kept my head down and my eyes diverted, I felt the eerie sadness that always lingers on a murder scene.

I drove back to my apartment, checking periodically for a tail, but so far as I could see, no one was following. I parked and trudged up to my apartment. I opened the door and ran into Ranger in my kitchen.

He looked me over and gave his head an almost imperceptible shake. 'Babe.'

'Food fight with Joyce Barnhardt.' I noticed Ranger had changed clothes and was looking comfy in washed-out jeans and T-shirt. 'I'm surprised to still find you here,' I said to him.

'Tank had to put a threatened witness in the safe house, so I'm going to need to stay here. We've got federal surveillance on the office.'

'I thought you were working with them.'

'I'm working with one man, and he's not sharing that information with anyone.'

'Morelli isn't going to understand this arrangement.'

'You can't tell Morelli I'm here. He's a cop. He's supposed to arrest me if he finds me.'

Ranger opened the refrigerator and took out a plastic-wrapped sandwich.

'Where'd that come from?' I asked him.

'Hal brought me some food and clothes and equipment.'

'Equipment?'

He unwrapped his sandwich and ate it standing. 'In the dining room.'

I looked in at the dining room and had to do deep breathing to keep from screaming. There were two computers, a printer and fax machine, four cell phones with chargers, two cases that I knew contained guns, four boxes of ammo, a large Maglite and a small Maglite, the scrapbook, a stack of folders that I knew were case files, and three sets of car keys.

'Two computers?' I asked.

'One's mine, and the other we took from the apartment in Virginia.'

'Anything interesting on it?'

'His surfing history is what you'd expect. Fascination with martial arts, guns, law enforcement, some porn. He has one basic search program. No information stored that would be of any use. He's done some blogging. Talking about wanting to be a cop. Then wanting to be a bounty hunter. Then he starts mixing fantasy and reality. He talks about working with a superstar bounty hunter. How he's learning a lot but has no respect for his mentor. There's a brief mention of a manhunt where he tracks his quarry to Florida. And the blog stops at that point.'

'I imagine you were the quarry he was stalking.'

'Yes. His scrapbook is filled with photographs from that visit. That's how he knew about Julie. He followed me, did his homework, and put the facts together.'

'You never suspected you were being stalked?'

'No. I try to always be vigilant, but I didn't pick this guy up. It was a complicated surveillance, too. He had to follow me when I left the office, and then follow me into the terminal, learn my destination, and then buy a ticket in time to get on the plane.'

'Do you think he had an accomplice?'

'There's no mention of anyone else.'

'What about Carmen?'

'He'd already assumed his Ranger identity when he met Carmen. He only uses her name once and then she becomes Stephanie. And that's the main reason I'm staying here. I'm sure he's going to come after you. I want to be there when he does.'

'You'll use me to get to Julie.'

'Are you okay with that?'

'Of course.'

Ranger picked a spaghetti noodle out of my hair. 'I'd like to think I was protecting you at the same time.'

'You mean I won't be a sacrificial virgin?'

'Too late for that, babe.'

My cell phone rang, and I looked at the screen. Morelli.

'How's it going?' I asked him.

'The ME is releasing Carmen's body today. We didn't get anything off the car. Doubtful if we'll get any DNA off Carmen. There wasn't a struggle. She was shot at close range through the open driver's side window. If you're reading the papers you'll see this is getting a lot of press. Daughter of Trenton bounty hunter is kidnapped and wife murdered.'

'Do you have any theories? Suspects?'

'I'm working on some angles. And I'm under a lot of pressure from above to bring Ranger in.'

'Understood.'

'Where are you?'

'I'm at home. There was an incident at the bonds office, and I ended up wearing my lunch. So I came home to change.'

'You aren't harboring a fugitive, are you?'

'Who, me?'

Morelli gave a disgusted sigh and hung up.

'Sounds like that went well,' Ranger said.

'Yeah. If I get caught with you I'll go to jail for a thousand years.'

Ranger gave me a smile that didn't quite make it to his eyes. 'I could make it worthwhile.'

'I'll hold that thought. Right now I need to take a shower and get the noodles out of my hair.'

I went into my bedroom, closed the door, and stripped

out of the spaghetti clothes. I hopped into the bathroom and stopped short when I looked at the sink. Ranger's razor and shaving gel, Ranger's toothbrush. I went back to the bedroom and looked in my closet. Ranger's clothes. Ranger had moved in. I locked myself in the bathroom and did some more deep breathing.

Eleven

R anger was slouched back in his chair, long legs stretched out under the dining-room table, his attention on the computer screen.

'How's the search going?' I asked him.

'It's going in slow motion. It feels like two lifetimes have gone by since he took Julie.'

'Anything new?'

'Pictures and background on Scrog. His mother is Puerto Rican. He comes by his skin and hair naturally. Nothing that has a big orange arrow on it saying Look Here. A profiler would find him interesting. Some of his makeup is classic and some is off the map.

'He's an only child. Early school reports are that he's smart, but he doesn't apply himself. He's a dreamer. Shy. Doesn't participate in class activities. Middle school, he does a nosedive. Failing grades. One of twelve boys questioned about molestation by a local priest. He receives counseling and the diagnosis is that he has low self-esteem and has difficulty separating fact from fiction, leading to a poor sense of consequence for his actions. High school, he's tracked with underachievers, doing some remedial work. At home he's spending hours playing computer games. His mother thinks he's a genius. His counselor thinks he might be borderline psychopath. His work history is erratic. He can't keep a job. He resents authority. Most of his jobs are sales. Music stores, movie theaters. Had a good run managing a comic book store with a gaming room. Took some computer courses at a community college but nothing came of it.'

'Were you able to find his connection to you?'

'Do you remember Zak Campbell? He was caught in a drug bust two years ago. He skipped and while he was in the wind they tied him to a double homicide. I tracked him to Virginia, and Tank and I made the apprehension in a music and video store. Scrog was working in the store at the time. I don't remember him, and I didn't have any contact with him that I remember. It was a quiet bust. We went in with mall security waiting at the store entrance. I approached Campbell, introduced myself, cuffed him, and walked him out.'

'No guns drawn?'

'No. Not necessary.'

'I guess you made an impression.'

'Apparently. That was the only connection I could find.'

I went into the kitchen and investigated the refrigerator. It was filled with Ranger food. Sandwiches, fruit, low-fat cream cheese, yogurt, and assorted snack vegetables all cut and washed. I selected a baby carrot and dropped it into Rex's cage. I looked at the phone on the counter by the cage and saw that I now had a working answering machine.

'I don't want an answering machine,' I yelled at Ranger.

'When this is over you can throw it away.'

I took a turkey sandwich and brought it to the table to eat.

'I thought you had spaghetti for lunch,' Ranger said.

'I wore it. I didn't get to eat any. The entire country's looking for Scrog. Hard to believe he hasn't been caught.'

'He's enjoying the game,' Ranger said. 'Probably has Julie stashed somewhere and goes out in disguise. He'll be careful at first, but the longer the game goes on the more chances he'll take.'

'Is there something I can do?'

'You can go about your business, so he has a chance to make a move on you.' He took a cell phone from the table. 'If you need to call me, use this phone. My number's programmed in. And make sure you're always wearing the panic button. It's tied into the RangeMan network. I can track you if you're wearing the button. If you catch someone following you, don't try to lose him.'

I looked at the car keys on the table.

'I'll be in a blue Honda Civic, a silver BMW sedan, or a silver Toyota Corolla,' Ranger said. 'And Tank will be in a green Ford Explorer.'

'I'll be in a black and white Mini Cooper,' I said. And my knees will be knocking.

I drove to the bonds office and parked at the curb where I could easily be seen. Stephanie Plum, psycho bait. Lula and Connie and Melvin were huddled around Connie's desk, debating the files in front of them.

'These people all creep me out,' Lula said. 'I don't want to work with none of them.'

'I liked the blond woman with the eagle tattooed on her big huge breast,' Melvin said.

We all turned to look at him, and he blushed bright red.

'Pickle, if you want to be a pervert you gotta stop blushing like that,' Lula said. 'You're gonna give perverts a bad name.'

The door opened and a woman walked in. 'I heard you're looking for someone to do bond enforcement,' she said.

We looked her over. No black leather, no tattoos that were visible, no gun strapped to her leg, no obvious missing teeth. Already she was ahead of everyone else. She was about my height and weight. Maybe a little chunkier. She had short brown hair cut into a bob. Not a lot of makeup. Some lip gloss. She was wearing a three-button collared knit shirt and tan slacks. She was perfectly pleasant-looking and amazingly forgettable.

She extended her hand. 'Meri Maisonet.'

'Maisonet,' Lula said. 'Isn't that a puppet?'

'That's marionette,' Connie said.

'I haven't got a lot of experience,' Meri said, 'but I'm a fast learner. My dad was a cop in Chicago, so I grew up around law-enforcement types.'

Connie gave her one of the forms we'd printed out, asking for name and vital statistics . . . like human being, yes or no. When she left, Connie punched her name into the computer.

'She looked sort of normal,' Lula said. 'What's with that?'

The information started flooding in.

'Everything checks out,' Connie said. 'Never been convicted of a crime, good credit. High school graduate. Waited tables for two years. The rest of her work history is on the line at a small brewery in Illinois. Relocated here two months ago, following her boyfriend. Twenty-eight years old.'

'You could start her in the office doing telephone work and computer searches,' I said. 'Then after she gets a feel for the job we can take her on some road trips.'

'Okay,' Connie said. 'If everyone's agreed, I'll call her and see if she can start tomorrow.'

'I'm getting restless,' Lula said. 'I feel like I need to go out and apprehend a scumbag.'

'Lonnie Johnson's still open, but I don't know where to begin with him,' I said.

'I'm chuffed over Caroline Scarzolli,' Lula said. 'We should have nabbed her. How does it look to get run over by a freaky old lady like that?'

'If we go back to the store she'll shoot us.'

'Not if we buy something.'

'No! I'm not buying any more dildos.'

'Don't have to be a dildo. They got lots of good stuff in that store. I might need a pair of panties.'

'Okay, fine,' I said. 'I'll wait in the car, and you can go in and buy panties.'

'I'm not just going for the panties,' Lula said. 'It's my cover. This here's serious shit. I'm gonna make an apprehension.'

I grabbed my shoulder bag and palmed my keys. 'I'll drive.'

I drove eyes forward, and I avoided checking the rearview mirror. If Ranger was following me to Pleasure Treasures, I preferred not to know. I parked on the street, two doors down from the store.

'I'm not going in,' I said. 'If she shoots you, you're going to have to drag your ass out the door, because I'm not going in to pick you up.'

'Hunh,' Lula said. 'I thought we were partners. How's

that for a partner to act? I'd go in there for *you*. I'd walk on fire for you. I'd bitch-slap the devil for you. You wouldn't catch me sitting in no car if my partner goes into the danger zone. If it was you in there getting shot for upholding the law of this great land, I'd be there right behind you.'

'Oh for crissake,' I said, wrenching the door open. 'Just shut up. I'll go with you.'

Caroline looked up and narrowed her eyes when we walked in.

'We're just shopping today,' Lula said. 'I was real happy with my dildo, and I thought I'd come back and browse.'

'We've got a one-day special sale on electronics,' Caroline said. 'In case you're interested.'

'I might be interested,' Lula said. 'I had a Madam Orgasmo, but I burned out the motor.'

I made an unsuccessful attempt to choke back a snort of nervous laughter. I turned my back on Lula and made a show of being engrossed in a display of erotic oils. There was Lickit and Luvitt Chocolate Love Cream. Kama Sutra Slick, rub it and it gets hot, blow on it and it gets hotter. Spank Me Peppermint Cooling Cream. Pleasure Jelly to minimize friction and avoid irritation, enriched with vitamin E and completely edible.

Here's the thing about all this stuff ... some of it I thought looked like fun. And truth was, I wouldn't have minded if Joe brought some of it home. I just felt like an idiot buying it for myself.

'She's got some good electronics,' Lula said to me. 'You want to come take a look?'

'No, that's okay,' I said. 'I'm trying to decide on these oils.'

'I think you should come take a look,' Lula said. 'I might need you to, you know, help me out here.'

'Those oils are all overpriced,' Caroline said. 'You're better off buying one of these vibrating miracle makers and they throw the oil in for free. It's a lot better bargain.'

'Gee, I really don't need a miracle maker though,' I said. 'I got a house full of them already.'

'Well, I need a miracle right now,' Lula said to me. 'You got any miracle makers in your bag? Do you see what I'm saying?'

'Sorry,' I told her. 'I left my miracle maker at home. It's in my cookie jar.'

'What's going on?' Caroline said. 'You two aren't thinking about trying anything funny, are you?'

Lula reached in her bag to get her gun but Caroline was faster. Caroline hauled the shotgun out from under the counter and pointed it at Lula's head.

'You better be reaching in that bag to get your credit card,' Caroline said.

'That's just what I'm doing,' Lula said. 'You sure are an untrusting person.'

'I'm thinking you both want to buy one of these Lady Workhorse cordless personal massagers. And I'm even going to throw in extra oil,' Caroline said.

I glared at Lula and forked over my credit card.

'It's not so bad,' Lula said when we were in the Mini. 'It's not like you got something useless. You'll get years of satisfaction out of this machine. Just don't go for thirds on account of apparently that's what freezes up the motor.'

I dropped Lula back at the office and sat at the curb for a while. I wanted Scrog to find me. I wanted to make contact and be done with it. I wanted the nightmare to be over for Julie and Ranger and everyone involved. After a couple minutes I called Ranger.

'Is anyone tailing me?'

'Not that I can tell.'

'Where are you?'

'Across the street, half a block south.'

'Now what?'

'Now we go home and order take-out.'

Fifteen minutes later, I opened the door to my apartment and Ranger followed me in.

'This is frustrating,' I said.

'He's out there, waiting for the right time to make his move. Probably he's enjoying the foreplay. We need to be patient. The police are scrambling, looking for him to be recognized. We're working from a different direction. We're playing the game with him.'

I tossed my purse and the Pleasure Treasures bag on the kitchen counter and rooted through the drawer where I kept all the take-out menus.

'What do you feel like?' I asked Ranger. 'Chinese, Italian, pizza, fried chicken?'

Ranger shuffled through the menus. 'Chinese. I'll have brown rice, steamed vegetables, and lemon chicken.'

And this is the problem with Ranger. I could spend a lot of time in bed with him, but he'd drive me nuts in the kitchen. I called the order in, adding Kung Pao chicken, fried rice, fried dumplings, and a piece of their Great Wall of Chocolate cake.

'When was the last time you talked to Morelli?' Ranger wanted to know.

'When I came home to change clothes.'

'You should check in with him. See if anything new is going on. Let him know you're working tonight.'

I slouched against the counter. 'I hate lying to Morelli.'

'You're not lying,' Ranger said. 'You're omitting some information. And if it makes you feel better, I'll make sure you work tonight.'

I did an eye roll and dialed Morelli.

'What?' Morelli said.

'I was just checking in.'

'Sorry, I'm still at work. Some big bad gangsta just took about fifty rounds in front of the B&B Car Wash and set a new world record for leaking out body fluids. They're not going to have to embalm this guy.'

'Anything new on Julie Martine or Carmen?'

'Nothing. We're waiting on DNA from Carmen. I'd like to spend some time talking to you, but I have to go. I'll be doing paperwork on this until tomorrow morning. Miss you. Be careful.' And Morelli disconnected.

'Some guy got ventilated in front of the B&B Car Wash,' I told Ranger. 'Morelli's working it.'

'Morelli's a good man with a sucky job,' Ranger said.

We were still in the kitchen and Ranger glanced over at the Pleasure Treasures bag. 'You must really like that store. You keep going back.'

'I don't want to talk about it.'

He looked in the bag and smiled. 'Lady Workhorse?' Ranger read the hype on the box. 'Hours of pleasure guaranteed.'

'You're going to torture me with this, aren't you?' I said.

Ranger took the gadget out of the box. 'I think we should take it for a test drive.' He turned it on, and it hummed in his hand. 'Feels good,' he said. 'Gentle action.'

'You're an expert?'

'No,' he said, shutting it off, setting it on the counter. 'I'm not really a gadget man.' He took the bottle of oil out of the bag. 'This holds more interest for me. Let's see what this does.' He opened the bottle, poured a drop into the palm of my hand and rubbed it with his fingertip. 'What do you think?'

'It's warm!'

'It says on the bottle it tastes like cherries.'

He touched his tongue to my oiled palm, and I felt myself go damp, and I worried my knees might buckle.

'W-w-well?' I asked.

'Cherries.'

The doorbell rang, and I sucked in some air.

'Are you expecting anyone?' Ranger asked.

'The food.'

'This fast?'

'They're just around the corner on Hamilton.'

Ranger capped the oil and got the door. And we carted the food into the living room to eat in front of the television.

'Scrog has been in Jersey for five days,' I said. 'He has to be staying somewhere. He has to be buying food. Why aren't we turning anything up? Where's he getting his money from?'

'You don't need money if you have a credit card. And he knows how to scam credit cards.'

I speared a dumpling. 'I'm not good at waiting.'

'I've noticed.'

Twelve

I woke up wrapped in Ranger's arms, our legs entwined, my face snuggled into his neck. He smelled nice, and he felt even better . . . warm and friendly. I enjoyed it for a moment before reality took hold.

'This is a little déjà vu,' I said to him. 'Didn't you start the night out on the couch?'

'No. I was on the computer when you went to bed. You were already asleep by the time I was done.'

'So you climbed in next to me? I thought when you moved in you'd be sleeping on the couch.'

'You thought wrong.'

'You can't sleep in my bed. It just isn't done. I have a boyfriend. He's a nice guy, but he's not good with sharing.'

'Babe, we're sharing a bed, not a sexual experience. I can control myself if you can.'

'Oh great.'

Ranger's face creased into a smile. 'You can't control yourself?'

I bit into my lower lip.

'Stephanie,' he said. 'You shouldn't tell me things like that. I'll take advantage.'

I blew out a sigh and rolled away from him. 'No you won't. You're Ranger. You're the guy who protects me.'

'Yes, but not from myself!'

I kicked the covers off and slid out of bed. I needed to find Edward Scrog. I needed to find him *now*! I couldn't manage another morning of waking up next to Ranger.

I took a shower and called Morelli.

'What's going on?' I said.

'I don't know,' Morelli said, sounding half asleep. 'Give me a hint?'

'With Carmen. With Julie Martine. Why hasn't someone found Julie Martine yet? What the heck are you guys doing? I don't understand what's taking so long.'

'What time is it?' Morelli wanted to know. I heard some fumbling and then swearing. 'It's seven-fucking-thirty,' Morelli said. 'It was after two when I got to bed.'

'Did I wake you?'

'Mmm.'

'Sorry. You always get up so early.'

'Not today. Talk to you later.' And he hung up.

I stomped out of the bedroom and into the kitchen where Ranger was making coffee. 'I'm going out,' I said.

'Where are you going?'

'I'm going out for muffins.'

'Give me five minutes to get my shoes on.'

'I don't have five minutes,' I said. 'I have things to do. I've got the panic button. I'll be fine. I'll bring a muffin back for you. What do you want, zucchini, no fat, no sugar, extra bran?'

I turned to go and Ranger scooped me up and carried me into the bedroom and tossed me onto the bed. 'Five minutes,' he said, lacing his shoes.

I lay there spread-eagle, waiting for him. 'Very macho,' I said.

He grabbed my hand and yanked me to my feet. 'Sometimes you try my patience.'

'You don't like it? You can leave.'

He slammed me into the wall and kissed me. 'I didn't say I didn't like it.'

'Okay, good to get that straightened out,' I said. 'Are we going to get muffins, or what?'

He walked to the lot with me, stuffed me into the passenger seat on the Mini and got behind the wheel.

'I thought you were supposed to be secretly following me. I thought I was supposed to be luring Scrog into action.'

'This morning, we're both luring him into action. Where do you want to go for muffins?'

'Tasty Pastry. And then Italian Bakery. And then Prizolli's. And then Cluck-in-a-Bucket for a breakfast muffin. And then the convenience store on Hamilton for a paper.'

'Trying to get yourself kidnapped?'

'Do you have a better idea?'

Ranger drove out of the lot and headed for Hamilton. 'Nice to know you're going proactive.'

By the time we got to the convenience store we had the Mini filled with muffin bags. 'Get coffee and a couple papers,' Ranger said. 'We'll have a picnic.'

Ten minutes later, we were on a bench in front of a used bookstore on Hamilton, next to the bonds office. The only way we'd have higher visibility would be to stand in the middle of the road.

'Anybody following us?' I asked Ranger.

'Three cars. Tank in the green SUV, a grey Taurus, and a mini-van.'

'Aren't you afraid you'll get arrested?'

'I'm more afraid I'll get shot by some good Samaritan citizen who saw my picture on *America's Most Wanted*.' He took a coffee and called Tank. 'Do you have a fix on the Taurus and minivan?'

I chose a carrot cake muffin and waited through a couple beats of silence while Ranger took in the information.

'Amateur bounty hunters,' Ranger finally said to me. 'Disable them,' Ranger said to Tank. 'I don't want Stephanie dragging that clutter around with her.' He disconnected, and we sat there for a half-hour eating our muffins, drinking our coffee and reading the paper. We were ready to leave for greener pastures when Morelli drove by, came to a screeching halt, and pulled to the curb. He got out of his SUV and walked over to us.

'You want to explain this to me?'

I told him about Edward Scrog and the scrapbook and the computer blogs.

'So you're sitting here trying to provoke him into making a move?'

'Yep.'

'This is a dangerous stupid idea. He shot his wife and there's no reason to think he won't shoot you.'

'Yeah,' I said. 'But I don't think he'll shoot me right away.'

'That makes me feel a lot better,' Morelli said. 'I'll tell that to my acid reflux.'

'I'll be fine. I swear!' I told him.

Morelli made a disgusted hand gesture. 'I didn't see this,' Morelli said. 'But I want to be kept appraised of the evidence you gather. And if you overstep boundaries with Stephanie and move in on me,' he said, turning to Ranger, 'I'll find you, and it won't be good.'

Morelli took a blueberry muffin out of a bag, jogged back to his car, and took off.

Ranger smiled at me. 'Just so you know, that's not going to stop me from trying to move in on him.'

'You and Morelli have an entirely different agenda. Morelli wants to marry me, and you want to . . .'

I stopped because I wasn't sure what word I wanted to insert. Not that any word was necessary. We both knew what Ranger wanted.

'Babe,' Ranger said. 'What I want to do to you is no secret. And I want to do it bad. But I can think with two body parts simultaneously, and I'm not going to do anything stupid.'

'That includes marriage?'

'Marriage, pregnancy, and anything nonconsensual.' He ran a finger under the strap on my tank top. 'I *will* make a move with partial consent.'

Ranger collected the bags and empty coffee cups and newspapers. He let himself into the bonds office, shut down the alarm, and dumped the trash into Connie's wastebasket. He reset the alarm, exited the office, and locked the door.

'I need to go back to your apartment,' he said. 'I have work to do this morning. Tank will stay with you, and I'll join him later in the day in a separate car. Try to move around and be visible. Remember to always wear your panic button.'

Ranger pulled me to him and kissed me before we got into the Mini.

'Just in case Scrog is watching I don't want to miss an opportunity to piss him off,' Ranger said.

Connie, Lula, and Melvin Pickle were in the office when I returned.

'Meri Maisonet is scheduled to start this morning,' Connie said. 'I'm going to have her run some of the simple search programs. If you have phone work or background checks, just put your file in the queue.'

I dropped Charles Chin, Lonnie Johnson and Dooby Biagi onto the Maisonet 'to-do' stack, writing a brief note for each. For Chin and Biagi, I asked for work and residence histories, followed by phone verification of the most current. For Johnson, I simply said, 'Find him.' Johnson's file was already thick with information. I didn't expect Maisonet to find him, but sometimes a new set of eyes saw things previously missed.

I paged through the remaining files and looked for jobs that didn't require the help of a partner. Edward Scrog would be more likely to approach me if I was alone.

I put Bernard Brown at the top of the list. He was low bond and low risk. His danger quotient was close to zero. Bernard had gotten drunk off his ass at Marilyn Gorley's wedding and in a display of ill-timed homage had set fire to a floor-to-ceiling drapery while holding his lighter aloft during a John Lennon song. The result was approximately $80,000 in damages to the banquet room of Littuchy's Restaurante. Probably no criminal charges would have been pressed but Bernard had panicked and punched out the maitre d' when the man had attempted to extinguish Bernard's flaming hair with a bottle of beer.

Bernard was a self-employed accountant working out of his house. Should be an easy catch.

'I'm going to help Bernard Brown get reregistered for court,' I said to Lula. 'It's not a two-man job. Maybe you want to stay here and help Meri get started. Tell her about being a BEA.'

'Sure, I could do that. I got a lot of things I could tell her.'

I avoided looking at Connie and whisked myself out of the office before I got stuck with Lula. I was on the sidewalk when I got a call from Morelli.

'I thought you should know we just towed an abandoned rental. It was rented at Newark Airport on Thursday around eight p.m. The name on the rental agreement was Carmen Manoso. That's why it bounced back to me. Not sure how it slipped through the FBI search. Maybe no one thought to look for something registered to Carmen. Anyway, I've got the car impounded and we're going through it. It looks like blood on the back seat. No way of knowing whose blood it is right now.'

'Is it a lot of blood?'

'Doesn't look like someone died there if that's what you're asking. The bad news is there was also a scrunchie on the floor of the back seat. You know, one of those things the kids use to tie up a ponytail. We photographed it and emailed it to Rachel Martine, and it's tentatively been identified as belonging to Julie Martine.'

'Where did you find the car?'

'It was by the train station.'

I called Ranger and gave him the news. Then I got into the Mini and drove to Hamilton. I was following Ranger's advice. Keep moving forward. Try not to think about the blood in the car.

Bernard Brown lived in a neighborhood that was adjacent to the Burg, just past St Francis Hospital. I drove down his street, checking off house numbers, parking when I reached his duplex.

Brown was forty-three years old and divorced. His house was neat but showing wear. A small sign next to Bernard's front door read BERNARD BROWN, CPA.

I rang his bell and waited, resisting the urge to burst into tears or frantically look around for stalkers.

Bernard answered the door in his pajamas and a knit cap. 'Yes?'

I gave him my card and introduced myself.

'I'll be a laughingstock if I go into court,' he said. 'I

know people. I do taxes for half the cops. I'll have to take my hat off, and I'll never live it down.'

My eyes went to the knit cap. Eighty degrees out, and he was wearing a knit cap. I looked at the mug shot on his bond agreement. Yow. Torched hair.

'Anything go up in flames besides your hair?' I asked him.

'The entire north side of the banquet room. Luckily no one was hurt. Except for the maitre d'. I broke his nose when he threw beer on me. That was before I knew my hair was on fire.'

'It's probably not so bad,' I said. 'Take your hat off. Maybe we can fix it.'

He took his hat off, and I tried not to grimace. He had patches of angry red scalp and tufts of singed hair. And it was all greasy with salve.

'Have you been to a doctor?'

'Yeah,' he said. 'He gave me the salve to put on.'

'You should shave your head. Shaved heads are sexy these days.'

He rolled his eyes up like he was trying to see the top of his head. 'I guess so, but I don't think I can do it myself.'

'Get dressed and we'll go to a hair salon before I take you to court.'

'Okay, but not the one on Hamilton. She's a big busy-body. And not the one on Chambers Street. My ex-wife goes there. And I don't want to go to the mall. Everyone looks at you. And it's all women in there. I'd feel funny. Maybe you could find someplace where men get shaved.'

'What's this?' Bernie asked. 'Why are we here?'

'This is the only place I could think of where men regularly get shaved.'

'This is a funeral parlor.'

'Yeah, have you ever seen anyone laid out with a two-day-old beard? No. Everyone's perfectly groomed when they get put in the box. And it's very private. And I just met these guys. They're new here. And they seem nice. And they make their own cookies.'

'It's creepy.'

'Don't be such a whiner. This is what I came up with. Take it or leave it.'

Bernie got out of the Mini and followed me into the funeral home. I walked through the lobby and saw that the office door was open. I could see Dave Nelson at his desk. He was wearing a crisp white dress shirt and navy slacks. He looked up and smiled when I got close.

'We have a problem,' I told him.

'Oh dear. I'm so sorry.'

'Not that kind of problem. Bernie here has had a hair disaster and needs someone to shave his head. I know you guys shave men all the time, so I thought maybe you could help us out.'

Bernie took his hat off, and Dave yelled for his partner.

'Scooter is here somewhere,' Dave said. 'He's wonderful with hair and makeup. He used to work at the Estée Lauder counter at Saks.'

'Estée Lauder,' Bernie said. 'I don't know. That's women's stuff.'

Scooter came up behind us. 'Estée Lauder has a wonderful line just for men. A dab of their eye serum each night would take years off your face,' he said to Bernie. He extended his hand. 'I'm Scooter. I was in the kitchen making cookies for tonight's viewing. I chose snicker-doodles for Mrs Kessman and big-chunk chocolate chip for Mr Stanko. I wanted something masculine for Mr Stanko. He was a truck driver. That's such a guy job, don't you think?'

Bernie shook Scooter's hand, and there was bolt-and-run all over Bernie's face, so I clapped a bracelet on him and attached the other half to my wrist.

'Just a formality,' I said to Bernie. 'Don't give it another thought.'

'Oh dear,' Scooter said. 'Is he a criminal?'

'No,' I told Scooter. 'He's having a bad hair month, and I thought he looked like he was getting cold feet. We were wondering if you could shave his head.'

'Of course I can shave his head,' Scooter said. 'He'll look wonderful. And I have some moisturizer which will be much better than that dreadful grease he's using now. Follow me back to my workroom.'

We crossed the lobby and trailed after Scooter into the new addition to the rambling funeral home. 'We'll use treatment room number two,' Scooter said. 'Number one is occupied.'

Bernie and I peeked into the room. Tilt-top stainless steel grooved table. Slight odor of formaldehyde. Carts filled with instruments best not seen in the light of day.

'This is an embalming room!' Bernie said.

'Isn't it wonderful?' Scooter said. 'State-of-the-art. And it has excellent light. Sit on the little stool by the table, and I'll get my razor. I've gotten used to working on people who are horizontal, so this will be a fun experience.'

'Oh fuck,' Bernie whispered. 'Get me out of here!'

'Chill,' I told him. 'He's going to shave your head, not drain your body fluids. It's not a big deal. And when he's done I bet he'll give you a cookie.'

'I guess congratulations are in order,' I said to Scooter when he got into position behind Bernie. 'Sounds like you've got a full house. Mrs Kessman and Mr Stanko. And a third body in prep.'

'The third body is just a holdover. It's poor Carmen Manoso. They autopsied her and released her, but we can't ship the body until Thursday. I had some free time, so I was trying to get her prettied up a little. Not much you can do to someone who's had their brain surgically removed, not to mention has a big bullet hole in the head, but I did what I could to soften it for her parents in case they open the casket.'

Carmen Manoso! And she was hanging out with nothing to do until Thursday.

'She needs a viewing,' I said to Scooter.

'Excuse me?'

'She's famous. The Burg loves a murder. You won't be able to shoehorn all the mourners in. You'll have to give out tickets like at the bakery.'

'I don't know. I'd have to check with her parents.'

'She doesn't belong to her parents. She belongs to her husband.'

'The murderer?'

'He's still her husband. And I bet he'd want her to have a viewing.'

'Interesting,' Scooter said. 'I'd have to bake *a lot* of cookies.'

I called Ranger on the special cell phone. 'You're not going to believe this . . . I'm at the funeral home on Hamilton, and they've got Carmen here.'

'Should I ask what you're doing at the funeral home?'

'No. It's not important. The important thing is, Carmen is here and isn't getting shipped off to Virginia until Thursday. And I thought since you're her husband you might want to hold a viewing so her friends and relatives who might be in the area could see her one last time.'

'Gruesome but clever,' Ranger said. 'Let me talk to whoever is in charge.'

I passed the phone over to Scooter.

'Is this Mr Manoso?' Scooter asked. 'The husband of the deceased?'

Thirteen

'Run this by me again,' Lula said. 'You took Bernie Brown to the funeral home to get his head shaved?'

'Yes. And it worked out great. And I checked him in at the courthouse after he got shaved, and he's already bonded out again.'

'And while you were at the funeral home, you ran into Carmen Manoso?'

'Yep. She was passed on to the funeral home for transport back to Virginia. Only they can't do it until Thursday.'

'And while you were there, Ranger called in and arranged for her to have a viewing?'

'He *is* her husband of record. And as such, he has a right to a viewing.'

'I don't suppose you got to talk to him?'

'Mostly he talked to Scooter. Financial arrangements and everything.'

Connie had been the one to rebond Bernie. She'd gotten back to the office minutes before me and was in the process of repairing a chipped nail. 'I don't usually go to viewings, but I'm going to that one,' she said, adding a fresh coat of fire engine red to her index finger.

Meri Maisonet was on the couch with a stack of files, making notes, not saying anything, but not missing much either. I wasn't sure how I felt about her. She seemed likeable enough, but something was off. Usually, people are a little nervous on a new job. They try too hard. Or they try to become background. Meri Maisonet didn't show any of that. She was dressed in running shoes, jeans, and another of the three-button knit shirts. No big hair lacquered with hair spray. Only lip gloss. Not exactly a Jersey girl, but then she hadn't been in Jersey for very long.

'How's it going?' I said to her.

'I have the information you asked me to get on Charles Chin and Dooby Biagi. I haven't had a chance to make the phone calls. I was going to do that now. I haven't done anything on Lonnie Johnson yet. Sorry.'

'It's okay. Lonnie Johnson is probably in Peru. I've run into a brick wall on him. I thought it wouldn't hurt to have someone new take a look. Don't spend a lot of time and energy on him, but maybe you can make a feeler phone call once in a while to one of the contacts.'

'I read about Ranger and Carmen in the paper,' she

said. 'And the little girl . . . Julie Martine. How terrible. What a tragedy.'

'Yeah,' Lula said. 'It's pretty freaky. Is there any information on the viewing yet?' she asked me. 'I don't want to miss that one.'

'Tomorrow at six.'

'Darn. I got a gig tomorrow at seven. I'm wearing my new feather outfit, and Sally and me got a new song rehearsed. I'll have to get there when the doors open, so I can fit it all in.'

'Isn't seven early for a band to play?'

'It's another old people's home. They get medicated at eight, and it's lights out at nine,' Lula said.

'It's a little creepy that her husband murdered her, and now he's arranging a viewing,' Meri said. 'Is he here in Trenton?'

'I don't know,' I said to Meri. 'He made the arrangements over the phone.'

'I never heard for sure that anyone said he murdered her,' Lula said.

'The paper said he was wanted for *suspicion*,' Meri said. 'Do you know him? Does he work for this office?'

'Yeah, we all know him,' Lula said. 'He's a good guy, too. If he does something bad it's because he has a good reason.'

'Hard to believe there's a good reason for murdering your wife,' Meri said.

'Maybe she was a spy,' Lula said. 'She could have been a secret agent or a terrorist.'

'Or an alien from Mars,' Connie said.

'Hunh,' Lula said. 'You're making fun of me, but I was serious. Who's to know if she was a double agent or something?'

'She wasn't a double agent,' I said. 'She was a woman on the edge.'

'She shot at Stephanie,' Lula told Meri. 'Put a ding in her car.'

'Why did she do that?' Meri asked.

'Frustrated because she couldn't find her husband,' I said. 'I approached her at the wrong time.'

'Now what are we going to do?' Lula wanted to know. 'You got someone on target for this afternoon?'

'I have some errands I have to run, and then tonight I'm going after Caroline Scarzolli.'

'I'm surprised to hear you say that,' Lula said. 'You must have some room left on your credit card.'

'I have no room left on my credit card, and I'm fed up with this woman. She's going down.'

'And how are you planning on doing this?'

'I'm going to wait outside and ambush her when she closes up shop.'

'You gotta be careful,' Lula said. 'She's seventy-two. You could break something that can't be fixed. Hard to find spare parts for something that old.'

A more likely scenario was that she'd beat the crap out of me.

'Are you riding with me for Scarzolli?'

'Hell yeah,' Lula said. 'I'm not missing you duke it out with a seventy-two-year-old porn peddler.'

'The store closes at eight o'clock. I'll meet you at the corner of Elm and Twelfth Street at seven-thirty.'

I left the bonds office and sat in the Mini for a couple minutes. I looked around and adjusted the rearview mirror. Didn't see anyone, but that didn't mean much. I edged out into traffic and drove toward the center of the city. I turned onto Ryder and then Haywood Street. Two blocks later I was in front of Ranger's office building. I nosed the Mini up to the garage gates, remoted them open, and slid into the garage interior. I sat there for ten minutes with my motor off.

I didn't have business here. I was simply riding around, trying to attract attention. The plan was to cruise every location Scrog might be watching and try to get him to follow me. I left the RangeMan garage and drove toward the train station. I turned onto Montgomery and got a call from Tank.

'You've picked up two more bandits,' Tank said. 'One of them is an idiot. And the other is a federal idiot. We're going to get rid of them for you. Don't look back.'

I didn't know exactly what that meant, but I didn't look back. I drove past the train station. I drove up and down

Hamilton. I stopped at Cluck-in-a-Bucket for a soda. I drove past the bonds office. I drove through the Burg, and I stopped at my parents' house.

'Did you hear?' Grandma Mazur said. 'There's gonna be a viewing for that poor Carmen Manoso. Not often you get to see someone's been autopsied.'

'I'm sure it'll be closed casket,' I said to Grandma.

'That would be a shame,' Grandma said. 'Of course, sometimes those lids just spring open.'

We were in the kitchen, and I saw my mother flick a quick look to the cabinet by the sink where she kept her emergency liquor stash.

'I might have to get a new dress for tomorrow night,' Grandma said. 'It's gonna be a big hoo-ha there. I hear they're thinking about giving out numbered wristbands if you want to get up by the casket. And there's a rumor that Ranger will show up. I bet the place will be crawling with hot FBI guys.'

I found myself wishfully staring at the liquor cabinet with my mother. Tomorrow night was going to be hideous. If there was any justice in this world, Edward Scrog would be caught and Julie Martine would be found unharmed before tomorrow night's viewing.

'I'm going with Lorraine Shlein,' Grandma said to me. 'You're welcome to come with us, if you want.'

'Gee, thanks, but I'm going to pass,' I told her. 'I might just pop in for a minute or two on my own.'

My mother latched onto my arm. 'You will get there on time, and you will watch your grandmother every second, do you hear me? You will not allow her to pry that casket lid open. You will not take her to a nudie bar after the viewing, no matter how much she begs. And you will not allow her to spike the punch bowl.'

'Why me?'

'You're responsible for this. It's one of your crime schemes. I can feel it in my bones. Myra Sklar said she saw you going into the funeral home today.'

'Coincidence,' I said.

I looked up and down the street when I left my parents' house. No suspicious cars in sight. I got into the Mini, drove to the cross street, and my phone rang. 'You just picked up a hitchhiker,' Ranger said. 'He's in a silver Honda Civic half a block behind you. He's wearing a black ball cap, and from this distance he's looking good. We're running the plate on the car. Take him home with you.'

I drove out of the Burg and turned right onto Hamilton. It was close to five, and Hamilton was clogged with cars and impatient Jersey drivers. I watched my rearview mirror and saw the Civic make the turn. He was four cars back. I went through a green light and the Civic got a red.

Ranger was still open on the phone. 'Don't worry about it,' he said. 'I've got a visual on him. I don't want him to suspect he's been spotted. Go home and park and go up to your apartment. We'll take it from here.'

An hour later, Ranger let himself into my apartment and threw his keys on the kitchen counter. 'We lost him. He turned around before he got to your apartment and drove to the government complex. Then he went into a parking garage and didn't come out. Dumped the car and left on foot and somehow we missed him.'

'Do you think he saw you?'

'Don't know.'

'You think it was Scrog?'

'Yes. The car was stolen. From what we could see he fit the description.' Ranger stood with his hands flat on the counter and his head down. 'I can't believe I lost him. I didn't want to get too close to him in the parking garage. I wanted him to lead us to Julie.'

'You'll have another chance,' I said. 'He's not going away until he completes his family.' I opened the refrigerator door. 'And look at this. Here's a piece of good news. While we were gone the food fairy arrived and filled the refrigerator.'

Ranger grabbed a beer and a roast beef sandwich.

'It's too bad this guy is crazy,' Ranger said. 'He's not stupid. And he has good instincts. If he was even the slightest bit sane, I'd hire him.'

Ranger took his beer and sandwich into the living room and turned the television on. He slouched on the couch and surfed until he found local news. His picture came up and then Carmen's. The anchor read a short clip about the viewing and the fact that there was still an alert for the missing child.

Ranger sunk lower into the couch. 'They said I was armed and dangerous.'

'Yeah,' I said. 'They got that right.'

Ranger crooked an arm around my neck and kissed me at my hairline.

'I talked to Rachel this afternoon,' Ranger said. 'She's falling apart. She had to be sedated after they showed her the hair scrunchie. I know this isn't my fault, but I feel responsible. I wish I could do more.'

'It looks to me like you have every resource available to you working to find Julie. I don't know what more anyone could do.'

'I feel guilty sitting here.'

'Make the most of it. In a half hour you'll be following me around again. I'm determined to get Caroline Scarzolli. I'm going to jump her when she closes the store tonight.'

'I think you should go shopping first. I like when you bring all that kinky stuff home.'

I walked out the back door alone, but I knew Ranger was watching. He'd gotten a ten-minute head start on me and was waiting to follow me to Elm and Twelfth where I'd hook up with Lula. Tank was there too. And God knows who else. Bad enough I was going to look like a moron running down Caroline Scarzolli . . . now I was going to do it in front of Ranger and his men.

I didn't get any warning phone calls, so I assumed the only people following me were good guys. I saw Lula's red Firebird parked on Elm. I pulled up behind her and got out of the Mini. I had cuffs tucked into the waistband on my jeans, and a stun gun and pepper spray stuffed into my two back pockets.

'Looks like you're loaded for bear,' Lula said.

'I just want to get this over and done.'

'I hope you know this is probably gonna ruin it for me to go shopping here. And I was starting to like this store.'

'Are you ready?'

'Sure I'm ready,' Lula said. And she hauled a Glock out of her handbag.

'Caroline Scarzolli is a first-time shoplifter,' I said. 'You can't shoot her.'

'Every time we see her she pulls a gun on us.'

'I don't care. You can't shoot her. That's the rule.'

'Boy, who died and made you boss?'

'I've always been the boss.'

'Hunh,' Lula said. 'I was just gonna scare her anyway.'

'From what I've seen so far, it's going to take more than you and me and that gun to scare her. This time we're going to try *surprising* her.'

We walked to where we could look into the store from the opposite side of the street. We were partially hidden behind a panel van, and we could see Scarzolli moving around, doing nothing. At five of eight she started to go through the closing ritual, and Lula and I crossed the street and hid in the narrow alley separating the store from the neighboring business.

The front lights went out, and we heard the door open and close and the dead bolt get thrown. I peeked around the corner and saw that Scarzolli was walking in the wrong direction. She was walking *away* from us. I popped out from the alley and tiptoed after her, closing the gap. She sensed I was there, turned and uttered an oath, and took off at a fast shuffle. I was almost within arm's reach of her when Tank stepped out of a shadow, blocking her way.

'Excuse me, m'am,' Tank said.

Scarzolli backed up a step and kicked Tank in the nuts. Hard to believe anyone that old could get her leg up that high, but Scarzolli scored a direct hit. Tank turned white and went down to his knees, hands at his crotch. Ranger was behind him, doubled over laughing.

I tackled Scarzolli and wrestled her to the ground. 'Someone friggin' cuff her!' I yelled.

'I'm trying,' Lula said. 'You gotta hold her still. She's like an octopus, waving her arms and legs around.'

I had at least ten pounds on Scarzolli, and I used my

weight to pin her. I saw Ranger's denim-clad legs straddle us both, saw his hands reach over and attach a cuff to Scarzolli's one wrist, and then the other. He was still smiling wide when he lifted me off Scarzolli and got me up on my feet.

'I can always count on you to brighten my day,' Ranger said.

'You just liked seeing Tank get kicked in the nuts.'

'Yeah,' Ranger said on a whisper of laughter. 'That was worth the ticket.'

Tank was up, trying to walk it off.

'Hope you didn't permanently damage anything,' Lula said to him. 'I always had an attraction to you.'

'Most women don't like me,' Tank said. 'On account of I'm too big.'

'I'm not most women,' Lula said. 'I could handle a big man. I *like* them big. The bigger, the better, is what I say.'

Scarzolli was still on the ground. She was making angry cat sounds, and she kicked out with her feet when anyone came near her.

'It's just a crappy first-time shoplifting charge,' I said to her. 'Get a grip.'

Ranger got her under the armpits, dragged her to the green SUV, and eased her into the back seat.

'Take her to the station,' he said to Tank. 'Bring her around to the back door. Stephanie will follow you in.'

'I'll leave my car here and go with you,' Lula said to

Tank. 'The crazy old lady might get out of control, and you might need some help. And after we drop her off, we could go get a burger or something.'

'I'm supposed to watch Stephanie,' Tank said.

'Don't worry about it,' Ranger said. 'I'll take care of Stephanie.'

Fourteen

I t was a little after ten when I finally walked into my apartment. No sign of Ranger, so I called Morelli while I waited.

'Long time no see,' Morelli said.

'Miss me?'

'No. Joyce Barnhardt is here with her trained dogs.'

'You're not going to get me going on that one. You hate Joyce Barnhardt.'

'Yeah, but Bob might like the dog part,' Morelli said.

'I just took down the old lady who runs the porn shop on Twelfth. Tank tried to help me, and she kicked him in the nuts.'

'I'm sorry I missed it. I'm not being sarcastic either. I'm *really* sorry I missed it. I assume you've got a full contingent of Ranger's Merry Men watching your back.'

'Yep. Mostly I pick up vigilantes, but we think Scrog followed me for a while this afternoon.'

'Ranger called it in to me, and we determined the car was stolen. I reached the parking garage shortly after Ranger. Scrog slipped through my fingers too.'

'Will you be at Carmen's viewing tomorrow?'

'Yeah. We've called in the National Guard to help with crowd control.'

'You haven't!'

'No, but we probably should. I was getting ready to go to bed,' Morelli said. 'I don't suppose you want to join me?'

'That would be nice, but I have to stay here and hope there's an attempt made to kidnap me.'

'Other men have girlfriends with safe normal jobs,' Morelli said. 'Like swallowing swords and getting shot out of a cannon.' And he hung up.

Ranger walked in and caught me with my head in the refrigerator.

'The food fairy left sandwiches, salad, fresh fruit, bagels and cream cheese and lox from Nova Scotia. But no dessert,' I told Ranger.

'I don't eat dessert.'

'Yes, but it's *my* refrigerator.'

Ranger removed the gun he'd been wearing and placed it on the kitchen counter beside his car keys. 'I'll pass the word to Ella.'

I nuked a bag of microwave popcorn and dumped it into a bowl. 'I talked to Morelli. He said you brought him in to help tail Scrog this afternoon. That was very classy.'

'Yeah, I'm a classy guy.' Ranger scooped up a handful of popcorn. 'A little girl's life is at stake. That doesn't leave much room for ego and turf wars.'

I brought the popcorn into the living room and turned the television on. 'Has anyone talked to Scrog's parents?'

'They're being watched, but no contact has been made. The feds are running that show, and they're playing it very quiet. My understanding is that Scrog was estranged from his parents. He wanted to be a cop, and they wanted him to go into a monastery.'

'Any news from the underground that he's trying to buy drugs or guns?'

'No. Nothing.'

'Sightings?'

'Constantly. They go to the hotline. So far they aren't seeing a pattern. There was a rash of sightings in South Beach yesterday, but it turned out to be Ricky Martin.'

I was working my way through my 472 worthless cable stations, and Ranger's cell phone rang. He answered and in a moment was on his feet, yanking me to mine.

'One of my men just got shot,' Ranger said.

He had his hand wrapped around my wrist, moving me through the apartment. He grabbed his keys and his gun off the kitchen counter without breaking stride. He was out the door and down the hall, his legs longer than mine, forcing me to run to keep up.

It's pretty much a straight shot down Hamilton to St Francis Hospital from my apartment building. If there's no traffic and you hit the lights right, it can be done in less than ten minutes. We were in the silver BMW with Ranger behind the wheel, his cell phone on drive mode.

Hal was on the line, fielding calls through Ranger's central dispatch. 'Manuel and Zero responded to a break-in at the bonds office,' Hal said. 'Manuel approached the office and was shot three times, through the plate glass window. The perp left through the back door. Do you want me to patch you through to Zero? He just arrived at the hospital with Manuel.'

'No,' Ranger said. 'I'll take it from here.'

We were a block from the bonds office and traffic was stopped in front of us. Police strobes pulsed beyond the traffic. Ranger turned off Hamilton and wove his way through side streets. Five minutes later, Ranger turned onto the street leading to the emergency entrance at the hospital.

'I can't go in,' he said. 'I'm going to drop you off, and then I'm going to loop around and park on Mifflin. Send Zero out to see me. Remind him to check that he isn't followed. You're wearing the panic button, and you have a secure phone. Call me when you know something about Manuel.'

I hopped out of the BMW and hurried to the emergency room entrance. I saw Ranger wait until I was inside, and then he took off. Zero was sitting in the waiting room. Easy to find him in his RangeMan uniform.

'How's Manuel?' I asked.

'He's in the back. He was hit three times, but he was wearing a vest, so the two he took in the chest just knocked him back. The third got him in the arm. He's waiting for a doctor. It's a zoo in here tonight.'

Zero was right about the zoo. The waiting room was packed with the walking wounded and their relatives. I sent Zero out to talk to Ranger, and I looked around to see who was on duty. Growing up in the Burg meant you almost always knew someone working emergency. Not that it mattered. There was always so much traffic in the ER area, if you knew the drill you could just walk through to the treatment area.

I got two cups of coffee from the machine and walked past the ER desk.

'Excuse me,' the woman on duty said.

'Just taking coffee to my husband,' I told her. 'I'll be right out.'

I went bed to bed, peeking around curtains, until I found Manuel. He was on his back, hooked up to an IV. His shirt was off and his bicep was wrapped in a bloody towel. Gail Mangianni was with him. I went to high school with Gail. Her sister is married to my cousin

Marty. Gail is an ER nurse and almost always works a night shift.

'Hey girlfriend,' Gail said. 'What's up?'

'Came to see my husband Manuel Whatshisname.'

'Lucky for you we allow wives back here,' Gail said. 'Otherwise you'd have to leave.'

'How's he doing?'

'He's going to be flying in a couple minutes. I just gave him a shot.'

'I need to talk to him before he takes off,' I said.

'You better talk fast. He's starting to drool.'

'Do you know who shot you?' I asked Manuel.

'It was weird. I looked into the glass and this guy looked back out at me, and it was like looking at Ranger. I sort of freaked, you know, like I was confused. And then he raised his gun and the whole time I swear he never blinked, he just kept staring into my eyes while he was shooting me.'

I felt the skin crawl along the nape of my neck. Edward Scrog had executed his wife and gunned down Ranger's man in cold blood. He'd looked Manuel in the eye and shot him without hesitation. And now, I imagined, Edward Scrog was returning to his hiding place and his ten-year-old hostage. Julie Martine was locked away somewhere, waiting for the monster to return. The horror of it all pressed against the backs of my eyes and clogged my throat. I was gripping the metal bed rail, and I looked down and saw that my knuckles were white. I made an effort to relax and focused on Manuel.

'You could see in the dark office?'

'I had a flashlight on him. I was right up to the glass, trying to see in.'

'What happens next?' I asked Gail.

'I'm waiting on a doctor. Probably we'll take him into the OR to remove the bullet, but I don't think it's major surgery. He's going to have some bruising on his chest from where the bullet impacted the vest. I imagine we'll monitor him and keep him overnight.'

'Can I see him when he comes out of surgery?'

'Sure,' Gail said. 'You're his wife.' She looked over at his chart. 'You're Mrs Manuel Ramos.'

I returned to the waiting room and called Connie. Since Vinnie was still out of town, Connie would get called in to check out the office.

I heard the connection open and there was a lot of back-ground noise and police band squawk.

'*Hello*,' Connie yelled over the noise.

'I imagine you're at the office.'

'Yeah, and you would be where?'

'At the hospital checking on the guy who got shot.'

'How is he?'

'He'll be okay. What are you finding at the office?'

'Guns and ammo missing. That's about it. He left the

petty cash. Probably didn't have time to look. It was locked away. Didn't want a George Foreman grill.'

'The police having any luck finding him?'

'No. He was long gone by the time they got there. My understanding is that he set off the alarm when he entered, and Rangeman responded fast because they already had men in the area. I guess he shot the one guy and then took off out the back door.'

'Is Morelli there?'

'No. We got a bunch of uniforms and two suits. A guy from out of state named Rhodenbarr. I don't know any of them. They tell me a lot of the men are at an awards banquet for Joe Juniak who was just appointed Emperor of the Universe.'

'Do you need help?'

'No. I'm fine. And Meri is here. She was on her way to pick up a pizza and she saw all the cop cars so she stopped.'

I called Ranger next and told him everything I knew. 'I'm going to wait until Manuel is out of surgery,' I said.

'Stay inside the hospital. Call me when you're ready to leave.'

'Is Tank back on the job?'

'Yeah. And he's smiling but completely wasted. I saw him run a half marathon once and look better than this.'

'He's had a tough day. First he got his clock cleaned

210

by an old lady, and then he had to buy Lula a burger.'

'Must have been some burger.'

I thought Ranger sounded a little wistful.

I was in my knit tank top and cotton boxers. My teeth were brushed, and my face was washed and moisturized. I was exhausted. I wanted to go to sleep. Problem was . . . there was a man in my bed. And I didn't exactly know what to do with him. I knew what I *wanted* to do with him. And I knew what I *should* do with him. Unfortunately, what I *wanted* to do and what I *should* do were two very different things. Even without Morelli, I'd have a dilemma deciding on a path of action with Ranger. I blew out a sigh. Stephanie, Stephanie, Stephanie, I said to myself. That's a big fib. You know exactly what you'd do about Ranger if Morelli wasn't in the picture. You'd ride him like Zorro.

Ranger was watching me. 'Are you coming to bed?'

'I'm thinking about it,' I told him.

'Come closer, and I'll help you decide.'

'Omigod,' I said on a sudden flash of sleep-deprived insight. 'You're the big bad wolf.'

'There are some similarities.'

I grabbed my pillow and took the extra blanket draped over the chair. 'I'm too tired to wrestle with this tonight. Since you can't sleep on the couch, I'll sleep on the couch.'

I stomped off to the living room with my pillow and blanket, flipped the lights off, and flopped onto the couch. Turns out the couch is too short. No matter, just curl up a little, I told myself. Turns out the couch is too narrow. And the cushions were sliding around. And there was a ridge of something sticking up into my back. I threw the pillow and blanket onto the floor and tried sleeping on the floor. Too hard. Too flat.

I stomped back into the bedroom, climbed over Ranger, and slid under the covers.

'The princess returns,' Ranger said.

'Don't start.'

I rolled around in the dark, trying to get comfortable.

'Now what?' Ranger said.

'I left my pillow in the living room.'

Ranger reached out and gathered me into him. 'You can share mine. Just don't climb on top of me like you did last night or those cute little pajamas you're wearing will be on the floor when you wake up.'

'I didn't climb on top of you!'

'Babe, you were all over me.'

'You wish. And your hand is on my ass.'

'My hand on your ass is the least of your worries.'

I woke up completely entangled with Ranger.

'Uh-oh,' I said. 'Sorry! I seem to be on top of you.'

Ranger kissed my neck and slid the strap to my tank

top off my shoulder. And then his hand was under my little knit top, his fingers skimming across my breast. He kissed me, and our tongues touched, and his mouth moved lower and lower . . . and lower! And this is the thing I knew about Ranger from the one time we'd been together. *Ranger made love.* And Ranger liked to kiss. Ranger kissed *everything. A lot.*

Ranger froze in mid-kiss.

'What?' I asked.

'Someone's at your door. I just heard the lock tumble.'

'How could you possibly hear the lock tumble? You had your head under the covers!'

He moved off me, slipped out of bed, and started for the door.

'Holy cow!' I said. 'You can't go to the door like that!'

'My gun's in the kitchen.'

'Yes, but your underwear's on the floor in my bedroom!' And that wasn't the biggest problem.

The front door to my apartment opened, and the chain caught with a snap. There was a moment's silence, and then Morelli's voice sounding impatient.

'Steph?'

There've been times in my life when I couldn't get a decent date. Long dry spells with no boyfriend, no sex, no relationship prospects. And now I had *two* men. Life was a bitch. I scrounged under the covers for my pajamas, rammed myself into them and jumped out of bed. I padded barefoot to my front door and peeked at Morelli over the chain.

'Hi,' I said.

'Are you going to let me in?'

'Sure.'

I slid the chain back and opened the door for him.

'I'm not staying,' he said. 'I'm just dropping off.' And he tossed a duffle bag into the foyer.

'What's this?' I asked.

'I'm moving in.'

Oh boy.

Morelli looked at the pillow and blanket in the living room. 'Who's sleeping on the floor?'

'Ranger's here.'

'Going to be tight in the bathroom in the morning,' Morelli said. And he kissed me and left.

I made coffee and ate a Pop Tart while Ranger showered. Then I went across the hall and swiped Mr Wolesky's newspaper. I was standing in the kitchen, reading about the shooting when Ranger strolled in. He was dressed in jeans and a T-shirt, his hair still damp.

'That was close,' he said, helping himself to coffee.

'Yeah, you almost opened the door to Morelli.'

'I wasn't talking about Morelli. I was talking about us.'

'That too,' I said.

Ranger sliced a bagel and looked for the toaster.

'It's broken,' I told him.

He turned the broiler on and slid the bagel into the oven.

'That's surprisingly domestic for the man of mystery,' I said to him.

He looked at me over the rim of his coffee mug. 'I like things hot.'

Fifteen

The sidewalk in front of the bonds office was wet from being scrubbed down and hosed off in an attempt to remove the bloodstains, and two guys were working to repair the front window. I parked the Mini in front of the used bookstore, carefully stepped around the men and the glass, and walked through the open front door.

It was after nine, and I was the last to arrive for work. Connie was at her desk. Meri was at a card table with a phone and a laptop, Melvin Pickle was a filing demon, and Lula was on the couch reading *Star* magazine.

'How's Ranger's man?' Connie wanted to know.

'He's okay. I stayed at the hospital until he was out of recovery. They wanted him to spend the night, but he refused. Lucky for him he was wearing a vest.'

'He told the police it looked like Ranger shooting him,' Meri said.

'Yes, but when I talked to him in the hospital, he said

that was a first impression. He said it freaked him out, and he didn't respond because of it. His second impression was that it wasn't Ranger. It was someone who was dressed in black and resembled Ranger.'

'How could he be sure it wasn't Ranger?' Meri asked. 'I mean, he was getting shot!'

'He said he was right up to the window, shining his flashlight on the guy. He said the guy looked him in the eyes and raised the gun and shot him without blinking.'

'Gives me the heebie jeebies,' Lula said. 'That's so cold. And I bet he's the one who's got the little girl. How terrible is that? That child must be terrified.'

'I don't know,' Meri said. 'I'm having a hard time with this. Everything always points back to this Ranger person. How can you be so sure it's not actually him? I mean, he could have gone nutso. From what I hear he was dark anyway, like Batman. Silent. Tortured soul. Always dressed in black.'

'The all black clothes just make things easy,' I said. 'He doesn't have to mix and match. He doesn't have any decisions in the morning. His housekeeper doesn't have to worry about colors running.'

Meri's eyes got wide. 'Do you know him *that* well?'

'Um, no,' I said. 'I was sort of putting myself in his place.' Okay, so that was liar, liar pants on fire, but there was something about Meri that had me on guard. Hard to say what it was, but she still felt off to me. Something about her manner, the way she looked, the way she asked questions, the way she showed up and was too good to be believed . . . too perfect for the job.

'Your problem is you don't know him,' Lula said to Meri. 'If you knew him you'd understand. He's dark in a good way. And besides, anybody *that hot* can't be all bad.'

'What's happening with Dooby Biagi and Charles Chin?' I asked Meri.

She handed the files over to me. 'They're both business as usual. I made some phone calls and neither seems to have skipped town.'

'Ready to ride?' I asked Lula.

'Yeah, I gotta talk to you anyway.'

We took my Mini, and Lula waited until we were away from the curb before she spoke.

'I got three things,' she said. 'First is, there's something bothering me about Meri. I don't know what it is. Second thing, where the heck did Ranger and Tank come from last night? Tank doesn't talk. He wouldn't say nothing. And third is, Tank don't need to talk because he was right about being big. It's like wrestling some prehistoric monster. Like having a go at King Kong. And he's big all over the place, if you know what I mean. I tell you I'm in love. I don't need to go visiting that Pleasure Treasures on account of I found my own pleasure treasure and his name is Tank. Probably he has some other name, but I don't know what it is. He wouldn't tell me that either.'

'Maybe it's just that Meri is new.'

'Melvin is new, and I don't feel like that about him. And it isn't that I don't like Meri. She's real likeable. I just don't feel comfortable somehow.'

I had Dooby Biagi's file on top. Dooby worked the counter at one of the fast-food places and got caught with his hand in the cash register. He said he was making change, but the day manager found more than change in Dooby's pocket. Dooby had a couple hundred plus a pipe and a dime bag of crack.

Dooby lived in a row house in the Burg. According to Meri's research, Dooby rented with three other guys. And needless to say, Dooby was unemployed.

I idled in front of Dooby's house, and Lula and I stared out at it, neither of us moving.

'I don't feel like doing this,' I finally said.

'Me either,' Lula said. 'I'm wore out with this job. I'm tired of dragging these people off to jail. Nobody's ever happy. I feel like the Grinch.'

'Somebody's got to do it,' I said, trying to convince myself of my worth.

'I know that,' Lula said. 'This here's for the good of society. It's not like the police have time to find these people. I just think I need a mental health day.'

I looked in my rearview mirror for Ranger.

Lula looked too. 'He's back there, isn't he? He's

following you around, right? That's how come they were at the Pleasure Treasures.'

'We're hoping the Ranger impostor will come after me. And then when he nabs me he'll lead us to Julie.'

'That's a pretty good plan,' Lula said. 'Unless the Ranger impostor decides to kill you instead.'

I slumped a little lower in my seat.

'It's gonna be a hot one today,' Lula said. 'You know what I'd like to do? I'd like to go to Point Pleasant and play the claw machine in the arcade and get one of them orange and vanilla swirly frozen custard ice creams.'

I put the Mini into gear, hooked a U-turn, and drove back to the office. 'We need to take your car,' I said. 'Is it parked in back?'

'Yep. It's in the lot. The glass truck was parked in my usual spot on the street.'

'Just changing cars,' I said to Connie, as we breezed through the office.

I selected a gun from the cabinet, took a box of rounds, and left the panic button in the gun cabinet. I dropped the gun and the ammo in my bag and Lula and I went out the back door.

'I know this is the wrong thing to do,' I said to Lula, 'but I need a break from all the sad scary things. And I need to get away from Ranger for a couple hours.'

'I don't see nobody back here,' Lula said. 'I think we tricked them.'

* * *

Ranger called when we were on the bridge, crossing the Manasquan Inlet. 'Where are you?' he asked.

'I'm taking a day off.'

'You removed the panic button.'

'Yes, but I took a gun. And it's even loaded. And I have extra bullets. And Lula is with me.'

Silence.

'Hello?' I said. 'Are you mad?'

'Mad doesn't come close. Are you going to tell me where you are?'

'Not when you're in this kind of mood.'

More silence.

'Are you trying to control yourself?' I asked. Easy to be brave when Ranger was in Trenton, and I was in Point Pleasant.

'Don't push me,' Ranger said.

'You can just keep going and going and going,' I told him. 'I'm not that strong. I'm running low on happy. And I hardly have any brave left at all. We were careful not to be followed. We're armed. We're sober. I'll be home this afternoon. I'll call you when I get to Trenton.' I disconnected and broke into a nervous sweat. 'That was Ranger.'

'No shit.'

'It gets worse,' I told her. 'He's been staying in my apartment, and this morning Morelli moved in.'

'Let me get this straight. You got Ranger and Morelli living with you. At the same time.'

'Looks that way.'

Lula pulled into the lot at the pavilion. 'Girl, you got a problem. You can't put two alpha dogs in the same kennel. They'll kill each other. It's not like those two are ordinary men. They got enough testosterone between them that if testosterone was electricity they could light up New York City for the month of August.'

'I don't want to talk about it. I want to get some ice cream and sit in the sun and listen to the ocean.'

Ranger was brooding in the parking lot in front of my condo when I pulled in. He was in a RangeMan SUV, which meant it was new, it was immaculate, it had the big engine, it was black with black tinted windows, and it had the big-bucks chrome wheel covers.

He got out of the SUV and silently escorted me to my apartment.

'Is Morelli here?' I asked him.

'No. Not yet, but it's almost five, so I imagine he'll be rolling in soon.' He unlocked the apartment door, stepped in first, and looked around before he motioned me in. 'Your nose is sunburned,' he said. 'They don't sell sunscreen at Point Pleasant?'

'Are you sure I was at Point Pleasant?'

'I knew it was either the mall or Point Pleasant, and

there were no background mall sounds when you talked to me.'

'You followed me down there?'

'No. I sent Hal and Roy.'

'I didn't see them.'

'That's my point. Hal doesn't blend in. It's like being followed by a stegasaurus. So if you didn't see Hal, you sure as hell weren't going to pick out Edward Scrog.' He tossed his keys on the kitchen counter. 'If you have an issue with me I expect you to tell me about it, not run away.'

'You don't listen.'

'I always listen,' Ranger said. 'I don't always *agree*. I have a problem right now that I can't seem to solve by myself. I need you to help me find my daughter. And there's an even bigger problem involved. I feel a financial and moral obligation to my daughter. I send child support, I send birthday and Christmas presents, I visit when I'm invited. But I've kept myself emotionally distanced. I'm *not* emotionally distanced from *you*. I couldn't live with myself if something happened to you because I was using you to find someone . . . even if that someone was my daughter. So I have to make every effort to keep you safe.'

'You're a little smothering.'

'Deal with it.' He looked over at Morelli's duffle bag still sitting in the foyer. 'This should be interesting.'

'You're not going to do something stupid and macho, are you?'

'I try hard not to do things that are stupid. I'm willing to make an exception in this case. I'm not leaving. And if you sleep with him while I'm here, I'll have to kill him.'

If anyone else had said that I'd burst out laughing, but there was a slight chance Ranger was serious.

I took a shower and spent a few minutes on makeup and used the roller brush on my hair. Then I spent a few more minutes on makeup. I wiggled into a little black dress and stepped into black heels. I sashayed out of the bedroom and found Morelli and Ranger in the kitchen, eating.

Ranger was eating a chopped salad with grilled chicken. Morelli was eating a meatball sub. I checked out the refrigerator and discovered Ella had dropped off a cheesecake . . . so that's what *I* ate. No one said anything.

I finished off the cheesecake and glanced at my watch. Six o'clock. 'Gotta go,' I said. 'Don't want to be late for the viewing.'

Ranger had the panic button in his hand, and he was looking my dress over. If we'd been alone, he would have slipped it into my cleavage, but Morelli was watching with his hand on his gun.

'Oh, for God's sake,' I said. 'Just give me the stupid thing.' I took the panic button and stuck it into my Super Sexy Miracle Bra.

'GPS,' Ranger said to Morelli.

'Probably I can find her breast without it,' Morelli said. 'But it's good to know there's a navigational system on board if I need it.'

I saw Ranger's mouth twitch, and I was pretty sure it was a smile. I wasn't sure what the smile meant. First guess would be he was thinking he had no problem finding my breast without GPS either.

I grabbed my handbag and swung my ass out of the kitchen, out of the apartment, and down the hall. I was thinking I might get into the Mini and drive to California. Start over. New job. New boyfriend. No forwarding address. I checked my rearview mirror. Ranger in the silver BMW. Morelli in his green SUV. Two RangeMan goons in a black SUV, too far back to see their identity. I was leading a friggin' parade. And the parade would follow me to California.

'Stephanie,' I said, 'you're in deep shit.'

The little lot attached to the funeral home was packed by the time I got there. I drove up and down the streets, but the curbside parking was taken for blocks. I double-parked and got out of the car. The shiny black RangeMan SUV rolled up to me, the window slid down, and Hal looked out from the passenger seat.

'RangeMan valet parking?' I asked.

Hal got out, rammed himself into the Mini, and I thought I saw the tires flatten a little. Both cars drove off. One mark on the tally for Ranger. *Employees available for valet parking.* On the Morelli side was *hates salad.*

I fought my way through the crush of people on the funeral home porch and wormed my way through the crowd in the lobby. I felt a hand at my back and heard Morelli's voice in my ear.

'Go do your thing, and I'll keep you in sight,' Morelli said. 'Ranger has some men in here who are also watching you. Probably there are a couple feds as well.'

I got into the viewing room, but there was a wall of people in front of me. I looked left and saw a head rising above all else. It was Sally Sweet, close to seven feet tall in his heels. I inched closer and saw he was wearing shocking pink platform pumps with a five-inch stiletto heel and a raincoat. Lula was beside him, also in pink heels and a raincoat. I looked at the ground and saw they were molting pink feathers.

'This here's a mess,' Lula yelled when she saw me. 'I can't go forward, and I can't go back.'

Grandma elbowed her way over to us. 'I lost my sense of direction. Which way's the casket? I can't see a darned thing.'

Sally picked Grandma up and held her over his head.

'Okay,' Grandma yelled to Sally. 'I got a fix on it. You can set me down now.' And Grandma took off, burrowing through the bodies.

Sixteen

I tried following, but Grandma was instantly swallowed up by the mob of mourners.

'Can you see her?' I asked Sally.

'I can't exactly see her, but I can see people moving to get out of her way. She's almost all the way up front. She should pop out any minute now. Yep, there she is. She's right in front of the casket. Looks like the funeral director standing firm to one side, and everyone else is milling around, jockeying for position. And there's Granny, holding her ground. I can only see the tops of heads,' Sally said. 'Hold on, something's happening. People are scrambling. The funeral director's waving his arms and bobbing around.'

I heard someone shouting to stand back. Then some hysterical screaming. And a loud crash. Someone yelled out, 'Get her!'

'What's going on?' I asked Sally.

'It looks like a riot. Someone just got knocked into a big

floral arrangement, and it all went over. And I think the funeral director's thrown himself on top of the casket. Looks like there's someone under him. I can see two feet sticking out. It's someone in patent leather pumps. Omigod, I think it's your granny.'

'I bet she tried to get the lid up,' Lula said. 'You know how she hates when she can't see nothing.'

My mother was going to kill me.

'Everybody looks real angry,' Sally said. 'We should probably try to rescue Granny.'

'Coming through,' Lula said, head down, plowing her way to the front. 'S'cuse me, move your bony little ass, outta my way, make way for mama.'

Sally and I rode in her wake, stumbling up to the casket, coming nose to nose with Dave Nelson.

Nelson grabbed me by the front of my shirt. 'You have to help me. These people are insane. Your grandmother is insane. She started it all. Somehow she got the lid up. And now *everyone* wants to see!'

'Is there a problem with that?' I asked.

'Carmen Manoso has been autopsied! She makes Frankenstein look *good*. She's had her brain taken out and weighed and put back in!'

'Oh yeah,' I said. 'I forgot.'

'I drove here from Perth Amboy,' some lady said. 'I'm not leaving until I get to see the body.'

'Yeah,' everyone said. 'We want to see.'

'They're going to take my mortuary apart, brick by brick,' Dave whispered. 'These people are all ghouls.'

'They just want to be entertained,' I told them. 'I bet you ran out of cookies.'

I stood on a chair and yelled at the crowd. 'Everybody quiet down. We can't open the casket, but we've got some exciting entertainment. Two members of the What band have agreed to do a special performance.'

'We can't do that,' Lula said. 'We don't have any music. And besides, we're professionals. We don't do this shit for nothing.'

'All kinds of people have come to see Carmen,' I told Lula. 'I wouldn't be surprised if a bunch of television crews were here. And I think I saw Al Roker when I walked in.'

'Al Roker! I love Al Roker. Do you think he's married?'

'I thought you were in love with Tank.'

'Yeah, but Al is so cute. And I hear he has his own barbecue sauce. You gotta love a man's got his own barbecue sauce. Boy, it'd be real hard to have to choose between Al and Tank.'

'There's a stage behind the casket,' I said. 'And there's even a microphone on that pulpit thing. This could be your big break.'

Okay, so I didn't really see Al Roker and this was probably a rotten thing to do, but I couldn't figure anything else out. And who knows, maybe there were television people in the viewing room. From where I was standing, it looked like half the state was here.

Lula and Sally took the stage and stood there in their pink high heels and raincoats and the whole room went silent. They took their raincoats off and the room went nuts. Lula looked like a big round pink puffball in her genuine domestic farm-raised fowl feather dress. Sally looked like nothing anyone had ever seen before. He was wearing the heels and the flamingo feather thong. The thong sack looked like dyed dead bird. And the rest of Sally made a strong case for full body waxing.

'Hey, all you fuckin' mourners,' Sally yelled. 'Are you fuckin' ready for this?'

Everyone cheered and clapped and hooted. Jersey's always fuckin' ready for anything. Especially if it's hairy and in a thong.

Lula and Sally started singing and waving their arms and dancing around and the mourners all backed up a couple feet. Feathers were flying, and Lula was sweating, and the room was starting to smell like wet water fowl. By the time Lula and Sally got through the second song the room had emptied out some.

'Thanks,' I said to Lula. 'That did the trick. Everybody's happy now. I think you can stop singing.'

'Yeah,' Lula said, climbing off the stage. 'We were pretty good. Too bad, I didn't see Al Roker out there.

But I think I saw Meri. Guess she didn't want to be left out.'

'I always wanted to be in a rock-and-roll band,' Grandma said. 'I could do all those dancing moves too. I'm old, but I still got legs. I can't play any instruments though.'

'Can you sing?' Sally asked.

'Sure. I'm a good singer,' Grandma said.

'I've been thinking now that we're playing all these geezer gigs we could use an older demographic in the band. You'd have to get some outfits, and we practice once a week.'

'I could do all that,' Grandma said.

'Sometimes we're not done until ten o'clock when we do assisted living,' Sally said. 'Those cats get to stay up later. Can you stay up that late?'

'Sure,' Grandma said. 'Sometimes I even watch the ten o'clock news.'

'We could dress her up like us,' Lula said to Sally. 'And I'll teach her my moves.'

'Do you wear these feather outfits all the time?' Grandma asked. 'They look real pretty, but they don't seem practical. Sally's doodle sack lost all its feathers. Not that it don't look good bald like that, but it must be a lot of work putting those feathers back all the time.'

'Yeah, the feathers didn't totally work out,' Lula said. 'I got feathers up my ass. I gotta go shopping again.'

'Looks like the crowd's thinned out,' Grandma said. 'I'm going to see if there's any cookies left in the kitchen.'

'Sorry about the casket getting opened,' I said to Dave. 'I was supposed to keep an eye on Grandma, but she got away from me in the crowd.'

'It worked out okay,' Dave said. 'But it was scary there for a while. I was doing the best I could to protect your grandmother and the deceased, but I couldn't have held them off much longer. Good thing you arrived with the band.'

'We gotta get going,' Lula said, looking at her watch. 'The old folks don't like when you're late. They get real cranky.'

Lula and Sally had driven a lot of people out of the viewing room, but there was still a huge bottleneck in the lobby. I pushed my way into the gridlock and inched forward. I looked over my shoulder and spotted Morelli. He was keeping watch over me with people five or six deep between us.

'Look *here*,' someone said directly behind me.

I followed the voice and experienced the same flash of confusion Ranger's security man had described. For a nanosecond I thought I was looking at Ranger. And then all the hairs raised on my arm and the back of my neck, and I realized I was looking at Edward Scrog.

'I only have a moment,' he said. 'I know you're waiting

for me to come get you, but there are too many people watching us here. You have to be patient. We'll be together soon enough, and then we'll never be parted again. We'll go to the angels together.'

'Where's Julie?'

'Julie is at home, waiting for you. I told her I was going to bring her a mommy soon. And then we'll be a family, and I can finish my work.'

'She's okay?'

'I love you,' Scrog said.

I grabbed hold of his sleeve and opened my mouth to yell for Morelli. I heard something sizzle, and everything went black.

Even before I opened my eyes, I knew what had happened. I felt the familiar tingle and then the feeling getting restored to my fingertips. The noise in my head went from a buzz to a hum and then disappeared, replaced by voices.

Morelli's face swam into focus. He looked worried. 'Are you okay?' he asked. 'I was watching you, and all of a sudden you collapsed.'

'I think I was stun-gunned by Scrog. Did you see him?'

'I saw you say something to the guy behind you. I couldn't see his face, and from the back he didn't resemble Ranger. The skin tone might have been the same, but the hair, and the build, and the clothes were all different. You had Tank two people away to the side of you, and he didn't spot Scrog either.'

Morelli helped me to my feet and wrapped a supporting arm around my waist. People had been cleared away from me. A paramedic had just arrived and was standing to the side.

'Thanks,' I said to the paramedic. 'I'm okay.'

'We had men at every exit,' Morelli said. 'The instant you went down we sealed the building. We're letting people out one by one. Do you remember anything about him? What he was wearing?'

'I didn't notice, but I don't think he was in black. For a split second I thought it was Ranger. I think it's the face shape and coloring and haircut from the front. He's shorter than Ranger. His eyes and mouth are different when you see him up close.'

'I'm turning you over to Tank,' Morelli said. 'He'll see that you get home. I'm going to stay here until they empty and search the building. It shouldn't take long. They're moving people out fast. Seventy percent of the people here are women.'

Tank was sitting in my living room, looking uncomfortable. Ranger had given him orders not to leave me alone, and I was worried if I had to use the bathroom he might follow me in. I had a ball game on the television, but Tank kept nervously looking around at me, as if I'd suddenly vanish into thin air. I'd made him stop at a convenience store on the way home, and I'd gotten a week's worth of comfort food. Tastykakes, Cheez Doodles, candy bars, Suzy Qs, barbecued chips. I'd just started working my way through the bag when Morelli and Bob came in, followed by Ranger.

Some sort of silent communication happened between Ranger and Tank, and Tank got up and left without saying a word.

Ranger threw his keys on the kitchen counter. Removed his gun and left it alongside his keys. Morelli did the same. At first glance this looked like they were safe at home, relaxed and unarmed, but I knew they both carried ankle guns. And Ranger always had a knife.

No one said anything. They were both wearing cop faces. Wary, emotionally inaccessible. Not hard to tell they were both in a vile mood.

'How did the search go?' I asked.

'We didn't get him. It looks like he went out a back window,' Morelli said.

I repeated the conversation I'd had with Scrog. No one said anything else. Morelli put a bowl of water on the floor for Bob, got a beer out of the refrigerator, and slouched in front of the television with it. Ranger went to the computer. I stayed in the kitchen and shoved butterscotch Krimpets into my face.

I couldn't imagine what was going to happen next. I had one bed and one couch. The numbers didn't add up. Even if the sleeping arrangements were resolved, I couldn't live with both of them under my roof.

'This is uncomfortable,' I said. 'I'm going to bed. And I'm locking my door.'

Both men looked over at me. We all knew a locked door was meaningless. Morelli and Ranger went where they wanted to go. I blew out a sigh and closed the bedroom door behind me.

I got a tote bag out of the closet, stuffed clothes and cosmetics into it, quietly opened my bedroom window, and climbed out onto the fire escape. I tossed the tote bag and my shoulder bag to the ground, lowered the ladder, and jumped the remaining couple feet. I turned and bumped into Morelli and Ranger, standing hands on hips, not amused.

'How did you know?' I asked.

'Tank called,' Ranger said. 'He's watching the lot.'

'I'm divorcing both of you,' I said. 'I'm moving in with my parents. You can stay here,' I said to Ranger. 'Remember to give Rex fresh water and food in the morning.' I turned to Morelli. 'You and Bob should go home. You'll be more comfortable there.'

Silence.

I gathered my tote bag and shoulder bag up from the ground.

'One of us should stop her,' Ranger said to Morelli, his eyes fixed on me.

'Not going to be me,' Morelli said. 'Have you ever tried to stop her from doing something she wanted to do?'

'Haven't had much success at it,' Ranger said.

Morelli rocked back on his heels. 'One thing I've learned about Stephanie over the years, she's not good at taking orders.'

'Has authority issues,' Ranger said.

'And if you piss her off, she'll get even. She ran over me with her father's Buick once and broke my leg.'

That got a small smile out of Ranger.

'Nice to see you boys bonding,' I said.

I hiked the tote up onto my shoulder and left them still standing hands on hips. I crossed the lot to the Mini and got in. I cranked the engine over and drove out of the lot. I looked in my rearview mirror. Tank was following. Fine by me. I was actually very scared. I was scared for me, and I was scared for little Julie.

It was a little after nine when I got to my parents' house. I parked in the driveway and looked around for Tank. I didn't see him, but I knew he was there. He'd probably work shifts with Hal or Ranger doing surveillance on me. My mother and grandmother were at the door waiting for me. How they always knew I was in the neighborhood was a mystery. Some female homing device that announced the approach of a daughter.

'I'm letting a friend use my apartment,' I told them. 'I was wondering if I could stay here for a couple days.'

'Of course you can stay here,' my mother said. 'But what about Joseph? I thought you two were . . . you know, almost married.'

I dropped the tote bag in the little hall foyer. 'He has a full case load and is really busy. He's spending a lot of hours on the Manoso murder and kidnapping.'

'The phone's been ringing off the hook,' my mother said. 'Everyone calling about the viewing. They said you fainted.'

'They had way too many people in the funeral home. It was hot, and it smelled like funeral flowers, and I hadn't eaten any dinner. I'm fine now. And Joe was there to catch me.'

The buzzwords in that explanation were *hadn't eaten dinner.* Those were the words that without fail got my mother up and running every time.

'No dinner!' my mother said. 'No wonder you fainted in that crush. Come into the kitchen, and I'll make you a nice roast beef sandwich.'

My mother pulled a bunch of dishes out of the refrigerator and put them on the small kitchen table. Cole slaw, potato salad, three-bean salad, macaroni. She hauled out a chunk of roast beef, bread, mustard, olives, pickled beets, lettuce, sliced tomatoes, sliced provolone.

'This is great,' I said, filling my plate.

'Good,' my mother said, 'and after you've had something to eat, you can tell me how your grandmother managed to get the lid open on the casket.'

Seventeen

Morelli and my parents live in houses that are almost identical, but Morelli's house feels larger. Morelli's house has less furniture, fewer people, and one more bathroom. My parents' house is filled with overstuffed couches and chairs and end tables and candy dishes, vases, fruit bowls, china doodads, stacks of magazines, afghans, area rugs, and kid things for my sister Valerie's three girls. My parents' house smells like pot roast and lemon furniture polish and fresh-baked chocolate-chip cookies. Morelli's house rarely has a smell, except when it rains . . . then it smells like wet Bob.

There are three tiny bedrooms and the bathroom on the second floor of my parents' house. At the crack of dawn my mother gets up and is the first in the bathroom. She's quiet and efficient, taking a shower, putting on her face, neatening up after herself. After my mother it's a battle between my grandmother and my father. They rush at the bathroom and the first one there elbows in and slams and locks the door. Whoever is left on the outside starts yelling.

'For crissake, what are you doing in there?' my father will yell. 'You've been in there for *days*. I need to take a crap. I need to go to work. It's not like I sit around watching television all day.'

'Blow it out your you-know-what,' my grandmother will fire back.

So it's not like I ever have to worry about oversleeping at my parents' house. Toilets are flushing, people are yelling and stomping around. And morning kitchen smells work their way upstairs. Coffee brewing, sweet rolls in the oven, bacon frying.

My room hasn't changed much since I moved out. My sister and her kids took the room over while she was regrouping after her divorce, but they're in their own house now, and the room has reestablished itself. Same floral quilted bedspread, same white ruffled curtains, same pictures on the walls, same chenille bathrobe hanging in the closet, same small chest of drawers that I left behind when I went off on my own. I sleep like a rock in the room. It feels safe . . . even when it isn't.

By the time I got down to the kitchen my father had already left. He's retired from the post office and drives a cab part-time. He has a few regulars that need rides in the morning, to work or the train station, but mostly he picks his cronies up and takes them to the lodge to play cards. And then he stays and plays cards too.

My grandmother was in the kitchen, hooked up to my mother's iPod. 'Before you break my heart . . . think it *oh oh ver*,' she sang, eyes closed, bony arms in the air, shuffling around in her white tennies.

'She tells me she's got a *gig*,' my mother said. 'Just exactly what's going on?'

'Sally has a new band, and they have a bunch of jobs playing for seniors. He thought Grandma was an appropriate edition.'

'Sweet Jesus!' And my mother made the sign of the cross.

I poured out some coffee and added milk. 'It might not be so bad. They get done early because everyone in the audience gets medicated and falls asleep. And no one can sing, so Grandma will fit right in.'

My mother watched Grandma gyrating and flailing her arms. 'She looks ridiculous!'

I got a cinnamon roll and took it to the table with my coffee. 'Maybe she just needs a costume.'

Grandma paused while there was a song change on the iPod, and then she started skipping and strutting around the kitchen. 'I can't get no satisfaction!' she yelled. '*No, no, no!*'

'Actually, she looks a lot like Jagger,' my mother said.

Ranger's cell phone rang, and I opened the connection. 'Yeah?'

'Your friend Scrog called early this morning. I have him on the machine. I want you to come over and listen to this.'

'I knew it was a mistake to get an answering machine.'

'The mistake was to leave last night. If you'd been here this morning you could have talked to him.'

'Omigod, what the heck would I say?'

'You could keep him on long enough for a trace,' Ranger said.

'My line is bugged?'

'Of course it's bugged.'

I looked at my watch. It was almost nine. 'Is it okay if I stop at the office first?'

'As long as you're here by noon. I want you to change your recording.'

'I have to go to work,' I said to my mother.

'It's Thursday,' my mother said. 'And I know you usually come for dinner on Friday, but Valerie and the girls and Albert are coming tomorrow. Would you and Joseph rather come for dinner tonight?'

'Probably. I'll have to ask him.'

I walked into the bonds office and noticed that for the first time in almost two weeks the inner-sanctum door was cracked open. I threw my shoulder bag on the couch and gave Connie raised eyebrows.

'He's back,' she said.

I heard rustling in the inner office, the sort of sound rats make running through leaves, and Vinnie opened the door wide and stuck his head out.

'Hah,' Vinnie said to me. 'Decided to show up for work?'

'You got a problem?' I asked him.

'I'm drowning in FTAs. What the hell do you do all day?'

Vinnie is a cousin on my father's side of the family, and it's not a comfortable thought that he swam out of the Plum gene pool. He's slim and boneless with slicked-back hair and pointy-toed shoes and Mediterranean coloring. The thought of him married and reproducing sends chills through me. Still, in spite of his short-comings as a human being, or maybe *because* of them, Vinnie is a pretty good bail bondsman. Vinnie is an excellent judge of sleaze.

'You're writing too much bond,' I told him.

'I need the money. Lucille wants a new house. She says the one we have now is too small. She wants one with a home theater. What the fuck is that, anyway?'

Meri was watching from her card table. 'Maybe I could start going out with Stephanie and Lula,' she said. 'I wouldn't be any help in the beginning but maybe eventually I could pick up some of the easier skips.'

'Maybe eventually,' Lula said.

'Not eventually,' Vinnie said. 'Now! Get out there *now*. I'm hemorrhaging money, for crissake. Lucille's gonna kill me.'

Connie, Lula, and I knew who would kill him, and it wouldn't be Lucille. It would be Lucille's father, Harry the Hammer. Harry didn't like when Lucille was disappointed.

'How did the nursing home go last night?' I asked Lula.

'We had to quit early. The feathers gave two people an asthma attack. I'm going out on my lunchtime to get us new outfits. We have a big job coming up Sunday night at the Brothers of the Loyal Sons, and we're calling an emergency practice so Grandma can learn the moves. We're doing a dress rehearsal and everything.'

A floral delivery van double-parked in front of the office and a guy got out and carted a vase of flowers into the office. 'Is there a Stephanie Plum here?'

'Uh-oh,' Lula said. 'Morelli must have done something wrong.'

I took the vase and put it on Connie's desk and read the card. TILL DEATH DO US PART. NOT LONG NOW.

'What the heck?' Lula said.

'One of my many secret admirers,' I said. 'Probably some serial killer who just broke out of prison.'

'Yeah,' Lula said. 'I bet that's it. Those serial killers are known for being romantic.'

'Did we get any new skips in?' I asked Connie.

'None this morning. The one high-end bond we still have out is Lonnie Johnson. I'd really like it if you could get a line on him.'

The front door banged open, and Joyce Barnhardt stalked in. She was still in black leather, wearing the stiletto-heeled black leather boots and the skin-tight, low-slung black leather pants and black leather bustier with her boobs squishing out the top. Her red hair was teased, her long artificial nails were polished and sharpened, her glossy red lips looked about to explode.

'I've got it! I've got the death certificate,' she said. She let the paper float down onto Connie's desk and she turned her attention to Meri. 'Who's this?'

'New BEA,' Connie said.

'You look like a cop,' Joyce said to Meri. 'Did you used to be a cop?'

'No,' Meri said. 'But my father was a cop.'

Joyce turned back to Connie. 'I want my money. This is as good as a body receipt, right?'

Connie wrote Joyce a check, and Joyce tucked the check into the pocket on her black leather pants.

'Aren't those pants hot?' Meri asked Joyce.

'Gotta look the part,' Joyce said. 'And nothing says bounty hunter like black leather. Toodles, ladies, I've got a date with a bad guy.'

'Maybe that's my problem,' Lula said when Joyce left the office. 'I don't look like a bounty hunter. But hell,

I'd sweat like a pig in those pants.'

'I have things to do,' I told everyone. 'I just wanted to check in. I'll be back in an hour or so, and then we should go after Charles Chin.'

Lula walked me to my car. 'It was the Ranger nut who sent you those flowers, wasn't it?' she asked.

'Yes. And he left a message on my phone this morning.'

'And what about the funeral home? We left out the back door, but Meri said she was there, and you fainted, and then they locked all the doors and let people out one at a time. They were checking for the Ranger nut, weren't they?'

'He got behind me in the lobby somehow. We had a short conversation, and then he stun-gunned me.'

'You saw him?'

'Yes. It's strange. For a second, when you first see this guy you think Ranger. But then when you actually look at him you know it's not Ranger. And apparently he doesn't look like Ranger from the back or the side. Morelli and Tank weren't that far from me and didn't pick him out.'

'You be careful,' Lula said. 'You sure you want to go off on your own? I could ride with you.'

'Thanks, but I've got RangeMan surveillance. I'll be okay.'

Lula went back into the office; I locked myself into the Mini and called Morelli on my own cell phone.

'How's it going?' I asked him.

'Bob misses you.'

'I bet. What's on your dance card for today?'

'I'm doing a follow-up on a gang slaying. Between the feds and RangeMan and the maverick bounty hunters, there are so many people working the Carmen Manoso murder I get lost in the crowd.'

'The maverick bounty hunters are a problem. They're clutter.'

'Rangerman is working to get rid of them,' Morelli said, 'but they're like lemmings. You push a bunch off a cliff, and there are twice as many behind them.'

'I got a call from an old boyfriend this morning. I wasn't home when he called, so he left a message on the machine. And then he sent flowers to the office.'

'You're not going out with him, are you?'

'I don't have any plans at the moment. If I change my mind you'll be the first to know.'

'Appreciate that,' Morelli said.

'Everyone at the office thought the flowers were from you. Figured you'd done something bad.'

'What about you? Did you think they were from me?'

'No. You don't send makeup flowers. You send makeup pizza and beer.'

Ranger was at the dining room table, watching the computer screen. 'Last night Tank noticed there were security cameras in the funeral home. Common practice to lower insurance rates. The cameras aren't monitored, they're just there to record in case a negligence claim is filed. We thought there was a chance Scrog got caught on video, so we got the cards out of the cameras last night and have been going over them.'

'Does Dave know you have these cards?'

'Dave looked tired. We didn't want to disturb Dave.'

'I'm surprised you didn't have to wrestle the FBI for camera access.'

'They have to follow procedure. And they don't have the specialists I have.'

'Cat burglars?'

'The best in the business, not behind bars. We copied the cards, and the originals are already back in the cameras. We want the FBI to have access to this.' Ranger pulled a frame up and started the video rolling. 'Here's our man. He comes in from the side and moves directly behind you the instant you enter the lobby. Tank is on the wrong side to see him. Morelli is behind two women who are partially blocking his view. And when Morelli can see Scrog, this is what he gets . . .' Ranger did a stop frame and isolated the man behind me. 'Scrog is shorter and slimmer and is partially bald at the crown. The skin tone looks similar, but the overall appearance is very different. And he's not in black. Hard to tell from the camera angle exactly what he's wearing, but he's not dressed in SWAT clothes.'

Ranger wasn't in black either. Ranger was in jeans and a washed-out, loose-fitting grey sleeveless Big Dog T-shirt. He looked comfortable in the clothes and relaxed in my apartment. His hair was growing out, curling around his ears and falling across his forehead. It was a younger, softer look for him, and it was disconcerting. I didn't know this Ranger.

'Who are you?' I asked him.

'I'm always the same person,' he said. 'Don't judge me by my clothes.'

He hit play on the video, and I watched Scrog approach me. Scrog and I had a brief conversation, I grabbed his sleeve and opened my mouth, and in the next instant I went down and Scrog moved off and was lost in the swell of people.

'This is helpful,' I said. 'We know what he looks like from the back.'

Ranger paused the video and pushed his chair back. 'Come into the kitchen, and I'll play the message back for you.'

'It was great seeing you last night,' Scrog said. 'I probably shouldn't have taken a chance like that, but I couldn't help myself. I wanted to get close to you. I know the police are looking for me. They don't understand why I had to rescue Julie from those people. That's okay. I'm used to being misunderstood and underestimated. Soon I'll be able to rescue you, and then we'll all be together forever. Sorry I had to stun you last night, but you were getting too excited. You would have given us away.'

I instinctively moved closer to Ranger. 'Listening to him makes my stomach cramp.'

'So far he's textbook. Cautious at first and becoming increasingly bold . . . and careless. I want you to record a new greeting giving callers your cell phone. I don't want you to miss another opportunity to talk to him.'

'He sent flowers to the office. The card read, 'Til death do us part. Not long now.'

'We saw the delivery and already checked it out. He phoned it in and paid for it with a stolen credit card. You have to give this guy credit. He's got skills.'

I recorded a greeting on the answering machine and gave my cell number.

'I should get back to work,' I told Ranger. 'Vinnie is in the office today, and he's on a mission to clean up the FTAs.'

'Keep in touch. And make sure you're always wearing the panic button,' Ranger said. 'And make sure it's hidden. If you get to talk to Scrog, I want you to push him. Tell him you like when he dresses in black bounty hunter clothes. Tell him they're sexy. Ask him if he's working, hunting anyone down. Let's try to get him out of his hiding place so he might get recognized. And ask about Julie. Tell him you're anxious to see Julie. Try to get to talk to her. Tell him you think he's lying to you, that he doesn't really have her. Now that he's made contact with you, things should move faster.'

'Okey-dokey,' I said.

Ranger hung my bag on my shoulder and looked at me. 'Are you okay with all this?'

'Actually, I feel like throwing up a lot.'

'It's the doughnuts.'

'It's my life.'

Eighteen

L ula wasn't looking happy. 'Meri got a line on Lonnie Johnson,' she said. 'Personally, I'd rather stick a fork in my eye than go after Lonnie Johnson. I have a real bad feeling about Lonnie Johnson.'

I took the file from Meri. 'What have you got?'

'You told me to check on him once in a while so I ran his credit and got a hit. He applied for a car loan two days ago and gave an address.'

I looked at the credit report and sucked in some air. Stark Street. Just about the worst possible address. Stark Street made Johnson's last address look like high rent.

'Were you able to do any phone verification?' I asked Meri.

'No landline given. He gave a cell, but I didn't know if you wanted me to call it. I checked the by-street address and there was no phone listed.'

'Probably a rooming house at that end of Stark,' Lula said. 'Either that or a cardboard box on the sidewalk.'

'What kind of car did he get?' I asked Meri.

'I don't know.'

'Find out. And then get the temporary plate number.'

'Boy, you're smart,' Lula said to me. 'I would never have thought to look for the car.'

Mostly I was a big chicken. I was on the same page as Lula. I didn't want to go after Lonnie Johnson. He was a scary guy, and I wasn't exactly at the top of my game. I was too distracted by Edward Scrog. It was now the eighth day for Julie Martine. Nine days that she was away from her mom. Eight days that she was held captive by a psychotic killer.

I noticed Lula looking at her phone. 'Expecting a call?' I asked her.

'Yeah, a certain big guy works all the time. I've been getting a lot of phone calls, but I'm not getting any action.'

'You've been getting phone calls? With the big guy actually saying something on the other end?'

'Well I gotta do most of the talking, but I can hear him breathing.'

'Big guy?' Connie said. 'What's that about?'

'Lula's having a thing with Tank,' I told her.

'Get the hell out,' Connie said. 'Shut up.'

'It's only the beginning stages,' Lula said. 'But I think this could be it. I tell you, he's a hunk of burning love. He's a sex bomb. He's a big ol' honey bear.'

'Who's Tank?' Meri wanted to know.

'He's Ranger's top guy,' Lula said. 'He watches Ranger's back, and he takes over when Ranger's away.'

'So I guess he's in charge now?' Meri asked.

'Yeah, sort of,' Lula said.

A black Corvette with red, orange and green flame detailing screeched to a stop in front of the office and angled into the curb in front of Lula's Firebird.

'Here comes Vampira again,' Lula said. 'Wouldn't you think once a day was enough? What did we do to deserve this?'

'Connie hired her,' I said.

We all glared at Connie.

'I gave her three impossible files. I didn't think we'd ever see her again. I thought I was getting *rid* of her. And anyway, you were the one who suggested giving her the impossibles!' Connie said to me, glaring back. 'I'm not taking the fall for this all by myself.'

Joyce Barnhardt shoved through the front door and stood in the middle of the floor looking like something fresh out of an S&M movie. She'd improved on the black leather outfit by adding a black leather utility belt that carried a can of Mace, a stun gun, a Glock and cuffs. Only the whip was missing.

'These two files you gave me are impossible,' she said, tossing the files onto Connie's desk.

'And?' Connie said.

'There are no leads. Everything hits a wall. These assholes aren't even dead. I want something else.'

'Everything else is assigned,' Connie said.

'Then reassign someone.' Joyce looked at the Lonnie Johnson file open on Connie's desk. 'I want this one. I saw this guy on the wall in the post office. This is worth something. Armed robbery. I could get my teeth into this one.'

'Yeah, but you're supposed to bring them in to get rebooked, not gnaw on them,' Lula said.

'Shut up, fatso.'

Lula was out of her seat, and Connie and I jumped between her and Joyce.

'Take it,' Connie said to Joyce. 'Just get out of here!'

Joyce snatched the file and swished out of the office.

'Never mind finding the make of the car and the license number,' I said to Meri.

'Boy, too bad,' Lula said. 'I was looking forward to going after Lonnie Johnson.'

'Me too,' I said. 'I'm real disappointed.'

Lula's phone rang. She looked at the readout, pumped her fist in the air, did a victory dance, and bustled outside to have some privacy.

'Is she really going out with Tank?' Connie wanted to know.

'Looks that way,' I said.

'How did that happen?'

'I think it was fate.' And Caroline Scarzolli.

'I guess we're left with Charles Chin,' Meri said.

I looked at Chin's file. White-collar crime. He'd embezzled close to $15,000 while working at one of the local banks. He had a house in a nice neighborhood in north Trenton. And he hadn't shown up for his court appearance.

'He answered the phone sounding *very* drunk,' Meri said.

'When did you call?'

'About an hour ago.'

I grabbed my bag and stuffed the file in it. 'Let's roll.'

Meri looked hopeful. 'Me too?'

'Yes. We shouldn't have a problem with this. We'll let Lula do her shopping.'

I took the Mini and didn't bother to check for a tail. Best not to know, I thought. Meri, on the other hand, kept checking her mirror.

'Don't look,' I told her.

'But what if we're followed?'

I didn't want to explain the whole process to her so I conceded. 'You're right,' I said. 'Let me know if we're followed.'

'I thought we were being followed when we first left the office but then the car disappeared.'

Imagine that.

I turned onto Cherry Street and Meri read off the house numbers.

'It's on the right,' she said. 'The grey house with the white shutters.'

I parked in front of the house and tucked my cuffs into the back of my jeans and slipped a small canister of pepper spray into my jeans pocket.

'Just stand behind me and smile like you're friendly and let me do the talking,' I told Meri.

We walked to the small front porch and rang the bell and waited. No answer. I rang again, and I heard something crash into the door. I stepped away from the door and looked into the front window. There was a man lying on the floor in front of the door.

'Try the door and see if it opens,' I told Meri.

Meri turned the knob and pushed. 'Nope. Locked.'

I walked around to the back of the house and tried the back door. Also locked. I returned to the front and started looking for a key. Not under the mat. Not in a fake rock alongside the step. Not in the flowerpot.

'Everyone leaves a key somewhere,' I said to Meri.

I felt on top of the doorjamb. Bingo. The key. The door opened a crack but wouldn't go any further. The body was in the way. I forced the door to open enough for me to get my foot in, and then I shoved the body with my foot.

We squeezed in, carefully stepping over the body. We compared the body to the picture on the bond agreement. Charles Chin, all right.

'Is he dead?' Meri wanted to know.

I bent to take a closer look. He was breathing, and he smelled like he just crawled out of a bottle.

'Drunk,' I said, clapping the cuffs on him. 'I love apprehending unconscious people.'

We each got under an armpit and dragged Charles Chin out of his house and stuffed him into the back seat of my car. I went back to lock up and my phone rang.

'He isn't dead is he?' Ranger asked.

'No. Drunk. Where are you?'

'I'm almost a block away. Tank was supposed to be keeping his eye on you, but he had a nooner, so I'm filling in. Who's riding with you?'

'Meri Maisonet. She's the new BEA. No experience, but she seems okay.'

I disconnected, locked up, and went back to the car.

'Now what?' Meri asked.

'Now we take him to the police station and get him checked in. If he was sober I'd call Vinnie or Connie and try to get him rebooked while court was in session. Since he's out like a light, he's going to have to sleep it off in a cell.'

It was mid-afternoon by the time we returned to the bonds office. Lula was out shopping. Melvin had gone through all the filing and was making new tabs for the file cabinets. Connie was surfing eBay. Vinnie's door was closed.

I gave Connie my body receipt. 'Anything new I should know about?'

'Nope. Nothing new. All the bad guys have gone to the shore for the weekend.'

'I'm heading out then. See you tomorrow.'

I slid behind the wheel and called Morelli.

'What's happening?' I asked.

'Murder, mayhem. The usual stuff.'

'Are you up for dinner with my parents?'

'Yeah, I'm afraid if I don't fill that seat you'll bring in the second team.'

'Very funny. See you there at six.'

Ranger followed me into my apartment. 'My radar is humming so loud it's giving me a headache. This guy is watching you. I know he's there. And I can't get a fix on him.' He removed his gun and put it on the counter next to his keys. 'What do you know about Meri Maisonet?'

'Almost nothing. New to the area. Didn't show up for the interview in black leather, and didn't say she wanted to kill people, so we hired her.'

'She has cop written all over her.'

'She said her father was a cop. Connie ran her, and she seemed to check out.'

Ranger punched her into his computer. 'Let's see what we get.'

Twenty minutes into the computer search, my phone

rang. I answered on speaker phone so Ranger could hear. There was a pause, and then Scrog's voice.

'I followed you around today. I saw you make the capture. Not bad, but I could teach you some things,' Scrog said.

'Like what?'

'I could teach you to shoot. I know a lot about guns. I could teach you about everything. And I don't like that you look so unprofessional. You don't look like a bounty hunter. If we're going to work together you have to dress better. You should look like that other bounty hunter who came to the office. The one with the red hair.'

'Joyce Barnhardt?'

'I don't know. The one in the black leather. She looked great. You need to dress like that from now on if you want to hook up with me.'

I glanced at Ranger and caught him almost smiling.

'Maybe,' I said to Scrog.

'No! You'll do as I say. We're a team. You have to do as I say.'

'Okay, I'll dress like that if you will. Is that a deal?'

'Yeah. Okay. It's a deal.'

'So, what are you doing these days? Have you made any captures lately?'

'I captured my daughter.'

'That wasn't a capture. She probably wanted to go with you.'

'Yeah, but it was tricky. I had to get her on a plane and everything.'

I could hear his voice ratchet up a notch. He wanted to brag about his kidnapping success. 'How did you do that?'

'You're going to love this. I drugged her, and then I wrapped her leg in one of those inflatable casts and put her in a wheel chair. Everyone thought she was drugged because she was in all this pain and flying to Jersey for special medical help. Pretty good, huh?'

'Is she there now?'

'Yeah.'

'Can I talk to her?'

'I don't think that's a good idea. You have to wait until you see her.'

'When do I get to see her?'

'I don't know. I have to figure a way to get you here. You're always being followed. It's starting to get on my nerves.'

'I don't believe you. I bet she isn't there.'

His voice ratcheted up again. 'Of course she's here. Where the hell do you think she'd be?'

'I don't know. I thought maybe she ran away.'

'Okay, you can talk to her but make it quick.' There was some fumbling noise, and I heard Scrog prod Julie. 'Talk,' he said off stage.

'Hello,' I said. 'Julie? Are you there?'

'Who's this?' she asked whisper soft.

'It's Stephanie. Are you okay?'

She took a moment, and I was unable to breathe, waiting for her answer.

'Yes,' she said. Her little girl voice wobbled. 'Do you know my father?'

'Yes,' I said. 'We're friends. I work with your father.'

She absorbed that for a beat. 'Well, I hope you come visit before we move on again.'

There was a yelp and the line went dead.

I looked over at Ranger. His face was devoid of expression, and his breathing was slow and measured. Ranger was in lockdown mode.

I didn't have a lockdown mode. Tears swarmed behind my eyes, and a large, painful undefined emotion clogged my throat. I blinked the tears away and blew out some air. 'Jeez,' I said.

Ranger cut his eyes to me and gave me a moment to get myself together. 'You have a goal,' he finally said quietly. 'The goal is to rescue Julie. You have to focus on the goal. If you give yourself up to unproductive emotion you can't focus on the goal. Let's think this through. Scrog wouldn't risk taking Julie in the car when he was following you around. So he saw you go into this building and then he returned to his hiding place. That means he's no more than twenty minutes away. And Julie said they were moving around. That might mean they're in a camper or a motor home.'

'Can you run stolen property checks?' I asked Ranger.

'Yes, but the police have faster access.'

I called Morelli on his cell. 'Can you run a stolen property check for me? I want you to see if any campers or motor homes have been reported stolen in the last two weeks. All of New Jersey and eastern Pennsylvania.'

I hung up and my phone rang again.

'I had to hang up,' Scrog said. 'If you stay on too long they can trace you.'

'How do you know all these things?' I asked him.

'I know everything. I'm the best bounty hunter in the world. Anyway, everybody knows about tracing. They always talk about it on television and in the movies. I called back because I have a plan. The feds are watching you so you have to act natural. I want you to dress like a bounty hunter so they think you're going to work all the time. And then I'm going to show you how to lose them. I want you to be in your car driving around at midnight tonight. I'll call you on your cell phone.'

'Can't we do this earlier? I don't stay up that late.'

'Midnight. It's so the people following you will be tired. Jesus, take a nap or something. What's your cell phone number?'

I gave him the number and he hung up.

'He's created an odd world for himself,' I said to Ranger.

'If the stakes weren't so high I'd probably think some

of this was funny.' Ranger returned to the computer. 'You need to get some bounty hunter clothes.'

'I don't know where to go to get bounty hunter clothes.' I looked at my watch. 'And I haven't got a lot of time. I'm supposed to be at my parents' house at six. Maybe I could wear your clothes.'

'You're welcome to wear my clothes any time of the day or night, but I don't think that's what Scrog had in mind. I'll send Ella out shopping. She knows your size.'

'Are you getting anything on Meri?'

'Not at first look, but I think her history feels constructed. It's too perfect. I'm going to give this to Silvio.'

Nineteen

'I made lasagna today,' my mother said. 'Your father wanted Italian. It's in the oven staying warm. And there's extra gravy on the stove. Maybe you can help your grandmother with the bread and salad.'

'I already got the bread and the salad,' Grandma said. 'And I got some antipasto going. We got salami and olives and anchovies and cheese.'

It was five minutes before six o'clock, and my mother was counting down. 'Grated cheese? Butter? Olive oil?'

I pulled the butter and cheese out of the refrigerator and got the olive oil out of the cabinet. I set them all on the table. The red wine was already uncorked. A bottle at each end.

The front door opened, and Morelli and Bob walked in, and *bang* we were off and running for the dining room. My father was first to sit. My grandmother skidded in right behind him.

'We don't want dinner to run over,' my grandmother

said. 'Sally's coming here at seven and we're going to rehearse.'

My father was concentrating on the dish of lasagna, tuning my grandmother out. He mumbled something, and we all leaned forward to hear.

'Say again?' I said to him.

'*Gravy.*'

My mother sent the red sauce down to him, and he poured it over everything and dug in, never raising his head. At first glance the best you might say for my parents' marriage is that my mother never stabbed my father in the ass with the carving knife. If you look closer, you see they've found a lifestyle designed for the long haul. My father makes a huge effort to ignore my grandmother. My mother has a few rituals that make my father feel like he counts. And there's an underlying affection that's expressed mostly through tolerance.

Morelli filled his plate and passed on the wine.

'Working tonight?' I asked him.

'I don't think these are days when I'd want to risk impaired judgement.'

I admired his work ethic, but I had no intention of following it. I *really needed* a glass of wine.

'Did you find any stolen property?' I asked him.

He pulled a file card out of his shirt pocket. 'I got two hits. I have the details here for you. And the license numbers. You might not want to put too much stock in the license. If you have a smart thief, he'll swap out the plate. Should we be working harder to find these vehicles?'

'Yes, but you should be careful when approaching. I'll explain it all later.'

I called Ranger and gave him the camper descriptions. I disconnected, and Morelli watched me clip the phone onto my jeans. I now had two cell phones and the panic button clamped onto my waistband.

'New phone?' he asked.

'Goes directly to the Batcave.'

Morelli reached across me for the bottle of wine. 'Maybe just one glass.'

Grandma jumped when the doorbell rang. 'That's my band!' she said, running for the door.

My father had a plate of Italian cookies in front of him and a cup of coffee. 'Band?'

'You don't want to know,' I told him. 'Eat your cookies. Enjoy your coffee.'

Sally and his crew trooped in, carrying instruments and amps.

'Man, this is so cool that we can rehearse here,' Sally said. 'We've been kicked out of every place else.'

Lula was the last in. She was carrying a bunch of bags, and she was wearing a blond wig.

'Wait until you see what I got,' she said. 'It's the

bomb. This is the best outfit yet. And it hasn't got any feathers.'

Sally started setting up in the living room, plugging the amps in, unpacking his guitar. The other three guys were working, hauling in a drum set, keyboard, bass.

'What the heck?' my father said. 'What's going on?'

'I thought Sally was coming over for dessert,' my mother said. 'Who are these people?'

'The *band*,' my grandmother said. 'Nobody listens to me.'

'Of course no one listens to you, you old bat,' my father said. 'I'd have to blow my brains out if I listened to you. How am I going to watch television? There's a ball game tonight. The Yankees are playing. Get these people out of my living room. Someone call the police.'

We all looked at Morelli.

'Do something,' my father said to Morelli.

Morelli slid his arm across the back of my chair and whispered into my ear. 'Help.'

'Wait a minute,' my grandmother yelled. 'I live here too. And this here's an important moment in my life. And you know how old I am . . . I might not have many more moments left.'

Clearly that statement represented the pot of gold at the end of the rainbow for my father.

'We gotta go upstairs and get dressed,' Lula said to Grandma. 'And I got a wig for you too.'

'Maybe you should go to the lodge,' I said to my father. 'I thought Thursday was pinochle night.'

'It's always pinochle night at the lodge. I wanted to see the ball game tonight.'

'Don't they have a television at the lodge?'

'Yeah, they got one in the bar.' He looked at his coffee and cookies. 'I'm not done eating.'

'A bag!' I said to my mother. 'For God's sake, put his cookies in a bag.'

'I have to get changed,' Sally said, going upstairs. 'I'll only be a minute.'

'*Hurry!*' I shouted to my mother. 'What's holding up that bag?'

The bass player started tuning, adjusting the volume on the amp. The first sound that came out was *Wangggggg!*

'Holy crap,' my father said. 'What in the beejeezus was *that*?'

'Bass,' Morelli said, eyeing a cookie on my father's plate.

'I see you looking at my cookies,' my father said to Morelli. 'Don't even think about it. Go get your own cookies.'

I poured myself another glass of wine.

'Okay,' Lula shouted from the top of the stairs, 'don't anybody look. Everybody close their eyes until we get into position.'

'I'm not closing my eyes,' my father said. 'The Italian Stallion here will eat my cookies.'

The drummer beat out a couple heart-thumping bars, the bass and keyboard came on at a deafening level, and the dining room chandelier jiggled and swayed on its chain. Plates danced across the dining room table. A half-eaten cookie fell out of my father's mouth. And Bob tipped his head back and howled.

My mother ran in from the kitchen with the bag, but it was too late. Lula and Grandma and Sally were onstage in front of us. Grandma and Lula were wearing black leather hot pants and ice-cream-cone bras. Grandma looked like a soup chicken dressed up like Madonna. She was all slack skin and knobby knees and slightly bowed legs. Her blond wig was slightly askew, and her ice-cream-cone bra hung low, not from the weight of her breasts but from breast location. Gravity hadn't been kind to Grandma. Lula's body spilled out of her outfit. The hot pants were reduced to black leather camel-toes in front and what looked like a leather thong in the rear. And the ice-cream-cone bra precariously perched at the end of Lula's basketball breasts. They were in big platform heels and they had spiked leather dog collars around their necks. Sally was in a dog collar, black leather thong with a silver zipper inexplicably running the length of his package, and over-the-knee swashbuckling black leather high-heeled boots with huge platform soles.

My mother made the sign of the cross and staggered into a dining room chair. Morelli had his teeth sunk hard into his bottom lip to keep from laughing out loud. My father's face was stroke red. And Bob ran upstairs.

Lula and Grandma went into their dance routine and Morelli broke out in a sweat from the effort of maintaining composure. Grandma wobbled into an amp, snagged her heel on the cord, and fell over into the drum set, taking the bass player down with her. She was on her back, under cymbals and the bass player, with only her platform shoes showing. She looked like the Wicked Witch of the East when Dorothy's house fell on her. We all jumped up and rushed to help Grandma, except for my father, who stayed like stone in his seat, his face still red.

We got Grandma up on her feet and fixed her wig and adjusted her breasts.

'I'm okay,' Grandma said. 'I just caught my heel on the wire and unplugged the thingy.'

Grandma bent to plug the amp back in and farted in the black leather hot pants.

'Oops,' Grandma said. 'Someone step on a duck?' She farted again. 'Broccoli in the salad,' she said. 'Boy, I feel a lot better now.'

I looked over at Morelli and saw that he had a cookie in his hand. 'Is that my father's cookie? You're in big trouble.'

'He's beyond noticing,' Morelli said. 'I've seen that look on people passing by horrific car crashes. Trust me, he's lost count of the cookies.'

'Maybe you should turn the amp back a little,' I said to Sally. 'I think I heard glasses breaking in the kitchen.'

My mother had her fingers curled tight into the front of my T-shirt. 'You have to stop her,' she said. 'I'm begging you.'

'Me? Why me?'

'She'll listen to you.'

'If this works out I think I'll try to get a gig with the Stones,' Grandma said. 'I'd fit right in with them. They could use a chick in the band. I wouldn't mind going on one of them tours. And I can do that walk like Jagger. Look at me walk.'

We all watched Grandma strut around like Jagger.

'She's surprisingly good,' Morelli said.

My mother's eyes cut to the kitchen door, and I knew she was thinking about the booze in the cabinet by the sink.

'What do you think of this outfit?' Lula asked me. 'Do you think it's too small? They didn't have my size.'

'It looks painful,' I told her.

'Yeah, I think I'm starting to get a hemorrhoid.'

'Maybe tomorrow we can go out together and look for new costumes,' I said. 'It would be fun to go shopping together.'

'That's a deal,' Lula said. 'We could have lunch and everything.'

'You name it,' my mother said to me. 'What do you want? Pineapple upside-down cake? Chocolate cream pie? I'll make any dessert you want if you can guarantee me that your grandmother won't wear that leather outfit.'

Twenty

A low cloud cover had rolled in, obscuring moon and stars. Morelli and I walked Bob in the dark, down sidewalks I knew inch by inch from my childhood. I'd rollerskated on them, drawn chalk pictures on them, biked on them, walked to school on them, spied on boys and skinned my knees on these sidewalks. I knew the people who lived here. I knew their dogs, their secrets, their tragedies, failures, successes, and bedtimes. It was just a little past nine, and dogs were being let out for the last tinkle of the night. Televisions flickered through front windows. Air conditioners hummed.

Morelli and I were holding hands, following after Bob, who happily plodded around blocks, sniffing bushes. I'd filled Morelli in on the phone call and my midnight appointment with Scrog. Now Morelli and I were walking Bob, and I was feeling a little like a heart patient waiting to undergo surgery. Nervous. Looking forward to the end. Hoping it ends well. Anxious to get started.

I looked up from the sidewalk and realized we'd walked for an hour and come full circle. We were in front of my parents' house, still holding hands, still silent.

'Now what?' Morelli said.

'I'm going back to the apartment. Scrog wants me dressed like a bounty hunter, and Ella went shopping for clothes for me.'

'Anything I can do to help you?'

'It's Ranger's daughter. I think this is his show, and he has his whole organization behind him. And probably the FBI is involved. Ranger seems to be communicating with them at some level.'

'We're all communicating with them,' Morelli said.

'Just do your cop thing. Whatever it is you're supposed to do. And then do your boyfriend thing and make sure there's cold beer in your refrigerator. When this is all over I'm going to need a few.'

'When this is over and I get you back into my house, you're not going to have time for beer. I'm going to get you naked and make sure all the scary, bad thoughts are pushed out of your mind. Be careful tonight. Put the panic button someplace where it can't easily be found. I'll be around if you need me.'

'I don't believe I'm in this outfit,' I said to Ranger. 'I feel like an idiot.'

Ranger slid a black nylon-web gun belt through the

loops on his jeans. 'You're dressed like a real honest-to-gosh bounty hunter, babe.'

I was wearing black biker boots, black leather pants that fit like skin, and a black leather vest that had a layer of Kevlar sewn into it. The pants were cut low and a swath of skin showed between pants and vest.

'Ella was optimistic about my weight,' I said. 'A size up would have been better.'

'Not from where I'm standing,' Ranger said, buckling his gun onto the belt. 'But you might want to remember to sit with your back to the wall.'

I felt the back of the pants. Yikes. I needed another inch of leather. 'This is embarrassing,' I said.

Ranger clipped *his* cell phone with earbud on one side of my pants. 'Once you start driving, you're going to have a lot more on your mind than these pants. Let's hope this works and everyone comes out healthy.' He clipped *my* cell phone with earbud to the other side. 'My phone is voice activated, and you can leave it on at all times. Where's the panic button?'

'Hidden.'

'I'm afraid to ask.'

'Good, because I don't want to say it out loud.'

'If this wasn't so deadly serious and we had more time, I'd find out for myself. Go out ahead of me. Everyone's in place. I'll leave through the side door.'

I took the stairs, crossed the lot, and angled into the

Mini. I had a route planned out. I was going to keep it simple and drive up and down Hamilton until I got the call. Once I was in the car and out of the lot I settled down. I had Ranger in my ear. He wasn't saying anything, but I knew he was there. Not a lot of cars on Hamilton. That made it difficult to follow and stay hidden. Ranger could do it because he had multiple cars on the job. Scrog would find it much more challenging.

I drove for fifteen minutes and was making my second pass on the bonds office when my phone rang and adrenaline shot into my system.

'I like the outfit,' Scrog said. 'Much better. Now as soon as you lose the people following you, we can be together. Don't worry about them. I have it figured out. Just keep following my instructions. The first thing you have to do is go to the municipal building parking lot at the corner of Main and Fifteenth Street. You're to go to the middle of the lot and wait.' And the line went dead.

'I'm going to the municipal building lot at the corner of Main and Fifteenth,' I told Ranger.

'That lot will be empty at this time of the night with the exception of a few maintenance workers. Take your time getting there. I'm sending someone to check it out.'

Ten minutes later, I was approaching the lot and Ranger came back on the phone. 'There's a lone car sitting in the middle of the lot. A blue Honda Civic. We didn't want to get close to it, but it looks okay from a distance. No one in it. Probably he wants you to swap out cars.'

I drove into the lot and stopped a short distance from the car Ranger had described. My phone rang.

'Good,' Scrog said. 'Now get out of your car and stand with your hands in the air and turn around.'

'Why?'

'Just do it!'

I took Ranger's earbud out of my ear, tucked it into my pants, and got out of the Mini and stood with my hands in the air.

'What have you got clipped onto your pants?' Scrog wanted to know.

I was in the middle of an acre of blacktop, washed in the eerie glow from overhead security lights. And somewhere beyond the light Scrog sat watching me. He could see the two phones, so he was using a scope. Probably binoculars, but it could as easily be a rifle scope.

'That's my phone,' I told him.

'There are two of them.'

'I have a backup.'

'I want you to take both phones and leave them on the ground. Then I want you to get into the Honda. The keys are in the ignition and there are instructions on the passenger seat. Follow the instructions.'

I unclipped the two phones and set them on the blacktop. I got into the Honda, cranked the car over, and read the instructions. Scrog wanted me to go to the parking garage three blocks down on Main. I was to park the car on the second level, take the stairs to the street, and walk east on Dennis Street, toward the center of the city. When I got to the condo building at 375 Dennis' I was to enter through the front door and go in the elevator.

Okay, I no longer had a phone, but I had my little tracker gizmo. And probably forty people were following me. And the FBI probably had a helicopter flying around with infrared equipment keeping watch on my every move. I stuck my head out the window and looked up at the sky. No helicopter. Cheap-ass FBI.

I followed the instructions and parked on the second level of the garage. I got out of the Honda and my heartbeat picked up. It was late, and dark, and the garage was deserted. I was lucky if I didn't get mugged before I made contact with Scrog.

I took the stairs to street level and went east on Dennis. I walked a block and a half and found myself in front of the condo building. I stood there for a couple minutes, trying to give Ranger time to get into position, trying to get my feet to move forward. My feet didn't want to go into the building. For that matter, none of my other parts wanted to go into the building either. It was five stories of mid-range housing. Probably constructed in the fifties and renovated a couple years ago when it switched from apartments to condos. I was able to look through the double glass doors to the small foyer. Dimly lit. Unattended. Elevator to the right. A bank of mail-boxes to the left. No Scrog.

It was in the seventies, but I'd started to sweat at my hairline. A little girl's life is at stake, I told myself. You can do this. It's important. Be brave. And if you can't be brave . . . fake it.

I took a deep breath and entered the foyer. Very quiet. No one there. I saw a piece of paper taped to the wall by the elevator. RIDE THE ELEVATOR TO THE GARAGE.

Damn. I didn't want to go to the garage. Garages were creepy at night. Anything could happen in a garage. I cracked my knuckles, got into the elevator, and pushed the button. I felt the elevator move, and I got another shot of adrenaline. I had so much adrenaline going through me I felt like my hair was on fire and I could hear a pin drop a mile away.

The doors opened, I stepped out, and a woman moved into view from behind a van. She walked toward me, and I realized it was Scrog. No wonder it was so hard to spot him. He constantly stole new cars, and he went out in drag.

I watched him come closer, and I thought he made a pretty decent woman. If I was looking at him in a car I wouldn't guess he was a guy. It was the walk that gave him away.

'Surprised?' he asked.

I nodded. And oddly relieved. Men in dresses don't inspire terror.

'It's all about packaging,' Scrog said. 'Now it's time to change yours. You're going to have to get undressed.'

'No way.'

'There's no one here. Just you and me.' He had a tote bag over his shoulder and a gun in his hand. He tossed the tote at me. 'I have new clothes for you.'

'What about dressing like a bounty hunter?'

'This is in case something goes wrong and someone sees you. Everyone will be looking for the bounty hunter in black leather. And not that I don't trust you, but I have to make sure you're not wearing a wire. So take your clothes off. All of them.'

'You're going to have to shoot me to get these clothes off, because the only way they're coming off is if I'm dead.'

Scrog thought about it. 'You have to at least let me pat you down. Turn around and put your hands on this car.'

'Just don't get too friendly,' I said, turning around.

Scrog moved behind me. 'You're going to have to get over this modesty. We're together now.'

There was a familiar sizzle, and it was lights out.

It took me a while to get smart, but I finally put it together. I was in the trunk of a car. Been there, done that. It was pitch black. I had no idea of time. The car was moving, turning corners. My hands were handcuffed behind my back. I was pretty sure I'd been stun-gunned again. I hoped I wasn't naked. I felt around with my hands and was relieved to feel clothes. Unfortunately, they weren't the clothes I remembered wearing. Scrog had undressed me while I was unconscious. How icky is that?

The car stopped. The engine cut out. A car door slammed shut. And then the trunk opened, and I saw Scrog again. Still in drag in the brown wig.

'Feeling better?' he asked.

'No, I'm not feeling better. I'm feeling pissed off that you keep stun-gunning me.'

'That's the reward for bad behavior. You have to learn to obey me.'

He hauled me out of the trunk, and I saw that we were in a wooded area. I could hear cars in the distance, but I couldn't see lights. The road was dirt. A motor home was parked in front of us. It wasn't one of the motor homes reported stolen. It was old and partially rusted out around the rear wheels.

'Home sweet home,' Scrog said.

'Where are we?'

'We're home. That's all you need to know. Get in.'

I was wearing a white T-shirt and lightweight grey sweatpants. 'Where are my clothes?'

'In the tote bag. Except for the little gadget you had

cleverly hidden in your . . . pants area. I thought it best to leave that behind.'

I felt myself go cold and my heart stop dead in my chest for a moment. I was so cold I was chattering inside, and I thought, *This is fear.* Debilitating. Gut-clenching. Cold fear. Ranger had no way to find me.

I climbed rickety steps and wrenched the door open. It was dark inside. No electricity. I toed my way into the sweltering-hot room and stopped when I ran into something that felt like a table.

'Don't move,' Scrog said. 'I have a battery-powered light.'

Stay calm, I told myself. At least this rattrap doesn't smell like death. Just keep thinking. Don't panic.

He switched on what looked like a small electric lantern. The light was dim, and I thought this was a good thing. Best not to look too closely at the motor home. It seemed to be composed of two rooms. I was in the living room, dining room, kitchen area. Upholstery was filthy and torn. The floor had been patched with odd pieces of linoleum. Water stains ran down walls. The Formica tabletop and kitchen countertop were riddled with cigarette burns and knife scars. A lumpy soiled pillow and threadbare blanket had been left on the bench seat behind the table.

'I figure once we get the business up and running we can get something nice, but for now this will have to do,'

Scrog said. There was a closed door at the end of the kitchen area. It had to lead to a small bedroom and maybe bathroom of sorts. I was hoping Julie was okay behind the door.

'Where's Julie?' I asked him. 'I'm anxious to see her.'

'She's in the bedroom. You can go on in. The door isn't locked.'

I called ahead. 'Julie? It's Stephanie. I'm coming in.'

No one answered, so I pushed the door open and peered inside. Too dark to see anything.

'Do you have another lantern?' I asked Scrog.

'No,' he said. 'You can have this one. I have eyes like a cat. I don't need light.'

He moved past me into the room and set the lantern on a small bedside built-in. Julie was huddled on the bed. Her brown hair was snarled and her eyes were huge. Her face was filthy and there were days-old tear tracks on her cheeks. I'd read a description of her when she was kidnapped, and it looked to me like she was wearing the same clothes. Maybe that was a good thing. At least he hadn't undressed her. Her feet were bare, and she was chained to the bed with an ankle shackle.

She looked at me, and then she looked at Scrog. She didn't say anything.

'It's late,' Scrog said. 'You girls must be tired. You need to go to sleep. Tomorrow will be a big day. Special things doing tomorrow.' He reached under the bed and pulled out another length of chain with a shackle attached. 'I'll just clamp this onto your ankle,' he said to me, 'and then I can unlock the handcuffs.'

He reached for my ankle, and I kicked him in the head as hard as I could. I booted him back about three feet. He landed on his ass, and I went after him, catching him in the side with another kick. He managed to scoot away from me; he reached behind him, his hand moved toward me, and I got another jolt from the stun gun.

Twenty-One

Whe I came around, I was on my back on the grungy floor in the bedroom. My shoes and socks had been removed, and the ankle shackle was locked in place. I waited for the noise to go away in my head and for everything to stop tingling before I tried to stand.

Julie was sitting up in bed, watching me. 'Good one,' she said.

That knocked me over. *Good one.* Julie Martine had grit. Maybe more than me at this point. I did a head roll and shrugged off the muscle cramps that come with taking a bunch of volts and crashing to the floor.

'It was lame,' I told her. 'Your father would have finished him off.'

'Do you mean Ranger? I don't know him real well.'

'He's very special.'

Julie lowered her voice. 'He's going to kill him. That's

what he meant by tomorrow being a big day. Chuck says he can't be whole until Ranger is dead.'

'Who's Chuck?'

'That man. He wants me to call him Dad, but I won't do it. I call him Chuck. I don't think he even cares about you and me so much. I think it's Ranger he really wants.'

I wasn't completely surprised. It had crossed my mind that eventually Scrog would feel the need to eliminate Ranger.

'Chuck's crazy, isn't he?' Julie asked. 'He told me he's killed people. Like he was bragging about it. Has he really killed people?'

'I think he might have.'

'That's so horrible,' Julie said.

'Has he treated you okay?'

'Yeah. I mean, I'm chained in here like an animal but he hasn't, you know, done anything to me. And my chain can reach to the bathroom.'

The sound of snoring carried from the other room. Murder and kidnapping obviously didn't weigh on Scrog's conscience. No tossing and turning trying to sleep. No late-night pacing.

So now what? Now you suck it up and look for a way out, I told myself. You do what Ranger told you to do. Focus on the goal. Push unproductive emotion away.

I got down on my hands and knees and looked to see how the chains were fastened. 'The bed is bolted to the floor and the chains are padlocked around the steel frame,' I told Julie.

'I know. I looked. I couldn't find a way to get free.'

I took the lantern and prowled the bedroom, looking for something that might be helpful, not finding anything.

'Tomorrow I'll look again when there's daylight,' I said to Julie.

'There's no daylight,' she said. 'He's blacked out all the windows. Half the time I don't know if it's night or day.'

'Rise and shine, ladies,' Scrog said, throwing a couple bags onto the bed. 'Breakfast is here.'

I looked in one of the bags. Twinkies, Ring Dings, Hostess pies, tiny bags of salted nuts, little boxes of raisins, candy bars. More of the same in the second bag.

'He robs convenience stores,' Julie said, selecting a box of raisins.

'It's an easy hit if you get there when they're opening up,' Scrog said. 'Problem is, they never have a lot of money. I need more money.'

'Where's the coffee?' I asked him.

'There's no coffee.'

'I can't get through the morning without coffee,' I told him. 'Do you have any idea how nuts I'm going to be without caffeine? *I need coffee in the morning!*'

Julie made a big pretense of opening a package of peanuts, but I could see she was enjoying my show.

'Jeez, don't go all PMS on me,' Scrog said. 'How was I supposed to know?'

I narrowed my eyes at him. 'Are you going to get me coffee?'

'No. I haven't got the time. I'm in the middle of something here. Boy, you think you're doing something nice for people and all you get is yelled at. I didn't have to rob that store, you know. I did it for you and the kid.'

He went back to the living area, leaving the bedroom door open. I heard him raise a shade, and some light filtered in to the bedroom.

'What are you doing out there?' I asked him.

'I'm building a bomb.'

Julie and I looked at each other, mouths open wide.

'What kind of bomb?' I asked Scrog.

'What do you mean? It's a bomb, for crissake. I got it off the Internet.'

'You have a computer here?'

'No. I went to the library. They have computers you can use.'

'So, what are you going to do with the bomb?'

'Shut up. I can't concentrate with you yammering. I'm almost done. I just have to connect a couple things. Eat a goddamn doughnut or something.'

'I already ate a doughnut and now I'm thirsty.'

'There's water in the bathroom. And anyway, we're going out, and you can get something to drink then.'

'Where are we going?'

'We're going to get money. I need more money.'

Scrog came into the bedroom carrying a packet that was about four inches by four inches and maybe an inch thick and entirely wrapped in duct tape. 'I'm gonna toss this onto the bed real gentle, along with the tape, and you're gonna strap it onto yourself,' he said.

'Is that the bomb?'

'Yeah. It's supposed to be pretty stable,' he said. 'It's not supposed to go off unless I push the button.'

'Not *supposed* to?'

'Hey, cut me some slack. This is my first bomb.'

'I'm not strapping a bomb to myself,' I said.

'Well great, then how about I shoot the kid in the foot?'

'You wouldn't do that. You wouldn't shoot your kid.'

'I would if I had to. I'd shoot her in the foot, so she wouldn't die, and maybe she'd walk with a limp, but she'd get over it. It's in everyone's best interest. I need more money, and I don't trust you to just go out with me yet.'

'Why do you need all this money?' I asked him.

'I got a plan. I figure now that we're together we'll escape to Australia. No one will find us there. And we can all be bounty hunters. All we have to do is lay low for a while and everybody will forget about us. Like, while we're laying low we can drive to California. Then we get on a plane and next thing, we're in Australia.'

'Yeah, that's a good plan,' I said. 'What about passports?'

'Passports?'

'You can't move between countries without a passport.'

'Are you sure? Even Australia?'

'Duh-uh,' Julie whispered.

'Shit. I didn't think about passports. Okay, we'll just change the plan a little. We'll go to Mexico. Hell, we could go to Mexico in a little boat. Just sneak in after dark. Or we could probably just walk across in Texas. It would be cheaper, too. I wouldn't have to risk robbing a bank. I could keep robbing these little stores. I've already got a couple hundred saved up.'

'I know how we can get some money,' I told him. 'There's a high-risk bond that I just got a line on. If we could capture him my BEA fee would be around five thousand dollars. But there's a catch. If I get the money for you, you have to let us go.'

Not for a single minute did I think Scrog would let us go. What I thought was that he'd use me to get the money and in the process feed his ego and fulfill his bounty hunter fantasy. I figured if he had his way, he'd come back to this piece-of-shit motor home, lure Ranger here, and then kill us all.

I was just hoping to buy some time and get us out in the open where we might be seen. Ranger was in tracking mode, sniffing the bushes like Bob on a rampage. And if I was lucky enough to make the capture, I'd have a chance to pass information on. I'd have to walk my FTA into the police station.

'Who is this guy?' Scrog wanted to know.

'Lonnie Johnson. Wanted for armed robbery. He didn't show for his court appearance. Lula and I went after him but he disappeared from the face of the earth. Then yesterday he popped back into the area. I have a new address for him.'

'And he'd be worth five thousand dollars?'

'Yep.'

'Maybe I should just ransom you for the money.'

'Ransoming takes time. All that back-and-forth negotiating. And then the FBI gets involved. And you have to give directions for making the money drop. Anyway, I thought you wanted to be a bounty hunter.'

'Is this address a sure thing?'

'I don't know. We couldn't do a phone verification. He tried to get a line of credit, and he gave an address.'

'Tell me how this is gonna get us the money again.'

'We make the capture. I turn him over to the police. Connie gives me the money I've earned.'

'I'm a little fuzzy on the part where we turn him over to the police. You don't think I'm going to let you walk into the police station, do you?'

'That's usually the way it works.'

'Boy, you must think I'm stupid. You'll go in there and blab everything.'

'Okay, I have another idea. Lonnie Johnson shot a guy who was servicing an automatic teller, and Johnson walked away with $32,000 and change. I'm betting he's still got most of it. Suppose we rob Lonnie Johnson?'

'You mean we like, take him down and force him to tell us where the money is?'

'Yeah.'

I knew in my heart that Lonnie Johnson pissed away every cent he stole. The fact that he was trying to get a loan to buy a car would seem to support my theory. No point bothering Scrog with this line of reasoning.

'Okay, I guess I don't see any harm in trying,' Scrog said. 'You're going to have to strap the bomb on though and I swear if you do anything stupid I'll blow you to bits.'

I got the bomb strapped on, and I looked over at him. 'Unlock the ankle bracelet. If we go out now, we might catch him at home.'

Scrog stepped back. He had the little detonator in one hand, and he threw the key onto the bed with the other. I unlocked the shackle and skated the key back to him across the linoleum floor.

'Now you have to get dressed in your bounty hunter clothes,' he said. 'If I'm going to do this, I'm going to do it right. We need to look like a couple bad asses.'

'Sure,' I said, 'but you have to get dressed up too.'

'Don't worry about me. I'll be dressed.'

I went into the little bathroom and wriggled into the black leather pants. I took the T-shirt off and put the vest on and stepped out. 'What about the bomb?' I said. 'You can see I have a bomb strapped to my stomach.'

Julie was on the bed behind me. 'That's not all you can see,' she said, giggling.

Scrog had changed into black leather pants and a black T-shirt and was wearing a black leather Sam Brown belt armed with cuffs and stun gun and Glock. It was better than the ladies' dress, but he sure as hell was no Ranger. Ranger would crack a smile at the thought of someone impersonating him in leather pants.

'Put the T-shirt on over the vest,' Scrog said. 'It's the best we can do right now.'

I dropped the T-shirt over my head and walked ahead of Scrog, out of the motor home. I stood blinking in the bright sunlight, waiting for my eyes to adjust, trying not to get hysterical over the fact that I had a bomb strapped to my stomach.

'Jeez,' Scrog said. 'Now that you're out in the sun you look like the Bride of Frankenstein. Can't you do something with your hair?'

'Maybe if you'd stop running electricity through me my hair would look better! Ever think of that? And what do you think, hair just happens? I need a roller brush. I need gel and hair spray and a hair dryer. Next time you rob something, make it a hair salon.'

'Cripes, just trying to be helpful. I figured you cared about your appearance.'

'If I cared about my appearance I wouldn't be wearing these butt-crack pants,' I snapped back at him.

'Yeah, they're kind of small,' he said. 'Maybe you should lay off the doughnuts.'

I thought this was a good chance to get hysterical and try to rattle Scrog.

'You have a lot of nerve,' I said, all emotional. 'All you brought me to eat for breakfast was cake and candy. If I'm so fat, why didn't you bring me some fruit? You didn't even bring me coffee. All I wanted was coffee. Was that so much to ask?'

And to my surprise I'd actually popped out a couple tears and gotten my nose to run a little.

'I'm sorry!' Scrog said. 'Hold it down, will you? I'll get you some coffee. I swear to God, this isn't turning out like I thought.' Scrog opened the trunk on the car. 'Get in, and we'll go get coffee.'

'I'm not getting into the trunk! I've got a bomb strapped to me,' I said, hiccupping back sobs that were only half fake. 'What if I roll around? And anyway, it's demeaning. How would you feel if I made *you* ride in the trunk?'

I couldn't believe I was actually saying this. *Demeaning.* How was I thinking of this crap?

'It's so you can't see where we are. It's for your own good.'

I wiped my nose with the back of my hand. 'It's not for my own good if I blow myself up.'

'Oh man, you have to stop crying. You got mascara running all down your face.'

'It's all your fault. You started it. You said I was fat.'

'I didn't say you were fat. You're putting words in my mouth. Hell, get in the car. I'm starting to think it would be a relief to go to jail.'

'This is a nice car,' I said, buckling myself in. 'Is it new?'

'Yeah, I picked it up this morning when I went out for breakfast.'

'You should steal a Lexus next time. I hear they're really comfy.'

'I'll keep that in mind.'

'We're coming out of the woods now, so I want you to close your eyes and put your head down so you can't see.'

'Oh, for crying out loud.'

'Just do it. I'm ready to blow you up just to shut you up.'

I thought I'd pushed him about as far as I could, so I bent in my seat and put my head between my knees. The car swerved off the dirt road and skidded to a stop in a patch of grass.

'What the heck was that?' I yelled.

'Shoot, I'm sorry,' Scrog said. 'But you haven't got much leather back there when you bend over like that.'

303

I pulled the T-shirt down. 'If you were a gentleman, you wouldn't look.'

'Wasn't my fault. I was just about blinded by all that white ass.'

I felt my eyes bug out of my head. 'Excuse me? All that white ass?'

'That didn't come out good,' Scrog said. 'I didn't mean it exactly that way. You're not gonna start crying again, are you?'

'Just drive. Just get the heck back on the road.'

'Actually, after looking at your uh, backside, I wouldn't mind taking some time here to get better acquainted, if you know what I mean.'

'Let me get this straight. You have me wired to explode and now you want to get friendly?'

'Well, yeah.'

'I am so sorry to tell you that as long as I am a walking bomb I am not engaging in friendly activities. If you want to get friendly you're going to have to take this bomb off me.'

'I can't do that. Last time I wasn't careful with you, you kicked me in the head.'

I wasn't sure what to say to that. First chance I got I was going to *shoot* him in the head, but I didn't want to spook him. I folded my arms across my chest and tried to look petulant. I'd never looked petulant before but it seemed like it fit the role I was playing.

'Is that *no*?' he asked.

I did an exaggerated pout. 'I've said my last word on the subject.'

Scrog blew out a sigh and backed the car out of the grass and onto the dirt road. 'Where are we going?'

'Stark Street.'

Twenty-Two

We were on East State Street, driving toward the center of the city, and we were looking for a Dunkin' Donuts drive-through.

'We passed a bunch of shit,' Scrog said. 'I don't see why it's gotta be Dunkin' Donuts.'

'They make the best coffee. Everybody knows that.'

'They just put a lot of cream in it,' Scrog said. 'All it does is clog your arteries up. And I don't ever remember seeing a Dunkin' Donuts here anyway.'

'Maybe if you go to Greenwood.'

'I hate to keep thinking ill of you, but I'm starting to wonder if you're making us drive around so someone sees us.'

'That's silly. You drive around all the time, and you're never spotted.'

'Yeah, but I'm mostly dressed up like a woman when I'm driving around. I have three different wigs, too.'

'Well I'm sure there's a drive-through on Greenwood.'

'Okay, but that's the last street we're gonna try. After Greenwood we gotta go after Lonnie Johnson.'

'This is it,' I said to Scrog. 'It's the building on the right with the door missing and the boarded-up windows on the ground floor.'

'It looks deserted.'

'Lots of these buildings look like this. Some are even condemned, but people still live in them. If you look at the windows on the second and third floors you can see signs that the units are being used. A sheet tacked up for privacy. A couple empty beer bottles on the window sill.'

Friday morning was a quiet time on Stark Street. Everyone was sleeping off something . . . drink, drugs, desperation. In another hour the bars would open, and the hookers would start to stake out corners. Traffic would pick up and security cages would get rolled back on local groceries, adult videos, pawnshops, hash shops, and liquor stores. And little by little the bedraggled, angry, lost souls of Stark Street would roll out of their sweat-soaked beds and make their way to cement stoops and street-side folding chairs and discarded sofas to enjoy the first smoke of this steamy summer day.

There was a new black Cadillac Escalade with temporary plates parked in the alley next to Johnson's building. So there was a slim chance Johnson was inside.

I had no idea how this would play out. I was with a man who floated in and out of varying degrees of insanity. He wanted to take over Ranger's life, but there was a corner of his brain that always knew it was a sham. He didn't mind shooting people, but I doubted he was much of a match for Lonnie Johnson. Scrog was nuts. Lonnie Johnson was *bad*. My real concern was that Johnson would unload a clip into Scrog, and Scrog would fall on the detonator and I'd be dust.

I suspected Scrog hadn't any idea what to do next, but I didn't think he'd want me running the show, so I sat back and let him wing it. He circled the block and parked in front of Johnson's building. He sat there for a minute, and I swear I could see him calling up his Ranger personality.

'Let's do it,' he finally said, and I had to look closely because the change was striking. He wasn't Ranger, but he wasn't Edward Scrog either. 'Do you know which unit this guy is in?'

'No,' I said. 'He just gave the address.'

We got out of the car and entered the building. It was dark and musty. No bulb in the overhead foyer light. The stairwell smelled like urine and fast-food burgers. Paint peeling off the wall. A dead roach, feet up, on the third step.

'You go first,' Scrog said. 'I want to keep an eye on you. Sniff this guy out.'

It wasn't a big building. Three floors. Two units on each floor. No one in the two ground-floor apartments. The doors were missing. It looked like they were using 1B to dump garbage. A stained mattress and a bunch of fast-food wrappers on the floor in 1A. A rat as big as a beaver rustled through the wrappers.

I hurried up the stairs. Doors were closed to 2A and 2B. I listened at the doors. Spanish coming out of 2A. I didn't have Lonnie Johnson pegged as bilingual. Nothing in 2B. I knocked, and no one answered. I was losing patience. I put my boot to the door, and the door crashed open. I was totally impressed with myself. I'd never kicked a door open before.

'Nice,' Scrog said. 'Now go in and look around.'

Someone was living there, but it was hard to tell who it was. Junkyard furniture. Mattresses on the floor. Empty beer bottles filling the sink. Didn't feel like Lonnie Johnson.

I went to floor three and did the same routine, listening at doors. A woman answered my knock on 3A. She was hollow eyed and rail thin. I looked beyond her to a man on a mattress. He was equally wasted. No Lonnie there. She didn't know who was across the hall. No one answered 3B, so I crashed that door open, too. The apartment was empty but neat. This felt more like Johnson. A pair of men's sneakers had been placed on the floor beside a small stack of clothes.

'If I had $32,000, I wouldn't be living in this dump,' Scrog said.

'I'm not the only one after him. Someone shot up his house and then burned it down. That was when he disappeared. Something brought him back, but this is probably just a short visit before he moves on.'

We went back down the stairs and out of the building. A man was walking our way, carrying a brown grocery bag. I looked him in the eye and I knew. 'Lonnie Johnson?' I asked.

'Yeah?'

'We'd like to talk to you, if you wouldn't mind stepping inside.'

Johnson was big. Late thirties and about 250 pounds. Lots of those pounds were fried dough and beer, but there was some muscle, too. His eyes were small and close set and radiated mean.

'Fuck off,' Johnson said.

I took two steps back and left Scrog standing face-to-face with Godzilla.

'We have a business proposition,' Scrog said.

'What kinda proposition? You look like that stupid bounty hunter on television.'

Scrog glanced over at me and smiled as if to say, *See? Now we look like bounty hunters!*

'We need to go upstairs to talk about it,' Scrog said. 'I don't want to talk about it here on the street.'

I heard the staccato tap of heels on the sidewalk behind me. I turned and saw Joyce Barnhardt striding toward us.

'What the hell's going on?' she wanted to know. 'This guy belongs to me. I was here first. I've had this building under surveillance since yesterday. You think I'm sitting in this shit-hole neighborhood for my health? Back off.'

'I need to talk to him,' Scrog said.

Joyce planted her hands on her hips and got into Scrog's face.

'And you would be, who?'

'None of your business. You can have him when I'm done.'

'Yeah, right,' Joyce said. 'That makes me feel all warm and fucking fuzzy. Like I'm going to hand this guy over to the Ms Plumber Butt and Mini Ranger. I don't think so. Go find your own meal ticket.' And she gave Scrog a hard shot to the chest, knocking him on his ass.

Scrog and Barnhardt both pulled guns. Scrog squeezed off two rounds. The first went wide of Joyce and blew out a tire on Scrog's stolen car. The second stovepiped and jammed the gun. Joyce's first shot caught Scrog in the foot, ripping off a chunk of boot. Scrog yelped and rolled. And Lonnie Johnson bolted, shoving into Joyce, sending her gun flying out of her hand, skittering halfway down the block.

Meanwhile, I was furiously working at the tape that

was holding the bomb to me. It was heavy-duty electrician's tape, and it was wrapped around and around my torso. Scrog had the detonator stuffed into his utility belt. I kept one eye on Scrog's hand to make sure it wasn't going for the detonator, and I clawed at the tape. Scrog had momentarily forgotten about me, more focused on Joyce and Lonnie Johnson. I had a length of the tape ripped free. One piece to go. Scrog looked over at me and went for his stun gun and not the detonator. I gave a frantic yank on the tape and the bomb broke loose and went sailing into the street.

Lonnie Johnson peeled out of the alley in his Escalade. He whipped the wheel around, put his foot to the floor, and laid down a quarter inch of rubber before he took off down Stark. His back tire ran over the bomb and there was a fireball explosion. The Escalade jumped up a couple feet and came down on its side, the undercarriage smoking.

I was now face to face with Scrog. He had the stun gun. I had a lot of rage.

'Bring it on,' I said to him. 'Come get me.'

Scrog cut his eyes to his car. Flat tire, and the Escalade was blocking his exit. The only way he was going to get me to go with him was to stun me and drag me. And if that wasn't bad enough, his foot was bleeding where he'd been shot.

He turned to leave, and I grabbed him by the back of

his shirt and took him down to the sidewalk, cracking his head on the cement. I punched him in the face and then the son of a bitch did it again.

I was struggling to get to my feet, my brain still fried, and I realized the hands helping me stand belonged to Morelli. After a moment his face came into focus. His eyes were red-rimmed and shadowed from fatigue. His shirt was soaked in sweat.

'Jeez,' I said. 'You look like crap.'

'This is nothing. You should see Ranger. We worked through the night looking for you.'

'I got zapped again.'

'I heard. I was a couple blocks away, following a lead, when the call came in on the explosion and shooting. Joyce called it in. She wanted to make sure she got credit for her capture. She had Johnson cuffed to his steering wheel when we got here.'

'How is he?'

'Let's just say it wasn't necessary to cuff him. And if he ever gets out of jail, he'll remember to wear a seatbelt.'

'You have to get to Julie before Scrog. I know where she is. He's got her in a rusted-out motor home at the end of a dirt road. The road goes off Ledger. It looks like nothing is down there. You go past an abandoned house with a tar paper roof and then it's the next left.'

Morelli called it in.

'He can't have that much of a head start,' I said. 'Joyce shot him in the foot. And he didn't have a car. He had to steal one.'

'He got a car right away. He flagged a guy down and yanked him from behind the wheel and drove off. We got a description of the car, and it's already gone out. The driver didn't say anything about Scrog's foot. He said Scrog was bleeding from the nose.'

'I punched him.'

'And would you know how the Escalade happened to explode?'

'I had a bomb strapped to me, and when Scrog and Joyce were arguing I managed to work the bomb loose, and when it ripped free it flew into the street, and Johnson accidentally ran over it.'

'You had a bomb strapped to you,' Morelli said, sounding a little dazed.

'Scrog made it. It was only supposed to go off when he pushed the detonator, but obviously getting run over by an SUV could do it too.'

'You had a bomb strapped to you,' Morelli repeated.

'Yeah. It was really scary at first, but terror is a strange thing. It's such a strong emotion it can't sustain itself. After a while a numbness sets in, and the terror starts to feel normal. And that's a good thing because it allows you to function.'

Morelli hugged me against him. 'I need a new girl-friend. I need someone who doesn't wear bombs.'

'You're squeezing me too tight,' I said. 'I can't breathe.'

'I can't let go.'

'Look at me. I'm okay.'

'*I'm not!* I thought . . . I don't know what I thought, but I'm not sure I ever got to the numb-and-functioning stage. I've been at the terror level ever since you dropped off the radar screen.' He blew out a sigh. 'And where the hell did you get these pants? Half your ass is hanging out.'

We slowed when we reached the entrance to the dirt road and maneuvered around the cop cars that had been first on the scene. We'd already heard the motor home was deserted, but I wanted to see with my own eyes. A uniform was ringing the area with crime scene tape. One of the first cars in was a black RangeMan SUV. No reason for Ranger to remain hidden. Everyone knew about Scrog.

Morelli and I ducked under the tape and went to the motor home. The door was open. There were blood splotches on the steps leading in. I went inside and raised the shades and pulled taped cardboard off windows. The shackles were still chained to the bed, but Julie was gone. Scrog had cleared out in a hurry. He'd left the wigs and the few pieces of clothing he possessed behind. It looked to me like he grabbed Julie and took off. Even at that, I was surprised he hadn't run into the police.

Ranger was standing hands on hips, waiting for me when I came out of the motor home. Morelli was right. Ranger didn't look good. Our eyes met and a very, very small smile played at the corners of his mouth.

'I'm okay,' I said to Ranger. 'And Julie was okay when I left her this morning.'

Morelli was behind me. 'Find anything?' he asked Ranger.

'Scrog had a back door. The green Dodge that's parked here is the car he took on Stark Street. It looks to me like he went through the woods with Julie. If you follow the trail he left, you come to another dirt road. He probably had a car stashed there. There are fresh tire treads on the road. Tank is walking the road. I'm going to drive out and meet him.'

Meri Maisonet and a guy in a dress shirt and suit pants walked toward us. I crooked an eyebrow at Ranger.

'Feds,' Ranger said.

I looked at Morelli. 'Did you know?'

'Yeah. I knew.'

'And you didn't tell me.'

'Nope,' Morelli said.

I gave him a raised eyebrow that shouted *angry* girlfriend.

'Keep me in the loop,' Ranger said. And he jogged to his car.

'What are you doing now?' I asked Morelli.

'This ties to my homicide. I'm going to stay here and get the crime lab started. I'll get a uniform to take you home . . . wherever that is.'

'I'm going to my parents' house. My mother owes me a cake.'

Twenty-Three

'Where were you?' Grandma asked me. 'You look like you've been on an all-night bender.'

'I was working. I'm going upstairs to take a shower and change my clothes.'

Here's one of the great things about going home. Whatever clothes happen to be left in my mother's care magically get cleaned and pressed. I don't leave a lot of clothes there, but whatever's in the closet is ready to go. Nothing stays left in a heap on the floor.

I stood in the shower until I ran out of hot water. I brushed my teeth three times. I fluffed my hair dry and pulled it back into a ponytail. I got dressed in jeans and a T-shirt and went downstairs in search of food.

I settled on a chunk of leftover lasagna. I took it to the table and forked into it cold. It seemed like a lot of effort to nuke it. I could see my mother trying hard not to interfere, but I knew she really wanted to heat the stupid lasagna. I dragged myself out of my chair and slid the lasagna into the microwave. My mother looked enormously relieved. Her daughter wasn't a total loser. She heated her lasagna like a civilized person. I took the warm lasagna back to the table and dug in.

My mother gave me a padded envelope. 'Before I forget, this just came for you. A young man dressed in black delivered it while you were in the shower.'

'One of them RangeMan hunks,' Grandma said.

I looked in the envelope and found the two cell phones I left in the parking lot, plus the keys to my Mini. I went to the living room and peered out to the street. The Mini was parked at the curb. I went back to the kitchen and finished the lasagna.

'Are you going shopping for a new band outfit today?' I asked Grandma.

'I gave up on the band,' Grandma said. 'I threw my back out with all that wiggling around. I had to sleep on the heating pad all night. I don't know how those rock-and-roll people do it. Some of those people are as old as me.'

'Nobody's as old as you,' my father yelled from the living room. 'You're older than dirt.'

'Yeah, but I'm pretty good for being so old,' Grandma said. 'I'm thinking I might be better with getting a gig as one of them piano bar singers. I could wear one of them slinky dresses with the slit up the side.'

When I was done with the lasagna I plodded upstairs

to my bedroom, flopped onto the bed, and crawled under the covers. I was exhausted. I needed a couple hours of sleep before rejoining the hunt for Julie. Probably there were better-equipped people than me out there, but I'd make whatever contribution I could.

Grandma hovered over me. 'Are you awake?' she asked.

'I am now.'

'We're eating. I figured you'd want to know.'

'I'll be down right away.'

I sat on the edge of the bed and called Morelli. 'Anything?'

'No. This guy is good at disappearing.'

'I think part of his success is that he thinks ahead and then he moves fast. He was already on the plane heading north before the word went out in Miami. He was out of the parking garage with me in the trunk of his car before anyone realized the panic button was left behind. And he had a car ready and waiting to make an exit from the motor home. And I'm betting he knew exactly where he wanted to go.'

'Most people at this stage would just keep driving. Put as much distance as possible between point A and point B.'

'He talked about going to Mexico to start a new life, but I don't think he can do that until he gets his fantasy together. I think he has to get rid of Ranger first.'

'I can identify with that one,' Morelli said.

I disconnected Morelli and called Ranger.

'Are you okay?' I asked him.

'I'm managing.'

'Any luck?'

'It's like the earth swallowed this guy.'

'He needs to eliminate you before he can move on.'

'Many have tried. None have succeeded. Tell me about Julie.'

'She was a little bedraggled-looking, but she seemed healthy. She's a lot like you. Brave and resilient. She said she hadn't been molested. I think women might be something Scrog needs to acquire to play his role, but I don't think he's a sexual deviant. He's constructed this weird world for himself. It's like he moves in and out of a game. And he kills people who get in his way. I think Julie will be safe with him. At least for a while.'

'Do you have any idea where he might be hiding?'

'I don't think he'll go far. He gets food and spare change by robbing convenience stores. He goes out early in the morning and brings back a couple bags of candy bars and snack cakes. You might be able to do something with that. And he's going to be stalking you. Aside from that, I just don't know.'

'What's your plan?'

'I don't have much of a plan. I'm at my parents' house right now, but I think I'll go back to my apartment tonight. Morelli's in his own house, and you don't need to camp out anymore. That leaves Rex all by himself.'

'Are you evicting me?'

'Yes.'

'We have unfinished business,' Ranger said.

'We *always* have unfinished business. Just out of morbid curiosity, how would you define your role in my life?'

'I'm dessert,' he said.

'Something that gives me pleasure, but isn't especially good for me?'

'Something that could never be the base of your food pyramid.'

See, here's where I was in trouble. Dessert *was* the base of my food pyramid!

I was holding a bag of leftovers from my mom, and a bag of clean clothes, plus the shoulder bag I'd left in the Mini when I changed cars in the parking lot. I juggled the bags, fumbled with the key, and let myself into my dark, quiet apartment. I maneuvered into the kitchen and dumped everything on the counter.

Rex was on his wheel, running, running, running. I tapped on the case and said, 'Hello.' It was good to be home. Good to be alone. Ranger had just very nicely uncomplicated my life. Don't count on me to be meat and potatoes, babe. Decent of him to be honest. Not that I didn't already know it. Still, it helped to have it articulated. I blew out a sigh. Who was I kidding? It didn't help at all. Any more than the attempt to come back to my apartment and normalize my life helped to erase Julie from my thoughts. Julie Martine was a dull ache in my chest. The ache was constant, and all the more painful since I had no clue how to help in her search. At least when I was bait I had some purpose. I was sidelined now, left with nothing to do but wait. I couldn't imagine what it must be like for her mom. Truly terrible.

I pulled a package of sliced turkey out of the leftover bag. Some rolls fresh from the bakery. A wedge of chocolate cake. And then . . . *sizzle*. Again. *Shit!*

I didn't have a lot of furniture. A table and four chairs in the dining room. A couch and a comfy chair in the living room. A televison on a low chest. A coffee table in front of the couch. When I came around, I was in the living room, facing in such a way that I could see people entering from the little entrance foyer. I was sitting on a dining room chair, held to it by electrician's tape, my hands painfully cuffed behind the chair.

Julie was slumped in the single comfy chair. Her face was ghost-white and slack. Her eyes were drugged slits, barely open, unseeing. Her hands lay loose in her lap.

'What did you do to her?' I asked Scrog.

'She's okay. Just knocked out. I had to leave the motor

home in a hurry. I didn't have time to make another bomb. Easier to zap her and give her a shot.'

'How did you get in here?'

'I used a pick I bought on the Internet.'

Scrog looked terrible. He had blood all over him from when I'd punched him in the nose. His eyes were black and swollen. His lip was cut. His foot was still in his shoe, and the shoe was wrapped around and around with the electrician's tape. He was sitting in the living room with me, in another of my dining room chairs, pulled to the side, out of view from the front door. He had a gun in his hand.

'I feel sick,' I whispered, head down. I was dripping drool and snot and my stomach was in a nauseous free fall. I was scared and horrified, and I'd been stun-gunned one too many times.

'Are you gonna throw up?'

'Yeah.'

He limped to the bathroom and came back with the wastebasket just in time for me to fill it with my mother's roast chicken and chocolate cake.

'That's disgusting,' he said.

'Maybe if you'd stop stun-gunning me . . .'

He limped back to the bathroom, and I heard him flush the toilet. He limped back and eased himself into his chair.

'You look like you could use some of the joy juice you gave Julie,' I said to him.

'I took some Advil.'

'Are you still going to Mexico?'

'Yeah. Maybe I'll work my way south and go to Guatemala. I think I heard they need bounty hunters there.'

If I didn't hate him so much, I might feel sorry for him. Poor stupid crazy moron.

'Why are you here?' I asked him. 'Why don't you just steal a car and start driving?'

'I can't. It won't work unless I get rid of him.' He rubbed his temple with his fingertips. 'Headache,' he said. 'I think I might have a concussion from when I hit my head on the sidewalk. That was really bad of you. You're such a bitch. I was going to take you with me, but now I think I'll get rid of you too. I even know how I'll do it. I'll execute you. I'll put the barrel of the gun to your head and *bang*. A bullet in the brain.'

'You don't need to get rid of anyone,' I said. 'It'll just slow you down. You should leave now before someone finds you.'

'I can't. Don't you understand? He's ruining it. I hate him. He's stolen my destiny. He has *my* identity.'

Oh boy. 'Why Ranger?' I asked.

'I was supposed to be him. The minute I saw him, I knew. I was working in this dorky record store, and one day he came in with his partner and arrested some slimebag. It was like a movie. He was all dressed in black like a SWAT guy, and he just walked up to this creep and cuffed him. He was wearing a gun, but he didn't draw. He just cuffed him and marched him out. Man, it was so cool. And the more I thought about it, the more I realized something went wrong. I was supposed to be *him.* I even look like him. So I asked the guard at the door who he was, and I started finding out about him. That he was a bounty hunter and all. I figured I had to find a way to get what was mine, you know, like my identity, my destiny. Before that I was going to be a cop. I was all set. I was working part-time at another mall doing security, waiting for my cop job to start. So it was lucky it all happened when it did, because I might have been a cop, and that would have been all wrong.'

'Couldn't Edward Scrog be a bounty hunter?'

'I guess, but it wouldn't be right. It got mixed up some-how. I just knew I was supposed to take over. I always knew I'd have to kill him. I always knew it was just a matter of time,' Scrog said. 'I had to get my ducks in a row first.' He squinched his eyes together. 'This headache is bad. I can hardly think.'

'Maybe you should lie down. Sleep it off.'

'I can't. I have to be ready. He's going to come here. I can feel it. He's living here with you. All his stuff's here. I just have to kill him, and then I can get some sleep.' Scrog had his head down, between his knees. 'As soon as I kill him it'll all get better.'

I glanced over at Julie and realized her color was improved. She was still slack-faced and slumped in the chair, but she was watching Scrog through slitty eyes. The drug was wearing off, I thought.

It had to be maybe nine-thirty. It was true that Ranger had his computer here, but that wasn't reason enough for him to return. I'd told him he was evicted. I wasn't sure what would happen as the evening wore on and Ranger didn't show. I worried Scrog would become more erratic, more desperate.

'Ranger isn't living here anymore,' I said. 'He was just staying here because the police were looking for him, and he couldn't go home. Now that the police aren't looking for him he'll go back to RangeMan.'

'I don't believe you. His clothes are here. His computer is here. He was staying here so I couldn't get to you.' His hands were at his head again, and he was rocking with the pain. 'I hate him. I hate him. And he isn't Ranger. Stop calling him that. *I'm* Ranger.'

I looked over at Julie, and her eyes tracked to me. Her lids were still lowered, but her eyes were clear and focused. Julie was faking the drug.

'My hands hurt,' I said to Scrog. 'You have me all taped up to this chair. Why do I have to be handcuffed, too? If you'd just take the cuffs off, I'll be good. I swear.'

'You broke my nose! You're a maniac. Those cuffs aren't coming off until you're cold and dead.'

'It was an accident,' I said. 'I was—'

'Shut up!' he said, pointing the gun at me. 'If you don't shut up I'll kill you now. The only reason you're alive is so you can see him die, but I'll kill you now if it's the only way to shut you up.'

We all sat in silence for what seemed like a long time. Julie was slumped in her fake drug-induced slumber. I squirmed in my seat, hoping to little by little stretch out the tape. Scrog stayed vigilant in his chair, breathing heavy, cradling his gun in his lap, never letting go of the gun.

The only sound in the apartment was the occasional squeak of Rex's wheel. And then we all heard the lock tumble on my front door.

Scrog was out of his chair, moving forward toward the foyer. He flattened himself to the living room wall and took the safety off the gun. 'If you say anything,' he whispered to me, 'I'll shoot the girl.'

His face was flushed, and his eyes were feverish and crazy, and I absolutely believed him.

I saw Julie's hand clench and then release. She was fighting to stay slack in the chair.

I had my heart in my throat. I thought chances were better that Morelli would walk through the door than Ranger. Someone was going to get shot, and I was powerless to stop it.

Twenty-Four

T he door opened and closed. There was a moment
of silence and then the soft sound of unhurried
footsteps. My heart was pounding in my chest,
and I didn't know what to wish . . . Scrog was going to
shoot whoever walked into the living room. He had the
gun raised and ready, two-handing it for accuracy. One of
the men in my life was about to be eliminated. I was
sacrificing him for a little girl. A sob escaped from
somewhere deep in my throat, disturbing the silence.
Scrog didn't hear the sob. Scrog was concentrating on the
slight rustle of clothes and scuff of shoes on carpet.

And then Ranger appeared in the living room. He was
back to his SWAT uniform of black cargo pants and long-
sleeved black collared shirt, rolled to the elbow. Our eyes
met and there was no shock of surprise in Ranger's eyes.
He had hands raised. He'd walked in knowing Scrog was
here. He turned his head and looked directly at Scrog.
And Scrog shot him.

I didn't know how many rounds went into Ranger. It was a blur of sound and movement. The force of the gunshot knocked him back. He crumpled to the floor and Scrog moved over him. Scrog looked at him for a moment, gun poised. 'Execution time,' Scrog said.

'No!' Julie shrieked, catapulting herself out of the chair. She flew into Scrog, clawing at him, eyes wild. They went to the carpet with Julie scratching and kicking and screaming. The gun fell out of Scrog's hand. They both lunged for the gun. There was a shot. Scrog scrambled away from Julie. She had the gun. She aimed and fired. A bloodstain flowered on Scrog's shirt. She was about to shoot again, and the room filled with people. Trenton cops, federal agents, paramedics. Morelli.

Morelli had me up and walking around. I couldn't remember getting the cuffs removed or the tape cut away. I clung to Morelli, and I couldn't breathe. They brought oxygen to me, but I still couldn't breathe. From the corner of my eye, I could see them working over Ranger. Hooking him to an IV, shouting orders, running with equipment. And I just couldn't breathe. I was crying and choking and there wasn't enough air in the room.

Morelli scooped me up and carried me outside to the hall, away from the insanity in the apartment. He was talking to me, but I couldn't hear what he was saying. He moved me flat to the wall, and they came through with Ranger. They had the elevator doors open and waiting.

They rolled him past me. His eyes were closed. Oxygen mask over his mouth and nose. Shirt cut away. Blood everywhere.

Julie was running beside the stretcher, her hand clenched onto the strap holding Ranger secure. Someone tried to stop her, and she slapped him away.

'This is my father,' she said. 'I'm going with him.'

Morelli turned to me with a small rueful smile. 'The apple didn't fall far from the tree with that one.'

I nodded.

'Do you want to follow them to the hospital?' Morelli asked.

I nodded again.

Morelli took me down the stairs and through the lobby. Ranger was already on his way out of the lot when we walked through the doors. A black RangeMan SUV followed the EMS truck.

Morelli buckled me in and ran around to the driver's side. 'He might be okay,' Morelli said. 'They'll know more when they get him into X-ray. He was wearing a vest. From what I could see, he took four in the chest. One of them penetrated. Maybe not entirely. Even if it hadn't, at that close range they'd knock him out. He took two more. One in the shoulder and one sliced into his neck. It was the neck wound that produced all the blood. Sunny Raspich was working EMT, and he said he thought it looked worse than it actually was. He said it looked like a clean slice that didn't hit anything vital.'

Morelli had his Kojak light on the SUV roof, but he didn't speed to the hospital. He drove sane and steady, and he kept an eye on me.

By the time we got to Hamilton, I was breathing almost normally. 'I'm okay,' I said to Morelli. 'I just had a slightly overdue panic attack back there.'

'I've seen you in the middle of a lot of disasters. I've never seen you in that bad shape.'

'I didn't know who was walking into my living room, but I knew it had to be you or Ranger. Scrog was hiding with his gun in his hand, and he said he'd shoot Julie if I said anything. It was like I had to choose who lived and who died. And I didn't know what to do. And then when Ranger was shot . . .'

Morelli pulled to the side and put his arm around me because tears were running down my face, dripping off my chin and soaking into my shirt.

'It wasn't your fault that Ranger got shot,' Morelli said. 'There were no good choices for you to make. It would all have played out the same. Except you probably saved Julie from getting shot. Ranger went in as a target. He had Tank still doing surveillance on you. When you went back to your apartment, Ranger swept the area and discovered the car Scrog had used. How he picked that car out is a miracle. It was parked two blocks away, looking like any other car in the dark. I think he's psychic sometimes. Scrog left some trace bloodstains on the seat. I would never have found them.'

'I was stupid. I thought Scrog didn't want to have any more to do with me. I should have thought he'd go to my apartment and wait for Ranger.'

'Sometimes it's the obvious that we miss. I remember you saying the reason Scrog succeeds is that he thinks ahead and moves fast. And that's exactly what he did. He went directly from the motor home, to the car he had hidden, to your apartment.'

I had myself back under control, so Morelli put the car in gear and pulled into traffic.

'Ranger called me and said he found the car, and he thought Scrog was camped out in your apartment with you and Julie. We pulled a task force together and decided on a plan. Ranger knew Scrog wanted him, so he thought the safest way to go was to give himself up. He went in hoping he could talk to Scrog. And he knew there was a good possibility he'd get shot. He had the vest on. We had the EMT parked around the corner. Maybe Ranger was a mess inside, but he didn't show anything. He was eerily calm. I think if it was me I might have at least had to make a trip to the bathroom.'

'Something became very clear to me when I was waiting to see who was going to walk into my apartment,' I said to Morelli.

He looked over at me.

'I love you,' I told him.

'Yeah,' Morelli said. 'I know. But it's nice to hear you say it. I love you, too.'

What wasn't said was that I also loved Ranger, but one thing at a time, right?

Morelli parked in a small lot reserved for emergency vehicles, and we went into the ER together. The waiting room was filled with guys in black RangeMan uniforms.

'Blood donors,' Morelli said.

And it was horrible, but true.

Tank was standing with an arm around Julie.

'How is he?' I asked Tank.

'Don't know. We're waiting to hear. They took him right into the OR. He was awake when he came in, so maybe that's a good sign.'

'Have you called your mom?' I asked Julie.

'Yes. I just got off the phone with her. She was really happy that I was okay. Her and my dad are going to fly up here to get me. She said she wasn't putting me on a plane alone. And she told Tank he wasn't to let me out of his sight.' Julie grinned. 'She's a little over-protective.'

I pulled Morelli to a quiet corner. 'Did she kill Scrog?'

'He wasn't dead when they hauled him out. I hate to bring this up, but you don't smell great.'

'I threw up.'

'That would do it.'

* * *

Melvin Pickle was in a state. He was sitting rigid on the faux-leather couch in the bond office with his hands tightly clenched in his lap. His hair was newly cut and combed. His shoes were polished. His badly fitting clothes were clean and pressed. It was Monday, and he was scheduled for court. He was armed with a verification of employment from Connie and a letter of apology to the theater.

I was on hand to drive Melvin to court and make sure he got through the ordeal without jumping off a bridge. I was dressed in my court outfit of black heels, a little black suit, and a white knit tank top. Melvin was first up, and with any luck we'd all be done by noon.

'Joyce got the money for capturing Lonnie Johnson, didn't she?' I asked Connie.

'It just about killed me to have to give it to her,' Connie said.

Lula was on the couch next to Pickle. 'She should have at least split it with you. You were the one who blew Johnson up. She would have never got him if it wasn't for you.'

'And we're keeping her on?' I asked, already knowing the hideous answer.

'Damn right, we're keeping her on,' Vinnie yelled from his office. 'She brought in two big bonds. Count them. *Two!*'

'Life is so unfair,' I said to Connie.

'I'm really nervous,' Pickle said. 'I don't want to go to jail.'

'You won't go to jail,' Lula said. 'And even if you do, it won't be for real long. I mean, how much time can a little chicken-shit pervert like you get? And then when you get out, we're gonna go look for an apartment for you, so you don't have to live with your mother. Now that you got a job here, you can move out.'

'We have to go,' I said to Pickle. 'We don't want to be late.'

Connie handed me two folders. 'New FTAs,' she said. 'Nothing exciting. A wife beater and grand theft auto.'

I shoved the files into my shoulder bag. Maybe I'd look at them tomorrow. Maybe never. Maybe I needed a new job. Problem was, I'd gone that route recently, and it hadn't turned out great. But maybe I'd just lacked direction. Maybe if I had a plan this time. Like opening a business. That could be exciting, right?

'You got that look,' Lula said to me. 'Like you're gonna start driving and not stop until you get to Hawaii.'

I eased the Mini to the curb in front of the bonds office, and I was smiling along with Pickle.

'Ten days of community service,' Pickle said for the hundredth time. 'And I can do it on weekends. And probably it'll be fun. Maybe I can work at an old people's home or an animal shelter. I can't wait to tell Lula and Connie.'

I was genuinely happy for Melvin Pickle. It turns out he's a nice guy. And I mean, who doesn't occasionally whack off in the multiplex? I've never tried it personally, but who am I to judge?

I dropped Pickle at the door, and I drove two blocks to Giorvichinni's Market and got some cut flowers. It was almost noon. Ranger was scheduled to leave the hospital this morning, so he should be home by now, back in his apartment at RangeMan. Morelli had taken Scrog's computer and scrapbook as evidence. I had Ranger's computer and various office machines in my trunk and back seat.

I let myself into the underground RangeMan garage and parked in one of Ranger's private spaces. I left the office equipment in the car, took the flowers and a bakery box, and stepped into the elevator. I waved at the security camera and used my passkey to get to Ranger's private floor. I keyed his apartment door open and stuck my head in and called to him.

'In my office,' he said.

He was at his desk, dressed in grey sweatpants and a sleeveless grey sweatshirt. A large square bandage was taped to his neck, and his right shoulder was wrapped in heavy gauze and held tight to his body in a canvas sling. I could see his chest was wrapped in tape where the bullet had penetrated the Kevlar vest and splintered a rib.

'I'd get up,' he said, 'but the rib is a killer when I move.'

'No need to get up,' I told him. I moved some papers out of the way, sat my ass on his desk so that I was facing him, and gave him the flowers and the gift box. 'I brought get-well presents.'

He looked into the box. 'Birthday cake?'

'I thought your food pyramid might need some cheering up.'

'It says "Happy Birthday Stanley".'

'It also isn't your birthday, but I don't see why that should stop us from eating cake. Have you had lunch?'

'No. Ella brought a tray, but I wasn't hungry.'

'Are you hungry now?'

He looked down at my bare legs and little skirt. 'I'm getting there.'

I slid off his desk and went to the kitchen. I prowled around and found some sandwiches and brought them in on the tray along with some forks. I set the tray on his desk and pulled a chair over for myself.

'Things are going to be pretty dull around here with only one Ranger,' I said.

Ranger forked an icing rose off the cake and fed it to me. 'One Ranger is all you'll ever need.'

JANET EVANOVICH
Ten Big Ones

So your car has been blown up (again).

A local gang has put a contract out on you.

And there's a psycho on the loose.

When did going out for nachos get so complicated?

When you're Stephanie Plum, kick-ass bounty hunter.

Life is never easy for this super-sassy Jersey girl and when Stephanie witnesses a robbery on her lunch break things start to get a whole lot tougher. She must not only keep the local bail-jumpers in line but also find a ruthless killer, known as the Junkman, before he finds her. And then there's the mother of all challenges – staying faithful to her cute cop boyfriend, Joe Morelli, by resisting the charms of her seriously sexy mentor Ranger.

Sounds like a tall order but this is Stephanie Plum. And when your partner's an ex-hooker with a penchant for lurid spandex and your grandma likes to pack heat, you take it all in your stride.

Praise for Janet Evanovich:

'Punchy, saucy and stacks of fun. I'm hooked' *Mirror*

'Crime writing at its funniest . . . classic black comedy' *The Big Issue*

'All the easy class and wit that you expect to find in the best American TV comedy, but too rarely find in modern fiction' *GQ*

'Pithy, witty and fast-paced' *The Sunday Times*

0 7553 2699 7

headline
review

JANET EVANOVICH

To The Nines

Stephanie Plum's got rent to pay, people shooting at her, and psychos wanting her dead every day of the week (much to the dismay of her mother, her family, the men in her life, the guy who slices meat at the deli . . . the list goes on). An ordinary person would cave under the pressure.

But hey, she's from Jersey.

Stephanie Plum may not be the best bounty hunter in beautiful downtown Trenton, but she's pretty damn good at turning situations her way . . . and she always gets her man.

Her cousin Vinnie (who's also her boss) has posted bail on Samuel Singh, who mysteriously disappears just as his work visa is running out. And Stephanie is on the case to ensure the elusive Mr Singh doesn't make his disappearance more permanent. But what she uncovers is far more sinister than anyone imagines and leads to a group of killers who give a whole new meaning to the word 'hunter'. In a race against time that takes her from the Jersey Turnpike to the Vegas Strip, Stephanie Plum is on the chase of her life.

The unforgettable characters, non-stop action, high-stakes suspense, and sheer entertainment of TO THE NINES define Janet Evanovich as unique among today's writers.

Praise for Number One bestseller Janet Evanovich:

'That girl has some class' *New York Times*

'Pithy, witty and fast-paced' *The Sunday Times*

'Hilarious reading, with a gorgeous fistful of believable and only occasionally murderous eccentrics' *Mail on Sunday*

'Punchy, saucy and stacks of fun. I'm hooked' *Mirror*

0 7472 6763 4 (A format)

0 7553 2908 2 (B format)

headline
review

Now you can buy any of these other bestselling books by **Janet Evanovich** from your bookshop or *direct from her publisher*.

FREE P&P AND UK DELIVERY
(Overseas and Ireland £3.50 per book)

Stephanie Plum Novels

Seven Up	£6.99
Hard Eight	£6.99
To The Nines	£6.99
Ten Big Ones	£6.99
Eleven on Top	£6.99

written with Charlotte Hughes

Full House	£6.99
Full Tilt	£6.99
Full Speed	£6.99
Full Black	£6.99

TO ORDER SIMPLY CALL THIS NUMBER

01235 400 414

or visit our website: www.madaboutbooks.com

Prices and availability subject to change without notice.